JEWELS OF ORANGE

SPIRITS OF LIANA, BOOK 2

SIMON PITTMAN

Copyright 2023 © Simon Pittman.

All rights reserved.

For dad, Franz Josef, for being my proofreader and role model.

Hopefully I captured you perfectly in the two characters named after you in this book!

Despite the great power Liana demonstrated after attaining her Red Aura, the princess is under strict orders from her mother not to be involved with pursuing her next Spirit.

Instead, the quest to find the Jewels of Orange in the city of Allicalidantè is a diplomatic mission contrived by the Queen's Table involving a doppelgänger in place of the princess.

Fed up with her over-protective guardians, it's not long before Liana joins the hunt for her next Spirit, but she soon finds out why The Dantè was off-limits to her.

PROLOGUE

Thirteen years previous, the volcano of Mount Indigo on the island of Coryàtès erupted and became known as the Day of Darkness. Piecing together the events with a rumour from a time-worn parchment, a passage of writing from the forbidden religion Aurora Visendus, Queen Adriya Langton sent her uncle Sir Tarak to scout for any unusual activity. At the foot of the eruption, on the site of the old mines, he found a babe lying on a grassy rock floating in a river of lava next to a strange looking dagger. That babe was Liana, and that dagger was the Dagger of Red.

Queen Adriya adopted Liana into Langton royalty and raised her as her own daughter.

With her vibrant, indigo-blue hair and title of princess, Liana found it difficult to make genuine friends as she grew up. That was until she met Saffina Greymore and Joel Ellwood.

Her teacher and aide to the Langton throne, Clerk Vivek, suggested she split her time between private study with him and attending a school in the Coryatès capital city of Swyre. This is where she met Saffina and Joel. Using her place in society, she put an end to their bullying from an older student, Yasmin Thornfalcon.

Yasmin's father, Zagan, was Master of the Mines. He had lost everyone except Yasmin in the Day of Darkness. However, he always believed his family could have been saved and blamed the Langton monarchy for a poorly organised rescue attempt in the Guild District where his family were located.

It was on the eve of Liana's thirteenth birthday when she began to have strange visions. Colourless visions of white's, grey's and black's. It was during one of these episodes when she was caught off-guard and captured by a man named Nalan, who was standing trial for the attempted murder of a city architect.

Her friends, Saffina and Joel, launched a rescue attempt but ended up being captured by a group labelled the White Robes. These White Robes turned out to be a private army that Zagan had been secretly building within the mines for years.

After managing to escape her captor and return home, the citizens celebrated the princesses thirteenth birthday with the opening of the city's first place of worship for the Aurora Visendus since the Queen had legalised the religion - the Tulip Temple. In her haste to gain followers, Priestess Yi Lang rushed the training of Yasmin and Eugene, Saffina's brother, to show off the abilities of the Visendi. They demonstrated the power of the religion's Inner Root Core by the way of producing a Red Aura.

Soon after this event, Liana learned of her friend's disappearance and of her own proclaimed destiny. She embarked on a mission to find a secret temple of the religion - the

Shrouded Temple of Roots, where she met the Old Priest, Master Shiro Hayashi.

Master H, as he preferred to be called, led a small faction of Visendi in the temple. After some deliberation, he led Liana to an area of the temple he was entrusted to guard, the Tomb of the Transcended. This catacomb was home to the Visendi's most powerful, who had been contained in suspended animation. They were the Spectra Children. It was here that Liana learned that she too was entombed in this temple for 200-years, and about the Artefacts and Spectra Orbs that kept her Aura Spirits safe all that time, but were now no longer there.

Before Liana herself could launch a rescue mission for her friends, Saffina and Joel appeared in the Shrouded Temple of Roots with the help of Amara Langton, the Queen's unruly sister, who had been punished and sent to the mines for continually disobeying orders whilst she was a general in the Langton army.

The group soon learned, with the help of Liana's captor Nalan, that Zagan and Clerk Vivek were working in partnership to destroy Liana and the Langton monarchy. They had built an 'Army of Immorals' to take them down and claim the island for themselves.

Events came to a head on the eastern beach of Coryàtès, where a fearsome battle took place, ending with Liana producing a magnificent dome of Red and White Aura, healing those who had been Turned into Immorals by Clerk Vivek.

Liana's quest now is to seek out the remainder of her Spirits and see through her destiny as the saviour of the planet Mikana.

1
CITY OF THE ARTS

"Without the creativity, imagination, and industriousness of those in the arts the feeling of joy would be imaginary itself."

King Shimon's opening words to his speech reverberated amongst the crowd. He spoke into a large, brass, horn-like speaker to those gathered before him. He had a natural ability to turn up the volume of his voice to a level like no one else could, but sometimes even his vocal cords needed a little help in reaching the citizens gathered at the back of the main high-street of Allicalidantè.

Banners, flagpoles and bunting of all colours lined the city streets each adorning the city's symbol; an abstract, dancing figure holding a paintbrush and a flute set upon a square diamond-shaped games board which formed the symbol's background.

It was the opening day of Allicalidantè's most prestigious fortnight of events - the Tournament of Tournaments. For many, especially those who resided in Allicalidantè, their whole year had been leading up to this week. It was the week when they would showcase their talents and win the most desired and acclaimed prize: the opportunity to perform their craft for the royal household for the next year and earn a lifetime of coin for the privilege in the process.

Each year, King Shimon, his wife, his son and the winners of the previous years categories would vote for their favourite contestant in each speciality of arts and games. Music, storytelling, painting, sculpting, dancing, performing, magic, board games, wrestling and archery formed the ten categories contestants could enter.

Arts and games were at the forefront of Allicalidantè's identity and attracted numerous visitors from all across the mainland. During the two weeks of the Tournament of Tournaments, it's said that the number of people in the city quadrupled. Visitors came to not only witness one of the greatest contests on the whole of Mikana, but to admire the beauty of the city itself.

Buildings that would simply be plain stone in any other city were instead decorated and painted in the most colourful and unique murals, landscapes and abstracts. The frontage of every entryway was a testament to the creativity of its owners' tastes, making the city itself a diverse piece of art. A variety of sculptures, horticulture, ornaments, paintings and animatronics would keep a person's eye entertained for hours as they wandered the city streets.

"Let the Tournament of Tournaments commence!" King Shimon threw his arms up as he ended his speech, with a wide smile of genuine joy on his face. Afterall, it wasn't just his citizens' favourite time of the year, but his as well. A huge roar erupted from the thousands in attendance as brass trumpets, bass drums and flutes sounded out a perfectly tuned and in-time ceremonial song.

The crowd began to disperse and reveal the cobblestone floor of the high-street. The Tournament of Tournaments contestants made their way to their designated zones for their respective category. Those who were attending to simply spectate wandered off leisurely to watch their favourite discipline. As the main high-street cleared, well-drilled citizens unfolded tables in several neat columns placing game boards on top. The high-street was the zone for participants of the strategy board game called Chantrah.

The tables were placed far enough apart so spectators could wonder and choose which contestants to watch. One skill of a successful Chantrah player is to be able to block out their surroundings and focus solely on the board in front of them, and that was none more so required than in the early rounds of Chantrah in the Tournament of Tournaments. Allowing a distraction from the bustling around them could easily result in a game-ending mistake.

One of the favourites for this year's Chantrah tournament was a man called Franklin Rozier. He had been runner-up two years in a row, and many in the city thought this would finally be his year.

A large crowd had already gathered around his table, eager to witness his opening round. He had been randomly paired with a young, first-time contestant. No one in the crowd had any doubts as to what the end result would be.

The game began and Franklin was surprisingly put on the backfoot early on. He had memorised the likely tactics of all the higher-level players as they frequently pitted themselves against each other throughout the year for practice, so he had to be wary of this newcomer despite the fact that the crowd were already convinced of the game's outcome.

A commotion from the game next to Franklin's caused everyone who was standing around his table to turn around.

"You cheated, old man!" shouted a boy with wavy shoulder-length brown hair, who could have been no older than twelve or thirteen years old.

"Did not!" replied his opponent, a bearded middle-aged man.

"Did too! You've done it twice now, moved two pieces at once! You sly old fool, you think I wouldn't notice? Afraid of getting beat by a kid?"

"You're lying, kid. And there ain't no way I'm losing this."

"With tricky hands like that, you would have more of a chance entering the magic contest instead!"

As the pair exchanged insults and accusations, one of the prior years winners, acting now as one of the tournament referees, came by and calmed the situation down and ordered for the game to restart.

The slight distraction worked in Franklin's favour. He could tell the newcomer's mind had become distracted and unfocussed. His opponent made an inevitable mistake and in a matter of three more moves, Franklin had won. Much to his relief.

The onlookers clapped and he raised a modest, half-hearted hand in the air in recognition as his opponent slumped back dejectedly into his chair. Franklin pushed his way through the crowd, eager to find a spot to relax his mind ahead of the second round being held later that day. As he pushed through, a hand caught his bicep and a female voice whispered into his ear with a shallow and sharp, yet sincere, tone in her voice.

"When this city is turned into a joyless casket, be sure to stay away. There will come a time when we need your skills."

Franklin spun around as the hand released from his arm. A streak of green hair is all he saw of the departing woman. He tried to catch up with her but she soon faded away amongst the jostling of bodies. *"When this city is turned into a joyless casket..."* he repeated to himself. He tried to shrug off the warning, but the words did nothing but linger inside his head from that day on.

2

DISPUTES AND DAYDREAMS

"It's so unfair!" screamed Princess Liana as she thrust down the Dagger of Red into the triangular-shaped table in front of her. A ray of early-morning sun caught the dragonfly engraving on the dagger's cross guard at just the right angle to recreate the insect as a reflection on the room's ceiling. The red light within the Spectra Orb nestled in the dagger's handle danced and swished like a shoal of happy fish. The cross-armed figure of the princess's mother, Queen Adriya, also reflected clearly in the red-tinted blade as it stood impaled in the mahogany timber.

"Liana Langton," replied the queen sternly. "We've been through this a thousand times already," the queen uncrossed her arms and now gestured with flailing arms and a 'don't start this again' frown. "The Queen's Table is in agreement. This is the safest way."

"It's supposed to be *my* journey, *my* quest, *my* responsibility," said the unhappy princess as she kicked away the chair she had been sitting on and stood up in one swift motion. "It's like you're treating this as a game of fetch with Cas, sending other people out to bring home my Spirits." The large ears of a wolf-like, soft white-furred dog pricked up at the sound of his name, although it wasn't enough to make him move from the pile of warm blankets he was curled up on. Cas had been found as a stray by Liana one day on her way back home from a lesson with Master H. at the Shrouded Temple of Roots, and because of his past hardships, Liana's four-legged friend particularly liked the home-comforts that came with being a royal canine. At least taking him in as her pet wasn't one thing Liana's mother argued with her about. The dog went everywhere with her, and it made the queen feel more secure about her daughter's safety knowing that Cas was by her side.

"It's easier to keep you out of danger if you remain in Swyre," sighed the Queen, tired of repeating herself. "It's not like finding the Temple of Shrouded Roots, when there was no idea what to look for, where to look, or even how to enter. We at least now have some knowledge of the dangers that lie ahead, all thanks to your birth mother."

Liana frowned, crossed her arms, and turned her back on her mother. She still thought of Queen Adriya as her actual mother even though she'd found out half a year ago that a 200-year-old Visendi woman called Candela was her birth mother. And also despite the arguments they seemed to have on a near daily basis now.

"Candela's knowledge is two-hundred years old, we don't know what happened in that time."

"All the more reason to keep you close to home." Queen Adriya said as she carefully approached her daughter and placed a hand on her shoulder. "Life outside of Coryàtès is very different."

"You haven't stopped saying that ever since the Battle of

Coryàtès," Liana said as she spun around and looked her mother in the eye. "Just tell me why it's so different outside of the island."

"No, I won't. Not yet. At this stage, the less you know the better. This undertaking to get your next Spectra Orb is just as much about reconnaissance and getting first-hand knowledge regarding conditions outside of Coryàtès as anything else, and that can be done by people other than yourself. I won't put you in needless endangerment."

Liana yanked the Dagger of Red out the table, along with a blurt of angry, garbled gibberish, and sheathed it into a scabbard on her waistband, leaving a splintered gash in the otherwise smooth and glossy wood. She moved towards the room's exit, but halted as she opened the door.

"Six months ago I was the one who saved you from being killed. I was the one who saved the city from what would have been a monstrous rule. I saved our citizens from being Turned, yet you still don't trust me."

Queen Adriya started a sentence to respond and reached out, but Liana quickly left the room with her head bowed, refusing to hear her mother out. She knew the words she said would hurt her mother, but she also knew they wouldn't change her mind either. Her mother was as stubborn as ever. Years of making decisions for the good of the city and its citizens (even though with hindsight, the majority of those decisions had been correct) had made her mother overprotective of what she'd built during her reign. The personalities of Liana's adventurous nature and the Queen's conservativeness came to a head more often than ever since the Battle of Coryàtès. *'If it's so dangerous outside the island, surely the strength of my Red Aura will only be a benefit in retrieving the next Spectra Orb,'* she procrastinated as she made the long descent down the spiralling steps of the Tower of Seeds. Her thoughts were disturbed by the sound of a quick pitter-patter of paws behind her as Cas skipped down the steps to join her at her side. She gave him a quick pat on the head and the angst inside her immediately evaporated away, almost as if the hound himself possessed a magic power that made her feel instantly happy.

"Oh, Cas," sighed Liana, scratching behind his ears once they'd eventually made it to the bottom of the tower. "What I'd give to be a care-free pooch like you right now." The dog wagged his tail excitedly and let his tongue droop out his mouth as he made the most of the love and attention. "C'mon, let's go see what Saff and Joel are up to," she said, and raced off through the Triunity Hall and out into the castle's courtyard. Cas bounded along beside her in youthful exuberance, his white fur shining in the early morning winter sun. The planets' three moons could still be seen as faint stamps high in the clear blue sky.

"Careful!" exclaimed Agatha, Castle Langton's head maid, as Cas got under her feet, almost causing her to trip over. "Where're you two off to?"

"Have you seen Saff and Joel? They mentioned to me yesterday that Master H was making them get here at first light for training," Liana said, panting.

"They're in your favourite conservatory at the back of the castle," smiled Agatha. Agatha's smile never waned. Sometimes Liana wished she could use her power of Sight when she was feeling low just to see the magnificent glow of White Morality that emanated from Agatha, but the day after the Battle of Coryàtes, after she had unturned the Army of Immorals, she hadn't been able to use her power of Sight. No matter how much she tried or how much she meditated, she couldn't go back to the Morality Realm.

"Thanks, Agatha!" her shout tailed off as the dog and owner sprinted off once more.

The pair ran past the stables, (briefly stopping to say good morning to Sherwin, Liana's golden-coloured steed), and into Castle Langton through the kitchen door. They dodged, ducked and weaved their way around cooks, stoves and steam whilst the day's breakfast was being prepared for the royal household. They barged their way out the other side and into the dining hall.

Liana paused and glanced up at the painting above the fireplace of her and her mother enjoying an idealistic picnic on the sands beneath the castle. Her vibrant indigo-blue hair contrasted the pale creams of the beach. She reminisced about that moment. It was one of the last memories she had before she turned thirteen. Before she found out she had the power of Sight and could see people's Morality. Before she was labelled the 'Light from the Dark' who would 'Restore the Spectrum' of the Aurora Visendus. Before she found out she was born with magical Aura's. Magical Aura's that were Peeled from her as a babe and where she was made to lay in stasis for two-hundred years before the eruption of Mount Indigo on the Day of Darkness released her from her entombed casket and adopted into Langton royalty. Before she found out her trusted tutor, Clerk Vivek, was in fact a traitor who wanted to use Liana for his own thirst for power. Oh, how she'd like to go back to being able to have a life where her only worries were learning correct etiquette and the challenge of making any friends.

A bark from Cas, who was eagerly waiting by the next doorway, shook her from her musing. The pair took off again. The grand, arching sandstone corridors echoed as they sprinted through hallway after hallway of Castle Langton. They arrived at one of the castle's many reception rooms, one that Liana particularly liked to frequent if she was in a particularly arty or creative mood. She paused again in thought, as she grasped the doorknob. She took a moment to picture in her mind the views from the rooms adjoining conservatory. Views that overlooked the sweeping sea waves, and at this early time of day, the tones of yellows, reds, and pinks of the dawning of the sun. It was a picture she had often put paint on canvas to, but in her own opinion, had never been able to do it justice. Her fondness of the scene was not a coincidence, she thought, considering her prophetic ties with the Aurora Visendus, but she couldn't help smile at the thought of seeing that early-morning view.

That smile was soon wiped away the moment she turned the doorknob and opened the door.

3

THE DOPPELGÄNGER

'*What is this place? It seems... familiar... yes, yes, I know where I am now. I'm not in a different place, no, I'm in the same place... but the place is different. It looks different, it feels different. What happened to me? Is... is this some sort of afterlife?'*

Liana's knuckles began turning white as she gripped the doorknob with an increasingly tighter and tighter grasp. She observed in silence as her best friends, Saffina and Joel, each let out a loud belly-laugh which could be heard through the conservatory's glass windows. *'I didn't know **she'd** be here,'* she thought to herself in a mixture of anger, jealousy and upset which contorted inside of her like strands of hair being braided. Feelings that wrapped and twisted around in her throat and chest to the point of physical pain. It was obvious to her what they were laughing about. She could tell by the body language and exaggerated movements. They were laughing at her. Mocking her. Not caring if they hurt her feelings, and it was all because of Lucille. Ever since she had been brought in to take part in the mission to Allicalidantè, Saffina and Joel had been infatuated with her. They found her funny, interesting, and gregarious. And they were spending more time with her, due to their training for their visit to Allicalidantè. The extended time Liana had spent in tutorship with Master H and Priestess Yi to prepare her in the Sacral Core ready for when her Orange Aura was retrieved also took time away from her from seeing her friends.

"It's not fair why do I *always* lose!" mocked Lucille, putting on a fake voice, pretending to mimic Liana as she lifted her hand and overstated a flick of her shoulder-length, cropped, blue hair, before slamming it down onto a Chantrah board, causing some of the game's pieces to topple over. Of course, Lucille's vivid-indigo blue hair wasn't her natural colour. Master H had created a dye out of tulip petals. After much experimenting he finally found a colour that was almost an exact match for the princesses.

It had taken over a month to find a girl whose features were a close enough match to Liana's. After an extensive search of Swyre, Lucille was found selling wine on a stall outside her parents' home. The Coulliard's owned vineyards located on the far-western outskirts of the city and were some of the last places that were scouted to find a suitable doppelgänger.

Because she lived so far outside of the main city, and because her parents' intended for her to take over the vineyard when they could no longer physically manage it, Lucille hadn't attended school since she was eleven. Despite the Queen's Table understanding the importance of education, the limited amount of migration to the island from other lands over the last decade meant that they could only enforce mandatory schooling up to that age. Schooling from twelve years onward was either a parental decision or mandatory for only those who showed particular skill in a certain academic area. Specialist schools for science, technology, mathematics, language and warfare tactics were scattered across the city for these academics. Even if Lucille's parents were willing to continue with her education, she would have ended up in a generic school. Her talents were certainly more suited to selling wine. When the scouts came across her, she was standing on an old wooden horse cart full of wine crates outside her home's front gate. A small gathering of prospective merchants were watching as she acted and gesticulated about the processes that their wine go through, telling the story of grape to bottle and why their produce was superior to their neighbours. Her acting clearly worked, as the horse cart was emptied by the end of the speech. It was a huge stroke of luck, the scouts thought, to find someone who could not only take the place of Liana visually but could be trained to portray her mannerisms.

Lucille continued to mock the Princess in front of Joel and Saffina. She raised her chin, symbolising an act to depict self-importance: "My name is Liana Langton. I am the Seventh Spectra Child. A descendant of the Transcended of the Aurora Visendus. Princess of Coryàtès and heir to the throne. I command you to release these prisoners, relinquish your title and surrender yourselves to your Queen." The mimicking of her now infamous speech after defeating Zagan and Vivek in the Battle of Coryàtès brought out a roar of laughter from the trio.

"Is there something funny about saving your asses?" Liana spoke up, scornfully.

Saffina's and Joel's cackling abruptly stopped, realising they'd been caught red-handed taunting their friend. Lucille also did her best to stop laughing but the jolts from her abdomen and pursed lips gave it away that she found her mocking so hilarious she couldn't stop.

"Uh," Saffina hesitated, "Sorry. We didn't mean to.."

"Didn't mean to make fun of me?" said Liana, finishing the sentence.

"It was just a harmless joke," shrugged Joel.

"Some friends," an angry burning in Liana's chest grew hotter and spread to her throat and stomach like she'd just ingested a sheet of sandpaper. "Let's hope this fake me can save your asses when you inevitably screw up in Allicalidantè." It was a harsh evaluation, and Liana regretted saying it almost as soon as she said it, but she was so angry with them. They knew the burden placed on her, yet they mocked her.

"Hey! That's not fair!" exclaimed Saffina, who took a confrontational step forward. "We risked our lives looking for you after your kidnapping!"

"And look how that turned out!" countered Liana.

"What do you think we're doing for you now? Allicalidantè isn't going to be a walk in the park," Joel stepped up bedside Saffina, backing her up. "It's not our decision to have Luci stand in for you." Liana's gut wrenched at hearing Saffina call her doppelgänger 'Luci' instead of her full name. Lucille had well and truly wormed her way into the friendship now, thought Liana. "We have to get to know her," continued Saffina. "We have to actually be friends with her, be as close with her as we are to you to make the whole thing believable."

"And mocking me is your way of doing that?"

"Come on, let's not fall out over this. We're sorry, okay?"

"No, Joel, I'm not okay. If I can't count on my two best friends, then who can I count on? It's not like I have a free reign in the city anymore to go and make new ones. I'm leashed like a dog for my 'own protection'."

"Or maybe it's to protect others from you," spouted Luci, accidentally vocalising her thoughts.

"And exactly what do you mean by that?!" Liana's raised voice echoed out of the conservatory room and down the stone corridor behind her.

"Well, you know. With your powers, people are, you know.."

"No I don't know, *Lucille*, why don't you enlighten me." Liana was purposeful to emphasise the pronunciation of her doppelgängers name to enforce the disdain she felt towards her.

"Everyone's anxious about how you will use them. You're more short-tempered and irritable than the Queen."

"Short-tempered and irritable? I'll show you how short-tempered and irritable I am!" shouted Liana, ironically raising her voice some more. She shifted to become nose-to-nose with her verbal sparring partner.

"Liana, she's right, ever since the Battle of Coryàtès you've become this fiery loose cannon. Ever since you've not been able to…"

"Typical Saff," interrupted Liana, "should've figured you'd take the side of your new best friend."

"Liana, she's not my new best friend," Saff pleaded. "Come on, you have to admit that ever since you produced that Morality Aura at the Battle of Coryàtès and returned all the Immorals good, you've not been yourself."

"Or maybe it's just because I'm just seeing things more clearly now. You just can't stand me having all the attention of being a princess and the proclaimed saviour of Mikana, can you? Face it, you're just jealous!"

The sandpaper-like feeling that had been rubbing her insides had worn down her boundaries and her frame started to glow with her Red Root Aura. Shimmering wisps of red light danced around her slender frame, slowly growing brighter and wider as her feelings intensified. Saffina, Joel and Luci cautiously and fearfully stepped backwards away from the Princess. The light swelled and began to fill the room. The trio in front of her backed into a corner, afraid of what would happen if Liana's Aura touched them. Her Aura moved to within a parchments-width of Saffina's nose when a thunderous voice boomed from behind Liana, shouting her name, quickly followed by the whip of a staff to the backs of her knees that knocked her off her feet. The red glow dissipated as Liana's focus shifted to the throbbing pain in her legs.

"Have I taught you nothing!" exclaimed the disappointed voice of Master H, standing over her. "Leave, now. I will deal with your lack of discipline at the temple later."

Liana gingerly picked herself up off the floor before taking off towards the conservatory exit where Cas was waiting in the doorway. The wolf-like pup growled fiercely at Saffina, Joel and Luci as they each breathed a sigh of relief before the canine bolted down the corridor after his keeper.

"They should make you keep him on a leash too," Luci shouted after them, "You two *are* dangerous."

4
THE FIVE F'S

Liana groaned as she walked into the Tulip Temple's ground-floor auditorium. Master H was already kneeling in the centre of the large circular arena floor. They hadn't trained much in the Shrouded Temple since burying Estrella and the rest of the temple's murdered occupants. Liana didn't press Master H on his feelings, but even after all these months, she could tell the pain of losing his comrades was still raw.

The Tulip Temple's stadium-style seating that encircled the arena floor, stretched up three tiers. Even now, six months after the Priestess opened the temple and was allowed to start teaching the religion of Aurora Visendus again, the arena would reach its full 80,000 capacity once a week when she would preach and demonstrate the teachings that had been passed down to her through the generations. Generations that had been repressed and hunted since the religion was outlawed two hundred years ago. That was until the old literature predicting the events of Liana's finding came to be true.

Even then, it had been a constant battle between her and Queen Adriya as to how much influence the religion could have on city politics and the argument whether or not to tell Liana that she was the proclaimed Light from the Dark that would restore the spectrum of the Aurora Visendus.

Liana sipped a cup of hot tea as she walked toward Master H and knelt down facing her mentor.

"I'm sorry about what I did in the conservatory, Master. I just feel so out of control of my own future, my own destiny. After the Battle of Coryàtès, you'd think my mother would trust me more."

"You talk about trust, and yet you frightened your friends half to death. There is a huge weight on your shoulders, all your mother wants to do is share that burden and risk. This is a desire shared amongst the entire Queen's Table."

"But I have the most powerful Red Aura of anyone thanks to my Root Spirit. It's not like I can get hurt."

"You are a beacon for the dark, Liana. Your power will only draw those who want it towards you. Do you understand the risk Luci is placing herself in, pretending to be you? Evil is surfacing and it is searching you out, Liana. Luci is risking her life for you in this mission."

Liana lowered her head, staring silently into her tea. *'When do you attain the wisdom of a Priest?'* she thought to herself as she reflected on her action's and her teacher's words.

"Reflection of one's actions is a good practice, child, but sometimes you just need to release your thoughts outwardly. Come, let's train, and I will teach you about decision making when you are faced with a reactionary choice, so you don't make the same mistake again."

The Old Priest made his way to a weapons cupboard and picked up just one dagger from a set of Twin Sai blades from and a flailing mace. He handed Liana the other twin sai blade, and a club.

"No Aura's," said Master H, setting out the rules of the contest. "Unless at risk of injury, in which case, it will be deemed that the use of an Aura is an admission to concede. The loser is the first to concede." He led the pair back to the centre of the circular arena. They bowed before each other to signal the start of the sparring contest.

The pair completed a full circle around each other, side-stepping, waiting for the other to make the first move.

"There are various responses to trauma. We call them the Five F's," said the Old Priest, beginning the lesson.

Liana, trying to catch the Old Priest off guard, attacked first, wielding the club above her head.

"The first F," grunted Master H, as he dodged Liana's attack, before lunging with his blade into a counter attack. "Is Fight." The blade narrowly missed Liana's upper right arm, the arm which held the club. "This is when a person's natural response to trauma comes out as anger."

Liana made a counter of her own, jabbing and thrusting at her mentor, forcing him back towards the arena wall.

"The second F," the Old Priest continued whilst running toward the wall, turning his back on Liana. *'A rookie mistake to turn your back on your opponent,'* thought the Princess, and she flung her twin sai blade. "Is Flight."

As the Old Priest neared the wall, he leapt and turned sideways, running horizontally along the vertical wall as a mere flash as he raced. Liana's flying dagger missed its target and bounced off the sandstone with a metallic clink as it fell to the floor. "This is when a person feels they must remove themselves and flee from their situation," he said, and landed into a crouch after running ten-paces along the wall flaunting an act of this gravity defying feat.

Starting to get out of breath, Liana raced to pick up her Twin Sai from the floor. As she did, the door to the arena opened. Waylon, a skinny bald man with thick-black rimmed glasses and one of the Temple's night watchmen, poked his head in to see what the commotion was. He wasn't a trained watchman like you'd find in the Swyre army, just a volunteer who rotated shifts with other followers to roam the temple and protect it against youthful vandals.

"The third F," said the Old Priest, turning to the opened door and flinging his blade toward the direction of the watchmen. The blade stuck, vibrating in the wood of the doorframe, less than an inch from the nose of the watchman. The watchman stood still, gulped, his eyes starting to water. "Is Freeze. When a person is too panicked to move."

Master H slowed to walking pace into the centre of the arena. "Would you like to concede now, before I end this?"

"Of course not," Liana replied. "I'm not just going to give up."

"But we can go back to our pleasantries, maybe we can share some more tea together," the Old Priest lowered his arms in front of him, an open-handed gesture of compromise.

Liana chuckled to herself, "I see, I'm guessing the fourth F must be Friend," deduced Liana from the exchange. The pair moved back to circling each other around the half-empty cup of tea that sat in the bullseye of the arena.

Master H reciprocated the chortle. "Indeed. When the automatic response is to seek help or an offering of peace from another."

"So, what's the..?" Liana started to say, but before she could finish asking the question, the Old Priest threw his flailing mace at the cup on the ground, leaving himself weaponless. The cup spun up in the air, a little over the head-height of the priest. The flailing mace also spun frantically, and the two objects met again in mid-air. The spikes of the flail caught the bottom of the cup sending a gush of hot tea towards Liana, causing her to flinch and stumble backwards. She lay on her back and protected her eyes to prevent herself from being burned and begged for the Old Priests' mercy, conceding the fight.

"...Is Flop," finished Master H, standing over Liana as he finished his sentence. "When the person decides they or their cause are no longer worthwhile and give up." Master H bent down and stretched out an arm. The princess reached up and they grabbed each other's forearm as he helped pull her back to her feet.

"And that is the five F's. Along with a little lesson in creative fighting as well. All good lessons for your Sacral Core." Master H smiled to himself as he pulled his twin sai out of the wooden door. The watchman still stood in the doorway, frozen and trembling at his near-death experience before Master H gently pushed Waylon back out and shut the door behind him.

"If you can identify in yourself how you unconsciously react to a potentially traumatic or emotional situation, you can instead begin to choose how best to respond, and turn your unconscious instincts into a superior, conscious act."

He carefully placed the weaponry back into the cupboard and locked them away.

Liana, still catching her breath from the brief yet intense fight, leaned against the wall.

"Which of these Five F's do you feel you have most to learn?"

"That's an easy answer," Liana replied, still trying to compose her breathing, "Friend."

"And why do you say that? You have friends: Saffina, Joel, Agatha, Benji, myself."

"That's two friends and a few adults who have a duty to look out for me. Making genuine friends is hard enough as a princess, let alone some sort of world saviour. Half the time people just want favours or money, the other half the time they're afraid of me."

"Mentors and adults can be friends too. Don't underestimate your ability to connect with new people. Remember how you befriended your captor, Nalan, and how he helped us defeat Zagan?" Liana suddenly had flashbacks after hearing Master H use those two names. Nalan, who took her captive with her own dagger and ended up an ally who died in her arms and Zagan, whose mining operation provided the perfect cover to train a secret army.

"Everyone has their strengths, child. You are a leader, whether you like it or want it. Either as a royal or a saviour, making connections with all types of people will serve you well. Don't dismiss those who you may not get on with straight away, they are often the ones who have qualities you lack, and therefore need. Now, I think you wouldn't forgive yourself if you didn't see off your friends from the dock. Their ship leaves for Allicalidantè in a little under an hour."

5
BON VOYAGE

'The crumbled walls around me offer little protection from the swirling winds of circling fine sand. This handful of dust I pick up and allow to pour out through the cracks in my fingers looks so dull. Everything around me is so colourless. Greys on greys, whites on blacks. Where has everyone gone? It is the same, but it is different.'

"There they are," said Liana, stroking the neck of Sherwin, her trusted equestrian companion. "Ready to take on my adventure without me."

She looked down from a cliff edge upon Swyre's bustling harbour of fishmongers, traders, merchants, sailors and navy persons as they jostled and jigged along the piers and quay's dodging both people and produce to get to their destinations.

The harbour waters were sectioned into a large, designated area where the royal fleet kept anchor and a smaller L-shaped wharf where the fisheries docked. The wharf was not used as a permanent dock for the fisheries and served only for unloading and delivering their catch to the fishmongers of

Swyre, before sailing back to their berths at the northern side of the island where the best schools of fish could be found.

Despite the franticness below, it was not hard to miss the parting of the crowd as her uncle, Sir Tarak Langton, led a royal entourage towards Admiral Remi's flagship vessel. Constructed out of the city's famous, blue-tinted glass, the words RNC Ascendancy adorned the hull of the boat (RNC an acronym for Royal Navy of Coryàtès). The reflective blue letters stood out in contrast to the soft-brown wood used to construct the largest ship in the fleet. Matching blue sails draped from the masts and on them embroidered in gold thread was the Langton crest of four equilateral triangles fitted together, making one large triangle, to symbolise the equal importance of the military, religion and royalty to protect the centre triangle - the citizens.

"I didn't realise being so powerful would be so lonely," Liana said, stroking Sherwin's golden fur. "I thought I was lonely just being a princess, but now I'm supposed to be the light that restores the spectrum of the Aurora Visendus, I'm even more alone." Cas barked and tilted his head up with classic puppy-dog eyes and a huge wide grin. "I know boy, you're my friend, aren't ya." He panted happily as Liana scruffed his snowy-white head and rubbed behind his ears.

"They're still your friends, Saffina and Joel," a voice behind Liana made her jump, not realising she had company, "like everyone else, they want to help you and protect you."

"Mother?" a confused look glazed over the princess. "Shouldn't you be down there, with the entourage?"

"New evidence arrived late last night that Allicalidantè is even more dangerous than we first feared."

"More danger? I don't even know why it was dangerous to begin with! So why are you up here and not down there?"

"The same reason you are. The Queen's Table thinks my life is in jeopardy if I go with them."

"So, who's going to lead the negotiations of the treaty with King Shimon?"

"Your uncle will act as my proxy."

"Great Uncle Tarak? He's not exactly the talkative type..."

Queen Adriya smiled, acknowledging the accuracy of the observation. "You might be surprised at the wisdom of your great uncle. Besides, it might work in our favour."

"Surely King Shimon won't even entertain the idea of an allegiance if you're not present?"

"Or he might think he has an advantage dealing with someone who is supposedly less skilled in the art of diplomacy."

"So, that should put us at a disadvantage? How does this work in our favour in any way?"

"Because the negotiations don't really matter. They're just our way in, to distract King Shimon. It's Saffina and Joel's job to find and obtain your Sacral Orb, so the longer talks go on - the more chance we have of succeeding without conflict."

"But you said Allicalidantè is dangerous, really dangerous?" repeated Liana.

"It is."

"So, Saffina and Joel will be searching for the temple between themselves?"

"That's correct."

"So, they're risking their lives to find my Spirit Orb?"

"Again, that's correct."

Princess Liana stood silently, watching as the entourage to Allicalidantè made their way up RNC Ascendancy's ramp to board her.

'They're risking their lives for me, again, and all I could do was

shout at them, frighten them, the day before they set off. I'm so clueless sometimes.'

"Master Hayashi says you didn't turn up for training yesterday afternoon," Queen Adriya said, changing the subject.

"I was tired. Besides, we got in a session just now," she said.

"Only to make up for you using your Aura on your friends. Master H informed me of your outburst this morning."

Liana bowed her head shamefully.

"You must keep up your studies with Master Hayashi. If you are unprepared to receive your Spirit Orbs, we don't know what could happen."

"You mean, I could be uncontrollably destructive and go on a killing rampage."

Queen Adriya smirked before replying: "Oh no, that's far too optimistic, you could blow apart our world into billions of tiny pieces." The mother and daughter let out a unified giggle at the queen's joke.

"Just how dangerous is it out there?" Liana's laugh turned to sincere concern. "Is it more dangerous than what Zagan and Vivek did here?" She physically shuddered at the memory of trusting the old clerk for her whole life, before he turned on her and the monarchy for access to her powers. If only she'd been able to put an end to him for good, she thought.

"It's that bad that your mother, your real mother, Candela," Queen Adriya paused, "I'll never get used to that," she thought aloud, before continuing, "is said to be making her way to Allicalidantè herself."

"Has she found her Artifact? The Mask of Indigo?"

"Her most recent Jackdaw didn't say, but it seems the threat in Allicalidantè is the priority now."

Liana didn't respond. She knew inside that if Candela was returning from her hunt for the Mask of Indigo Artifact, something serious must be happening in Allicalidantè, and that's exactly where her friends were heading.

"I'd best make my way down to see them off, are you coming?"

Liana shook her head. "I don't think so. I'm probably the last person they want to see before they set sail. I'll watch from up here."

Queen Adriya lifted the front of her red dress to stop it dragging on the ground as she made her way across the clifftop grass and down several flights of wooden steps that sat against the cliff-face towards the harbourside. Liana watched her mother the whole way, as the throng of fishermen and merchants parted and bowed before her.

A flash of red light emanating from a side alley between a row of warehouses that lined the quay suddenly caught Liana's attention. The flash was unmistakably that of an Aura Screen. Of course, it wasn't as bright, wide or intense as Liana's, but someone was using their Aura powers. Soon, another flash, and then another. Both Master H and Priestess Yi taught their students, no matter how old they were, that you must only use your Aura powers as a last resort in public, for example if your life was in danger. This was to prevent division between practitioners of the Aurora Visendus and those who either could not achieve their Root Core, or who chose not to practise the religion. So far, since the religion's resurgence after its two-hundred-year outlawing, Swyre had remained united. A few skirmishes had been known to break out, usually drink related, but all-in-all, the transition of migrating the religion into society had proven to be successful.

This smooth transition was in part due to having two religious leaders on the island. Priest Shiro Hayashi's methodical and traditional approach balanced out Priestess Yi Lang's impatient and forceful outlook. The Priestess was less than impressed when the Queen's Table voted Master H into its decision-making processes, but as Queen Adriya so clearly conveyed at one Queen's Table meeting, the choices were to either accept him as an additional member, or replace her. Afterall, in Visendi standing, he was a more senior figure to her since he was the Priest of a Founding Temple. The queen and the priestesses' relationship had always been frayed around the edges. The contrasting opinion of Master H on the running of the religion was greatly welcomed by Queen Adriya. Yes, it meant there were more disagreements around the Queen's Table than before and meetings seemed to almost always overrun, but the balance of opinion and personalities around the Table kept the notoriously peaceful island, peaceful.

The flashes of red continued, so Liana decided to go down and investigate. She kept an eye on the alleyway until the tall, stoney walls of the warehouses shielded the light. The buildings around the harbour were rare in the fact they weren't constructed of golden sandstone like the rest of the city but of quartzite, a material that was also readily available since both quartz and sandstone were native to the island. The choice of building materials was something to do with them being less corrosive against the salty air and water, Liana remembered, from one of her lessons with Vivek. Strange how someone whose intention to use her powers for evil also taught her so much, she thought.

She made her way toward the end of the alleyway, Cas in tow. Behind a stack of large wooden shipping crates stood a group of four boys, similar looking age to her. They were each showing off their Aura Screens to another younger boy who was watching on, mouth wide open, jaw-to-the-floor, like an anchor caught on the seabed. Children were quicker learners than adults. Their brains sucked in new information like a flower catches the rays of the sun, so it's no surprise that many of Swyre's children had already attained their Root Core and could produce their own Red Aura. However, the look of shock and awe on the youngest boy's face made it obvious he had never seen such powers before.

"What are you all up to?" Liana appeared from behind a stack of shipping crates, making the boys jump in shock as she asked the question.

"Yer majesty!" blurted the oldest-looking boy, who was wearing a red tunic. "We, we were just playing." he said, nervously, clearly afraid he would be reprimanded for his actions.

"It's okay," reassured Liana, "I still slip up every now and then." *'Only this morning, in fact,'* she thought to herself.

"Say… can you show us your Screen, yer Majesty? I've heard it's totally amazing!"

"You know we're not meant to use our Visendi powers outside of planned events and teachings," said Liana, thinking to herself how much of a hypocrite she was as she said it. The boy's shoulders dropped as they looked visibly disappointed with the rebuttal.

"It's just, we've not come across another kid, even another person, who has never seen an Aura before," said the boy in the red tunic, continuing to explain the group's actions. He pointed to the youngest boy, who had managed to up anchor his jaw off the floor.

"You've never seen an Aura before?" asked Liana, quizzically.

The boy shook his head. His shoulder length, matted brown hair stayed strangely in situ rather than the usual side-to-side swaying you'd expect with hair of such length. Looking at him, his hairs were probably stuck together with a copious amount of dirt, thought Liana.

"Then you can't be from around here, can you?"

The boy bowed his head and shook it again with a look of guilt on his face.

"How did you get here?"

The boy pointed to a vessel in the harbour which had the name 'King Shimon's Maiden II' carved into its wooden hull. The vessel wasn't nearly as grandeur as the RNC Ascendancy. In fact, there were fisherman's boats docked beside it which nearly matched it for size.

"You arrived on the King's escort vessel?" Liana continued to enquire.

The boy nodded.

"You don't look like you belong on a royal ship."

"Okay, lady, you got me! I'm a stowaway!" The boy's shy facade disappeared in an instant as he became animated and very talkative. "Look here, ship's only leave Allicalidantè a handful of times a year. Even less since Zagan stopped his secret side hustles of trading Quartaltium for men and women, and this was too good an opportunity to miss! Sailing right into the harbour of Swyre! Look at all this fresh food!"

"'Ere!" shouted one of the other boys, "This ain't no ordinary lady. This is the Princess, Princess Liana. You address her properly, you hear?"

"What, you expect me to be impressed? Royalty ain't worth nothin', especially where I'm from."

"You can't talk to 'er like that!"

"I'll talk to 'er how I want!"

"Apologise to her right now!"

"Got no reason to apologise!"

"Boys, boys, calm it down!" Liana interrupted before fists and feet went flying. "I understand it's not easy where you come from," she said, turning back to the boy from Allicalidantè, secretly hoping the boy could shed some light on what Allicalidantè was like, and why it was so dangerous.

"Not easy? Not easy! I ain't had nothing but boiled water to drink, fish leftovers and seaweed soup for months on end."

Liana looked at the boy's ripped and stained navy-blue shirt which also matched his trousers in both colour and dilapidation. She thought he probably wasn't lying about his less than palatable diet.

"Look, things are different here, that's all, and I get it. I don't mind if you don't know how to address me. If you want food, I'll go fetch you something, okay?"

"I don't need your charity, lady. I'll look after meself. 'Ave done all my life."

"Is that so?"

"Yeh, 'tis."

"So what, you're just going to stay here all alone, begging and scrounging off my citizens?"

"No, I got people at home who I care about. Said I had no food, not no friends."

"So you're going back to Allicalidantè then?"

"Yeh, figured I'd loot what I can here and take it home to my crew."

"And you can look after yourself, right?"

"Yup. 'Ave done the whole eleven years I been on this planet."

"Is that why the royal ships are sailing off without you, then?"

The boy turned around to the sight of King Shimon's Maiden II and RNC Ascendancy sailing off into the distance. His jaw weighed anchor, again, as the other boys fell about in hysterics behind him.

Liana laughed inwardly at the irony, but maintained a dignified exterior, before turning to the laughing boys rolling around in fits of laughter on the floor. "Don't know what you're laughing at," she said to them, "I'm leaving him in your charge now. He's going to have to bunk up with one of you for a while. Might be some time until another ship sets sail to Allicalidantè." The boys immediately stopped laughing and began arguing amongst themselves as to who was (or wasn't) going to bring this foreigner home with them.

"I didn't catch your name," she said to the forlorn looking Allicalidantè boy.

"Josef," he said. "But my crew calls me Seff."

"Well, Seff, looks like you'll be enjoying the sights of Coryàtès for a little while yet."

Liana, Seff and Cas watched on as the royal ships sailed out of sight over the faint line of the horizon.

"Bon Voyage, my friends," Liana whispered to herself.

6

THE GAME OF CHANTRAH

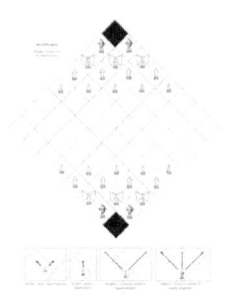

'I hold my hands out in front of me and push myself up from the sandy dunes but my hands don't feel the same. I instinctively move in the same way I've done all my life, but my whole body is numb. Pushing up from the ground without being able to feel my heart beating is… unnerving. I head towards the city and notice the difference in texture between the gritty grains of sand on the beach and the soft blades of grass in the forest. I notice a change in the air. The sea breeze against my cheeks is no longer there, but I don't know how I know. I cannot feel the change in temperature. I cannot feel moisture in the air. I have to find some answers.'

Benji slid a Shooter into Liana's half of the board as he edged closer to the target. With just one of each type of piece left on the board, the princess was already well on the back-foot. She rushed in and took the newly advanced piece with one of her Wingmen, but in doing so exposed a clear path for Benji's second shooter to advance into the target square and claim a third victory in a row.

"Argh!" she shouted, slamming the table with her fist,

knocking over a number of the game pieces. "Why do I always lose?" As soon as she heard the words come out of her mouth, she recalled the same five words being spoken in their mocking tone by Luci in the conservatory yesterday morning and immediately felt the anger rise at both herself and her doppelgänger.

"There's an art to the game, princess. You 'ave to think ahead and put yerself in the other player's shoes, try to work out what they're planning and what their next move might be. If ya don't have the natural skill, ya gotta observe. Watch yer opponents. Reflect on where ya go wrong each time ya play. Learn from experience, yer mistakes. You'll soon get the 'ang of it."

Benji's ageing but toned figure slumped back into the torn leathers of the tavern's corner seat, sipping his beverage. Stamped on the side of his tankard of ale read the establishment's name, Swyre's Rest. His cuffs were still stained with blood from another hard day's work chopping up pigs carcasses and glugged happily following another resounding victory.

Chantrah was played on a rotated square board, with one corner facing each player. The board was divided into squares of an 8x8 grid with four rows of different pieces. Shooters, Wingmen, Jumpers and Infantry. Shooters could move in any direction. Wingmen could move along the axis. Jumpers could move across one square in any direction and infantry could move one adjacent place. The closest square to each player was shaded. The aim of the game was to get one of your Shooters into the opponent's shaded square - the Target.

It is a game of tactics, with varying plays and strategies having been devised by the best players over the years. The traditional game had seen a sudden resurgence since the

Aurora Visendus had been decriminalised. The Visendi's Sacral Core teachings were based on joy, creative thinking and puzzle solving. This resulted in games, particularly those which challenged the mind, being popular amongst the Visendi to help boost their progress in attaining their Orange Aura's - the Sacral Core.

"It 'elps if ya can cut the cord on those little passengers jumping 'round in that mind o' yours!"

Liana raised a confused eyebrow.

"Even I'm feelin' weighed down by what's goin' on in that lil head. Ya can't be playin' a game about strategy unless you can put everythin' else to one side and really focus your thoughts on the game." He took another large swig of his drink, before setting it down and resetting the game pieces to their starting positions. "Let's go again!" he announced, but Liana folded her arms and looked away sour-faced. "How 'bout we play slightly differently this time?" Liana glanced sideways, intrigued at his proposition.

"Differently?"

"A variation of the game they used to play on Allicalidantè. I learned it in my years on the sea when the Island used to do business with them."

"Allicalidantè?"

"Tis called Speed Chantrah. Rather than the game bein' turn-based, it's played in real-time. Ya still move one piece at a time, but yer don't need to wait for yer opponent. Ya move onto the next move ya want to make. There's jus' one extra rule - yer can only touch your Shooters twice each. Each game is so quick, the winner is the first to win ten rounds."

"If the rounds are so quick, how do you know your opponent isn't cheating?"

"Ya nominate a Watcher who, unsurprisingly, watches yer

opponent to make sure they don't make any wrong moves. If they do, the round is called in favour of their opponent."

"Alright then. Let's choose our Watchers." Liana scanned the room looking for someone who she thought would make a good Watcher. The tavern was bustling with early evening business. Patrons, who had just finished work for the day, crowded around the horseshoe shaped bar that jutted out into the square room. Slanted squares of faded blue light stretched across the dark wooden floor as the low evening sun shone through the blue tinted Quartaltium glass windows that was synonymous with the island of Coryàtes. A few of the more well-off families that could afford to eat out sat at the tables which lined the walls enjoying their evening meals. A door beside the bar flew open as a waitress delivered a whole cooked chicken on a wooden slate to one of the families. The appetising aroma of cooking meat momentarily wafted through from the kitchen and delighted the princess's nose. As that door swung shut, taking the pleasant scent with it, the tavern's entrance swung open, and a jolly Agatha bounced into the tavern with a few of her colleagues.

"Agatha!" Liana shouted across the bustling noise of the tavern. The portly maid beamed at the princess and made her way to the far corner where she was sitting.

"Liana, what are you doing here? You don't normally venture out into the city these days."

"Benji suggested it, he says I've been cooped up within the castle grounds too long."

"She may need protectin', and people may be wary of 'er powers, but tis good for both her an' everyone else for her to be seen out an' aboot mingling."

"Well, you won't hear any arguments from me," Agatha smiled, her dimples pushing out her cheeks, and if Liana wasn't mistaken, cheeks that had turned a slight shade of red as she replied to Benji. Liana cleared her throat to end a small, but poignant, silence.

"Uh, Agatha, would you kindly be my Watcher?"

"Oh, Liana, I've watched over you your whole life!"

"No, it's a role in the game of Speed Chantrah."

"Speed Chantrah, I'm not sure I'm familiar with this variation on the game?"

Benji set out explaining the rule differences again. His and Agatha's eyes locked together for the whole time he was speaking, almost completely forgetting that Liana was even at the table with them.

"Sounds much more… lively," commented the maid after the explanation. After another short and, for Liana an awkward silence, the princess asked again if Agatha would be her Watcher.

"Of course, my dear! What about you, Benji? Who are you going to choose?"

Benji clicked his fingers and shouted to one of the two workers behind the bar. "Fetch me that new lad, will you?" The barkeep nodded in response to the request and headed into the kitchen. The smell of cooking meat drifted into the taverns front-of-house once more. A few moments later, the barkeep returned. Emerging from behind him, a familiar looking face appeared, his clothes covered in large patches of water.

"Josef?!"

The boy's shoulders slumped as he rolled his eyes.

"Ya know this boy?" Benji questioned.

"We met yesterday down at the harbour."

"Ah, so do ya know why I choose this lad ta be me Watcher then?"

"Yeh, he's from Allicalidantè. Probably knows the game."

"Who's 'he'? I'm standin' right here ya know. And yeh, I enjoy a game of Chantrah. Kind of have to, considering the circumstances."

"Circumstances?"

"Er, right, let's get on with this game, shall we?" interrupted Benji.

"Wait, I don't understa-"

"Focus, Liana! Remember what I said. Put everything else in that head of yours into its own little box. You gotta keep ya wits up in this game of speed!"

Liana huffed but took a moment to shut her eyes and take Benji's advice. She called on her knowledge of meditation to calm herself. She remembered the words of guidance that Candela taught her so she could enter the Realm of Morality and harness her ability of Sight. After a few moments, she controlled her breathing and blocked out any internal or external distractions that she could. She was ready.

"Okay, let's start."

Agatha and Seff sat across from each other on the two vacant sides of the table. Seff counted down from three and on the word 'Go!' Liana and Benji set about moving around their pieces. Agatha struggled to keep up with the pace. She admitted as such after the first round, after Benji wiped out Liana in just under fifteen seconds. The board was reset and the princess reassured Agatha, reminding her to just watch the movements of the pieces, not how the game was being played. Seff counted down for the beginning of round two and, again, Benji was victorious. Twenty seconds.

"A'ight, two nil to the big guy!" Seff joyfully bounced on his chair, going for a high five with his partner. Benji lifted a somewhat condescending eyebrow and inevitably left him hanging. "C'mon, show me some love," he pleaded.

"Are ya forgettin', lad, how I also wiped you out nine to one last night?" The boy recoiled in embarrassment into his seat.

"So how'd you two meet?" asked Liana.

"The boy 'ere was sneakin' round me shop, snoopin' for a chance to pocket some eggs. Caught him slippin' em into his pockets."

"That's just his way of taking care of himself," joked Liana, remembering their first encounter. "I thought the Turton brothers took you home with them?"

"They did. I didn't like it though, did I? So I left. Their old man tried to get me to stay but I told 'em I'm an independent lad who sets his own direction."

"And that direction has led you… here?"

Benji laughed as he finished resetting his pieces. "I did me usual when I catch a kid thieving. Instead o' scolding them, ask why they need it, how can I help, ya know." Liana nodded, knowingly. She might not have ever needed to steal, but she's certainly needed Benji's support once or twice when she's been in a fix. "Well, this clever lad thought he'd challenge me to a game of Speed Chantrah in exchange fer the eggs, so I made a deal with 'im. I lose, he keeps the eggs. He loses, he has to wash dishes in the tavern's kitchen, makeup fer his error of judgement."

"And here he is."

"And 'ere he is." laughed Benji and Liana. Even the kind natured Agatha couldn't hide a small chuckle at the kids expense.

"You know, he's only here because he missed his boat back.

The ship he stowed away on. We watched it sailing out of the harbour together," Liana said, adding insult to injury.

"Okay, enough!" said Seff, before muttering "I thought this city was s'posed to be welcoming..."

"Oh tis, boy!" Benji said, patting the boys back a couple of times, as if to reaffirm it was only a joke and there should be no hard feelings. 'Now, let's finish this game."

Benji won the next two rounds, but the victory time was growing. It took almost a minute for Benji to secure victory on the fifth round, before Liana saw through a defensive error and took the sixth round. She clenched her fist in excitement and let out a little shriek of joy at finally winning a round.

"Now yer seeing the game, ain't ya. Yer more aware of my pieces. Not just focussing on yer own agenda. Ya kept yer Target well protected forcin' me into a bad move," said Benji, complementing his opponent.

The seventh round was also awarded to Liana, after a call from Agatha that Benji moved an Infantry piece incorrectly, accidentally moving it like a Jumper.

"See, yer already doin' better than the boy," joked Benji. Liana suddenly realised she was feeling more relaxed. The adrenaline of moving in real-time heightened her senses and she had forgotten about all the things playing on her mind. She was enjoying herself. The ninth round was slightly delayed in starting, as Benji and Seff argued about a missed call. Benji thought Liana had moved an Infantry piece more than two places, but Seff didn't pick up on it. This distraction led to an easy victory for Liana.

"Five to Three," confirmed Agatha, who herself had become quite animated each time Liana won.

The Ninth round was the longest game so far. Rather than making immediate moves, both players reverted to a back-

and-forth tactical teasing of their opponent, waiting for each other to make their move. It wasn't quite as slow as traditional Chantrah, but eventually Liana had forced Benji into a situation where no matter which move he'd make, would leave an angle exposed and she claimed a fourth straight victory.

Agatha grabbed Liana's arm excitedly. "This one for the draw!"

She took a deep breath and moved out her Infantry in the same way she had done the last two games, but Benji must have predicted this and seen it coming, as he moved straight on the offensive, taking her first row of defence with his Wingmen and despite sacrificing a Shooter in the process, it left Liana exposed. With so many pieces already off the board, she was soon defeated, six to four.

The butcher breathed a sigh of relief. "'Twas a great game! I think yer getting the hang of this. I need another ale after that match!"

"Congratulations," said Agatha. "I'll go get the winner his liquid prize."

"And s'pose I'd better get back t' the kitchen before that chef has a go at me. I thought things were tough in Allicalidantè, but jeez, she's a real toughen." Seff disappeared, complaining as he slumped back to the kitchen.

"So," started Benji, his tone taking a more serious turn. "You heard back from yer real mother yet?"

Liana shook her head. "You'd probably know before I would."

"Wonder what's takin' her so long. I thought she were going to Allicalidantè with the rest of 'em."

"She wasn't at the docks yesterday. Guess she's gotten distracted. Visiting each Founding Temple in search of the other Spectra Children and Artefacts will take time."

"Aye, suppose ya right. Ya know, the Ascendancy should arrive in Allicalidantè in the middle of t'night. This time next week, you might be sat back 'ere with the Jewels of Orange gracing yer hand if all goes to plan. From what Candela said before she left, it sounds like a real fine handpiece."

"Yes, so I've heard. Let's just hope the handpiece is still paired with the Orange Spectra Orb and the two haven't become separated like the Dagger of Red and my Red Spectra Orb did."

"Well, let's 'ope that old man Vivek ain't involved again, 'ey?"

"Hmm," Liana murmured doubtful. "We've no idea where he escaped to. He could already be in Allicalidantè for all we know."

"Wherever he went, you gave 'im such a beatin' I'm sure he's still recovering." Benji said, straightening himself up as Agatha returned from the bar and placed a fresh tankard of ale in front him. Liana huffed despondently.

Agatha sensed a downturn in Liana's mood as she sat down and flicked Benji's arm with the back of her hand. "I leave you with her for two minutes and all of a sudden she has a face like one of your dead animals!"

Benji shifted awkwardly in his seat. Normally he wouldn't give two hoofs about someone else's opinion, but when it came to Agatha it clearly seemed to matter to him. "Aye, er, sorry," he apologised slightly unconvincingly. "Sorry fer raising the subject, princess. Whaddya say you two scrap out a game of Speed Chantrah, and I'll do me best to be a Watcher fer yer both, eh?"

7
ALLICALIDANTÈ

The RNC Ascendancy glided effortlessly through the choppy waters as the entourage of royalty neared the Allicalidantè shoreline. The same couldn't be said for the Maiden II as it bounced and lurched on the cambers the waves created.

In the midnight sky, the light from planet Mikana's trio of moons struggled to break through the cotton-like clouds. Thin streaks of silver, tekhelet and burnt yellow tentatively grazed the sea and created a shimmer of glinting flecks on its surface.

"Saff, wake up. We're almost there," said Joel shaking the shoulders of his friend as she lay asleep in one of the cramped crew cabins. Saffina groaned and pulled the thin blanket over her head. Since none of them were used to being aboard a ship long enough to have to sleep on one, it had taken her most of the night to drift into some kind of decent slumber.

"I said wake up!" Joel repeated. "Hurry up and get dressed, we're about to dock."

"How are you not tired?" she replied, with another groan of complaint.

"You know me, I can sleep anywhere, now get yourself sorted and I'll meet you on the deck." The wooden door creaked as Joel closed it behind him.

'The whole of this ship creaks,' Saffina thought to herself. *'How did Benji spend so many years at sea? How did he sleep with all this bobbing and noise?'* She rubbed her eyes and struggled to push herself upright from the wooden framed bed. *'More creaks!'*

The occupants of the other bunk bed, which was within an arm's reach of Saffina's bunk, had already vacated. Joel had slept in the bunk above her. She slid out a small, flat, wooden chest from underneath her cot and unlatched it. A navy-blue dress, lined with decorative silver threads in the shapes of tulips, lay neatly folded. She rubbed the fine cloth between her thumbs and forefingers as she admired its beauty, scarcely believing she was about to wear such a beautiful garment. Despite the fact one of her best friends was heir to the Coryàtès throne, Queen Adriya had always been consistent (and insistent, for that matter) that no friend of Liana's would be gifted anything for the sake of it. That stance hadn't changed despite all their years of friendship, and even after the events related to the Dagger of Red and Zagan's Army of Immorals. The only exception was the receipt to her and Joel of retired (but still incredibly athletic) horses from the Swyre Army and even then, Liana had to persuade, beg and grovel to her mother not to send them instead to general auction. Since Saffina's parents could only afford modest commodities, handling such fine embroidery was a rare opportunity for her. She couldn't understand why Liana spent most of her time wandering around in black shirts and grey trousers when she had such refined options at her disposal, until she realised the princess probably didn't want to laud her wealth around at risk of making her friends jealous and others envious of her position.

Saffina felt a sudden twinge of regret at how they had parted, and the role she played in the incident in the conservatory. How they had made fun of Liana, and how isolated it must have made her feel. She found herself wishing how she should have apologised before leaving, but Saffina being Saffina, she had been too stubborn.

Forcing herself to shake these thoughts from her head, she changed into the elegant dress and made her way up the open tread stairs to the deck, being sure to lift the hem to prevent it from dragging on the floor and risk catching it on a loose nail or splinter.

She chuckled to herself as she spotted Joel dressed in his finery. She couldn't recall a time seeing him look so sophisticated. The charming swallowtail jacket and matching waistcoat, coloured in the same navy blue as her dress, almost made him look dashing and handsome, she thought. The shape and colour of his attire suited his curly blonde hair and matched his light blue eyes. It even made his scrawny figure look a bit more stocky. *'Or perhaps he is getting bulkier with all the Visendi training we've been doing?'* Saffina wondered, before an elbow nudged her arm and distracted her from her thoughts.

"So, how was your beauty sleep?" Luci said, cheerfully.

"Had better," Saffina replied, honestly.

"Well, I slept like a dream. In fact, if I had a dream about sleeping, it probably still wouldn't have been as good. My bed on this ship was five times more comfortable than what I got to sleep on at the vineyard. It's amazing how royalty lives, isn't it?"

Saffina raised her eyebrows and nodded with sarcasm as

the fake princess strutted over beside Sir Tarak who was on the other side of the deck.

"She looks happy," said Joel who had crept up next to her.

"Wouldn't you be, if you got to sleep in the royal cabin?" the folded arms and retention of one raised eyebrow suggesting more than just a hint of jealousy.

"Here," said Joel, handing over a brush, somewhat tentatively. "No offence, but I think you need to use this before we meet the royalty of Allicalidantè."

Saffina paused, first staring at the brush and then at Joel. If it had been anyone else, she may well have taken offence, but she knew he was just trying to help. He was always trying to help, well, most of the time anyway. She took the brush. In the slight moment their hands touched as it passed over, she felt a slight flutter flap inside her chest, like a butterfly emerging from its cocoon for the first time. She pursed her dry lips as she fought to brush out the natural tangle of curls of her hair.

"Looking good," said Joel, admiring the wavy locks as they gently fell against Saffina's dark skin, the complement making her blush slightly.

Suddenly, a blanket of darkness draped over the vessel replacing the winsome gradients of moonlight ambiance with a cautionary blindness. The pair moved assumingly in the darkness towards Luci and Sir Tarak, trying not to trip over any barrels and crates.

"What's going on?" Joel asked Sir Tarak.

"We've entered a narrow canyon. The cliffs on either side are so tall they block out what little moonlight exists."

The ship's crew scrambled to light any unlit lanterns as they struggled to see the escort vessel ahead of them, not wanting to inadvertently shunt their stern. The warm, flickering glow of lantern flames grew brighter. The scale of their surroundings quickly became apparent. Columnar rock formations stood so high, if ten ships the height of the RNC Ascendancy were stacked together, there would still be room to spare. The layers of columned rock folded over each other like the ruffles on a maids apron.

"It's magnificent," commented Saffina, eyes wide in awe at the grand landscape bearing over them.

"It's unnerving," stated Joel, with much trepidation in his voice.

"I share your analysis, lad," agreed Sir Tarak, twirling in circles as he gazed upwards trying, in vain, to see the top of the cliffs. "A single ship containing royalty, tall cliffs, the cover of darkness. The perfect formula for an ambush," he said with a lowered voice. The darkened surroundings came coupled with a quiet acoustic. The ship continued on slowly through the canyon 10, maybe 15, ship lengths more. "There's something very discomforting about this place."

"Do you think we're going to be attacked?" Saffina asked, hugging her bare arms as the air around them began to chill.

"No, if they were to ambush us, I think they would have done so already," Sir Tarak shook his head, although not very convincingly, Saffina thought. "It's something else though. Can't you feel it? That strangeness?"

A long, high-pitched whistle of wind blew through the air, penetrating any gaps in the ships wooden construction it could find creating an interlacing of cold drafts. The sounds made Joel jump like a frightened cat, causing him to fall towards Saffina, knocking them both over.

"Jeez, Joel!" screamed Saffina, holding the back of her head. The shout of pain echoed and bounced back and forth several times between the canyon walls.

Joel grabbed his right buttock and writhed in pain on the

deck. The tough bristles of the hairbrush had pricked him, leaving several small red indentations on his skin.

"I hate these posh clothes," he complained, still holding his butt cheek. "They might look nice but they're damned thin!"

Forgetting about the small bump on her head, Saffina couldn't help but laugh at the scene before her. It wasn't long before Joel joined in as the initial shock of pain faded away. In fact, the incident seemed to relax the rest of the crew who were all having a good chuckle at Joel clutching his behind and the echoes of 'Jeez, Joel!' resounding out around them.

The easing amongst the crew didn't last long. As they helped the pair back to their feet, an ominous chant reverberated around them.

"A-lli-calidantè! A-lli-calidantè! A-lli-calidantè!"

A few glints from metallic armour and arrow heads sparkled in random places along the cliff faces. The echo chamber of the canyon made it difficult to tell exactly how many soldiers were chanting their city's name, but nonetheless, it made for an intimidating welcome.

The RNC Ascendancy passed through an orange shimmer of light as the canyon opened out. The layered rocks, still as high as the narrow entrance, spread outwards and formed a large, square-shaped recess from the ground above. In front of them, stone buildings had been packed into the crater-like area and were arranged disorderly in various levels and mezzanines. Built onto, and partly into, the back wall of the crater was a more imposing structure. It didn't take a genius to realise that it was the palatial home of King Shimon. The statue of a figure sitting on a throne, presumably of King Shimon himself, was carved into the cliff face. Bulbous domes sat upon four towers, in pairs either side of the sitting statue.

Several arched windows lined the wide building that connected the towers.

Joel and Saffina's view of the stone palace though was partially obstructed. A large, black cuboid pillar sat imperiously in the centre of the ramshackle city. From the pinnacle of the pillar, a steady stream of Orange Aura flowed directly upwards before fading out of sight.

"Well, I think we might have found Liana's Spirit," joked Joel nervously.

Saffina nodded, "Yeh, but why do I get the impression it's not going to be as easy as just walking up to that thing and asking for it?"

8

GUARDIAN OF LIGHT

Finally, I've made it to the city. The forest trees have been replaced with scattered stone buildings of the vineyard farms. I reach out and touch the first wall I come to, a low wall flanking a wooden gateway to one of the farmhouses. I should not be able to hold my hand against the wall for more than ten seconds before having to remove it because of the sun-soaked heat it should be harbouring, but I leave my hand there, resting my palm flat against it for well past a minute, and feeling nothing. "Hello!" I shout to a woman working in the field behind the wall, but they ignore me, or perhaps they did not hear my shout. "Hello!" I shout again, as two children come running out of the gate, but they run across my path acting like they have not seen me. I walk up to a small crowd of merchants picking out cases of wine from the vineyards stall. I walk up to one of the old men. "Hello?" I look him straight in the eye as I say it. If he knows I am here, he does not show it, not in his eyes or any of the muscles in his face. He simply proceeds to pay the woman behind the stall and sets off on his way. I *wave my hand in front of the woman's face. She does not blink. These people cannot see me, I realise. I flinch, as two other men start fighting over the last case of white wine. I instinctively jolt my head away and stumble to avoid being caught by a flailing arm, and in doing so, collide with the woman behind the stall. Except, this collision is different. Our skin and bones do not touch one another. The coming together does not force her to fall or catch herself, no, instead I pass right through her. A collision of our essences. "Oh!" she exclaimed, "I just got a sudden chill down my spine. Someone must've walked over my grave!" She rubbed her arms, hugging herself, before berating the two jostling men.*

After taking a few moments to gather my thoughts at this new development I realise what I must do next. I must find our saviour.

It does not take me too long to reach Castle Langton, but by the time I do, the sky is dark. I pass through the rooms and hallways of the castle, observing the strengths of Morality in all those around me. As the hubbub of servants carrying out their duties are beginning to wind down, I think to myself about the fact that no one knows I am watching them go about their daily business. I'm sure if they knew, they would be bothered by the intrusion of privacy.

After a few wrong turns and a dead-end here and there, I eventually find Liana's room.

She looks so peaceful, but I can only imagine the turmoil going on in her mind. I need to find a way to get her attention, but I don't want to scare her. I need to speak with her, not fight her. Or maybe I should just follow her? Wait patiently until she uses her ability of Sight?

But wait, what's happening? Is that her spirit falling into her body? Can she willingly separate her body and spirit? If she can, then surely she can help reunite me with my physical self?

I stand frozen to this spot. She's looking at me. Staring at me in confusion. She looks terrified. She surely can't be afraid of me, she has already beaten me once, when I... when I wasn't myself. I must stay close to her.'

~

'**M**y eyelids feel like they have an anvil weighing them down. I feel drowsy, but not like I've barely been asleep, more the opposite, like I've been asleep for too long. Like I've become so used to being asleep my body wants to do nothing else. I force myself to blink, slowly at first. In my upper arms and lower back, an aching numbness comes into my conscious thoughts. Now, a pounding throb in my forehead rises to the top of the list of painful ailments. It seems to use every ounce of effort to even move my joints. My knees creak as I stretch out my legs.*

I manage to sit up and slide myself around so that my feet dangle off the side of my bed. I roll my head, stretching my neck muscles. My eyes finally start to focus on their bland surroundings. The black and white walls of a tiny stone room. A room that isn't mine. A room that's not even in Castle Langton.

In my head, I want to move towards the door opposite my bed but instead I stand beside my cot and look out of a small, barred window. That's when I realise, it's not even me controlling this body. I'm just a passenger. I've had this same, powerless feeling before, when I regressed to being a babe, watching myself have my Aura's stripped from me in the Tomb of the Transcended. But this isn't an early childhood memory. The pair of hands of the body that I'm riding grasp the window's metal bars. To my surprise, the hands in front of me aren't even female. No, they are that of a man, but the wrinkled digits are engulfed in a flickering black flame. I knew at this moment that this figure had been here in this small room for a time longer than I could imagine.

Beyond the bars lay sweeping, rolling dunes of black sand. In just this line of sight I see four huge tornadoes of the black sand swirling high into the dark sky. Wind whistled around the small room and through the tiny window. Waves of sand blow in, the particles disintegrating as they touch the flickering black flames of this body.

I feel scared. Fearful of the place I find myself in. Fearful of the body I am a part of. Fearful of what this all means. The fear becomes more intense when the body speaks.

"Finally, it is time," the voice said in a low-toned rasp. Coarse, like the particles of sand had corroded it over the time this body had been here. "I feel you inside me. Your Spirit gives me the power to finally escape this damnation. I will see you soon, Guardian of Light."

Now he's laughing. A cackle of terrifying laughter. He lets go of the bars and holds his hands up in front of him, staring at his palms. They start to dissolve into a black dust, as if he were being cremated. His laughter grows louder, more ominous, as the rest of his body breaks down and surfs on the waves of the blowing sand back out of the barred window.

What if I dissolve with him? I have to get out of here! Think, Liana, think. Concentrate on your body. Your body back in your room at Castle Langton. Think of how you move between Realms using your ability of Sight. Quickly! The figure is now limbness, just a head and torso floating in the air. You must relax, Liana! Think of where you really are. Concentrate...

A flash of light. A ringing in my ears. Cold air brushes my cheeks. A sinking in my stomach. I'm falling!

But not for long. My spirit returns to my body. I lie still for a moment before quickly opening my eyes to check my surroundings. I breathe a sigh of relief as they are surroundings of familiarity. A familiar looking figure stands across the room, but I soon drift back into my physical self.

Thank Aurora for returning me.'

"Liana!" shouted Agatha, bursting onto the room. "Liana, are you okay? You were shouting and screaming for someone to let you go!"

"It's okay, Agatha, I'm okay." Liana sat up, the colours of the room blended back into existence, and the colourless figure across the room faded out. She felt for the Dagger of Red under her pillow. It was still there. She let out a sigh of relief and brought her heavy breathing under control.

"Was it a bad dream, little one?"

"No, not exactly. I think I was in the Morality Realm."

"But you've not been able to use your Sight since the battle?"

"I don't think I did use it. I think I was taken there."

"Taken? By who? Who could do such a thing?"

"I-I don't know," Liana hesitated as she collected herself. She stared into the eyes of Agatha in a desperate plea for reassurance. "They were the form of darkness, like they were made from darkness itself. You know that sinking feeling in your stomach when you're scared? Like when you're looking over a cliff or about to head into a fight or confrontation? It was like that, but somehow a hundred times more powerful, and all over my body."

Liana could see the concern in Agatha's eyes, like the maid herself was in physical pain seeing how scared she was. She didn't want to burden Agatha with any more of her thoughts and feelings, although she was now shaking in terror and afraid of what she'd just experienced. A few teardrops rolled slowly down her cheeks.

"It's okay, child. I'm always here for you," Agatha wrapped her arms tightly around the princess and stroked her blue hair. "No matter what, Auntie Aggie will always be here to give you a hug."

Liana eventually released her grip. "Do you know where I can find the Priestess? I must confide in her."

'Because I think my powers have just been used to free something deeply evil...' she thought to herself.

9
PILLAR OF SANCTUARY

The entourage of servants and diplomats disembarked the RNC Ascendancy being careful not to slip on the wet wood of the gangplank that joined the ship to the dock. It had taken the captain a few back-and-forth attempts to suitably align the ship, such was the tightness of the port that they'd entered. It was no wonder the Maiden II was so small in comparison.

Not being fond of politics, Admiral Remi was insistent on remaining aboard her flagship vessel for the entirety of their stay and watched on as Luci and Sir Tarak headed the group down the gangplank. Despite her training and natural talent for acting, Luci felt a churn of nerves in her stomach as a wave of unpreparedness washed over her. Feelings of doubt, and the fear of being caught, seeded in her mind. Had she studied Liana enough? Was she a believable substitute? Did she remember all the etiquette royalty seemed to instinctively know, even if they were from different lands?

Nerves and anxiety were of course to be expected. Like a hunter coming face to face with its prey, the rush of adrenaline focussed the mind. First impressions were immediate and most important, especially if she were to be unquestionably convincing, but what made her more anxious than she should have been was the welcoming party, or rather, the lack of welcoming party - which unnerved her.

The arrival of an esteemed monarch from another land would usually be cause for an elaborate party with much fanfare and exhibition from the host land showing off either its culture and wealth, or a demonstration of its military might with some sort of parade, but as she and Sir Tarak stepped onto the pier all they could see were the sceptical looks of the port's grubby inhabitants. Fishermen and women lined the pier in front of them. Their rows of feet dangling over the edge as they held their poles hopeful of a catch. Beyond the pier, people went about their daily business carrying buckets of dirty water and half-empty crates, uninterested in the guests who had just docked. Lop-sided buildings stood precariously on the ground floor, whilst layers of wooden shelters had been built up above, joined by rickety bridges and scaffolding held together by dried seaweed. A narrow street directly in front of them made a gap between the buildings where the thin orange funnel of spiralling light from the city's (if you could call it a city) pillar projected upwards and disappeared into the night sky.

Luci leaned into Sir Tarak and whispered: "We were definitely invited, right?"

Sir Tarak confirmed with a mumble and a nod as he took in the surroundings, assessing the environment for potential threats, such was his role and his nature.

It wasn't long before the people who packed the narrow

street in front of them parted, or rather, were forcefully shoved to the side of the street to make way for a small group of Allicidantè's soldiers. The people were not backwards with coming forward at the soldiers behaviour, most of whom shouted profanities and made rude gestures in their direction, but the soldiers ploughed on through the crowd unperturbed. The middle two soldiers in a row of four stepped out of line, and a young man stepped forward from the human shield that surrounded him.

Luci's churn of nerves turned to flutters of infatuation. She looked up at the young man before her. He was no more than two years her senior, still a teenager. His shoulder-length black hair, perfectly parted in the middle and framed his light brown face. Thick, dark, eyebrows sat square above his pair of chestnut-coloured eyes, giving him an air of seriousness. Silver armour glistened under the teenagers red tunic.

"Sir Tarak Langton and Princess Liana Langton?" he asked, offering no apology for either the lateness or underwhelming welcome.

"Correct," said Sir Tarak, responding as directly as he'd been spoken to. "Prince Kendrix, I presume? Where is King Shimon?"

"I apologise on behalf of my father that he could not be here to greet you. A last-minute engagement needed his immediate attention. Follow me to the palace. We have your rooms prepared." Prince Kendrix turned his back on the entourage and resumed his place inside the human shield.

"Well, isn't he full of sunshine and rainbows?" Joel whispered to Saffina.

"As bouncy as throwing a rock into water," Saffina joked back, the pair snickering. Luci shot them a look that reminded

Saffina of the one Liana had given them in the conservatory a couple days earlier.

"What's her problem?"

"I think somebody likes our new acquaintance," replied Saffina, suggestively. "I mean, just look at him," she bit her bottom lip as she watched Prince Kendrix stride authoritatively away. Joel frowned, annoyed at Saffina's lust, before she realised what she was doing and straightened her dress. "Let's not get left behind," she said, stepping forward and changing the subject,

The entourage of Swyre royalty and attendants outnumbered their escort three-to-one and dovetailed behind Prince Kendrix and his small group of personal guards. They weaved their way through the narrow, crooked streets. Above their heads, the bridges which joined the layers of buildings creaked in a breeze that was so sedate, it was barely noticeable even on bare skin. Around them, inhabitants gazed down from balconies. Wet rags they used for clothes dried slowly, draped over any suitable wall or railing. There was not a single smiling face among them, possibly because of the raw, foul smell that attacked the noses of anyone in the crater-like city. The contents of the gutters that lined the crooked streets evidence of a lack of a sewage system.

Soon, the convoy neared the centre of the city and the narrow, foul-smelling streets opened out to a much wider, cobblestone road.

Outside one of the buildings which lined this wider street was a carpenter's shop. Outside the shop, wooden stands supported several toy-like objects. There were boxes of various sizes, shapes, and configurations as well as boards for playing Chantrah, tubes with wooden balls inside and puzzles and brainteasers. It was the only remotely appealing place they'd passed on their journey.

Emerging from the shop doorway, a large woman waded out. Poking out from underneath her black flat cap, dirty ginger bangs curled down either side of her face. She wore a ripped, dark blue waistcoat which didn't match the brown, long sleeved blouse. The woman held her arms folded, but in her left hand she held a carpenter's mallet, suggesting she worked in the shop.

Saffina and Joel shared a disconcerting look with one another as they passed the heavyset woman. Her stern look, firm stance and defensive body language gave them a chill.

They soon passed by, and came to a wall which stood as tall as Joel. The wall seemed to have been constructed as a border and framed the cube-shaped pillar.

"Prince Kendrix," Luci tried to get the prince's attention. "Prince Kendrix," she repeated louder. "Prince Kendrix!" she shouted for a third time, which resulted in the square formation of personal guards coming to a halt.

"Yes, Princess Liana?" came the prince's voice from within his protection.

"What is that building?"

"Nothing to be afraid of."

"I'm not afraid of it," snapped Luci. Sir Tarak nudged his elbow into her arm to remind her of the role she was playing. "I mean, I'm more curious. What is that orange light coming out of it?"

"We call this the Pillar of Sanctuary, but I'd rather you didn't concern yourself with our landmarks or sightseeing. Whilst you are in Allicalidantè your time will be spent inside the palace where it is safe."

"Safe, safe from what?" Saffina interjected. Sir Tarak glared at Saffina for her outburst and there was a brief pause whilst the prince considered his answer.

"Do you often allow your servants to speak for you, Princess Liana?"

"Saffina's not a servant, she's a friend. My apologies, she won't speak out of turn again. She's not used to being part of royal engagements. They are so rare, and the voyage was long, I thought I could use the companionship," Luci said, thinking quickly to try and remedy the situation before their plan had imploded before it had even begun.

"Not to worry. I suppose engagements of these sorts are rare." Inwardly, Sir Tarak breathed a sigh of relief. Luci handled the situation well, he thought. Hopefully a sign of this all going smoothly.

"But we must get moving. As you said, you've had a long journey and I'm sure you'd like to settle into your new surroundings." Prince Kendrix's guards hadn't broken formation for the whole conversation and the guards soon marched on.

Joel leaned into Saffina and whispered: "I bet that's how Master H feels when he's trying to teach us something, like he's talking to the back of our heads behind a human shield."

"Only when I'm talking to you," said Master H, as he bopped Joel on the side of the head with his staff, whilst mimicking a hollow-wood sound with his mouth as he did. Saffina giggled as Joel frowned again and rubbed his head.

"So, do you think that's it, Master H? Do you think that's the temple with Lianas' Spectra Orb and the Jewels of Orange?" asked Joel.

Master H, who was attending the negotiations under the guise of Sir Tarak's clerk, stroked his grey handlebar moustache as he always did when he was deep in thought. He pulled Saffina and Joel out of the entourage formation to get a closer look. The Master and his pupils stood staring up at the black glossy-surfaced cube from the perimeter edge of the wall. Finally, the Old Priest answered Joel's question: "It definitely has something to do with the Aurora Visendus. Do you see Aurora's Eye at the top on each of its sides?" Aurora's Eye, the religious symbol which consisted of two curves and a circle forming an eye shape, was indeed etched into the obelisks' surface.

"What about the Orange Aura it's casting?" asked Saffina. "You don't think that's Liana's Spirit, do you? What is it being used for?"

Master H shook his head. "Unfortunately, I don't have an answer to any of those questions." He stroked his moustache a few more times before continuing. "An Orange Aura - the Sacral Core - is achieved through joy, creativity, fun…" he paused and did a full circle on the spot, holding out his arms as he did so, forcing Joel and Saffina to duck to avoid being hit. "But do you see any of that here? If this is the homeland of the Neoteric Temple, this place should be full of children playing games, goldsmiths forging jewellery, author's writing riddles. There should be laughter, joy, people having fun together. That's the meaning of the Sacral Core, but this couldn't be further from those ideals." Master H. let out a long sigh. The past six months had been the best moments of his life, watching the Aurora Visendus grow on Coryàtès once more, imparting his knowledge and teachings onto thousands of eager students, the feeling of hope he kept for Liana's mission. Seeing the state of this founding temple and the city in which it lay, knowing that at one time it must have been such a vital part of it, only made him realise how much of a challenge it would be to restore Liana's Spectrum.

"What do we do now?" Saffina enquired.

"We must be patient. Find out what we can without alerting any authorities. It's clear the Prince doesn't want to divulge much information, which usually means they are either hiding something, or do not trust us."

10

THE BOOK OF H'WA

'I look down at myself and wonder what Morality I am. The brightness of my hands, my torso and my legs would indicate I am of Good Morality. But not so long ago I used to be Immoral, albeit through no choice of my own, poisoned and manipulated by Vivek for his own immoral schemes, but Immoral, nonetheless. What had happened for me to suddenly change back to my natural state?

A question to be answered another time, for right now, I do not care. I stand in this newly built temple in the shape of one of our most celebrated symbols, the tulip, watching her with awe. She is a sponge for knowledge. Her thirst for learning our ways is remarkable, and necessary, if she is to be our Guardian of Light and Restorer of the Spectrum.'

Despite her recent spectral experience, Liana bounced around the second floor of the Tulip Temple from one area to another, trying her hands at the different disciplines.

The Sacral floor was separated into a number of different sections around its edge, all to inspire a person's creativity.

There was a craft area with workbenches and drawers full of jewellery making nik-naks like leather ropes, clasps, and an array of colourful beads and pendants. Another area contained large water buckets for dying materials and lessons on sewing were taught to turn the creations into clothing suitable for harnessing armour plating. A thick layer of sawdust covered the woodworking area where lathes were spinning, and chisels were knocking. The most noise could be heard from the smithing section, where followers were encouraged to create their own moulds for forging new weapons. The sound of metal-on-metal hammering echoed around the large, open plan room, much to the annoyance of two sets of players who were trying to concentrate on their games of Chantrah. The players were situated in an area which contained a number of tables and chairs with shelves full of various other board games.

It was the first time Liana had been onto this floor of the Tulip Temple. Since she wasn't enrolled into the Tulip Clan, she had no need to visit it. All of her training, facilitated by Master H, was conducted in the founding temple of the Red Aura, the Shrouded Temple of Roots. As such, she, along with Saffina and Joel, were Shroud Clan members.

There had been conversation of organising an inter-Coryàtes tournament between the two clans, but other priorities always seemed to take precedence. Benji and Sir Tarak were both in agreement that a new annual tournament would be a perfect distraction from recent events which could galvanise the city, but the other members of the Queen's Table were focussed on more serious matters, such as the plan to get Liana's next Spectra Orb. Designing a new tournament now would take too much time - time which they did not have - they said. Master H and Priestess Yi also noted that none of their worshipers had achieved their Orange Sacral Aura's yet and so the games would have little versatility.

Only those who had been part of the small, underground rebellious faction led by Priestess Yi had attained more than just their Red Aura. These were people who had continued practising Visendi teachings throughout its 200-year prohibition, but this also meant they would also be the ones who have to officiate and judge on the tournament if it were to go ahead. The members of the old rebellious faction were also the ones who helped around the Tulip Temple. They held Visendi classes, looked after the gardens and did housekeeping, to name but a few of their tasks. It was a far cry from having to practise and learn from Priestess Yi in an old smugglers cave in the far south-western corner of the island.

"Waylon, how many times have I told you? Pull the shutters when there are people smithing and woodworking!" ordered Priestess Yi, who walked into the room, carefully hugging a thick, antique book.

"S-sorry, Ma'am," said Waylon, bowing his head and slinking away. The bottom of his black, gold-trimmed robe teased the floor as it flicked up and down behind him. He went and spoke to another, shorter man with unkempt shoulder-length hair. After a short conversation, the pair of helpers each unlatched a twelve-foot-long pole which were attached to the far wall by a series of horseshoe-shaped hooks which only sprung open with a bit of brute force. Screwed into the top of the poles was a hook. Both men walked gingerly along a circular line that was marked out along the floor, before reaching up with the poles and using the hook to grab onto a ring in the ceiling. Waylon pulled on the ring above him, and a wooden partition concertinaed down, creating a wall in front of the smithing area. The men moved around each of the areas and repeated the process, bringing down the large partitions. It didn't completely eradicate the smithing noises, but it certainly dulled their effects.

"Thank you, Waylon. You may leave us now." Priestess Yi waved her hand, gesturing the man away. She guided Liana to the sixth area in the room, opening a door in the newly formed wall in front of them. "Every floor, no matter what its Core teaching is, has an area dedicated for meditating to Aurora."

Liana hadn't even noticed this space whilst she'd been jumping from one space to the next. In this area, a three-dimensional rainbow of tulips had been planted in a flowerbed. Sunlight from the long, high windows above shone brightly over the feature. Around the flowerbed, cushions lay for followers to sit and meditate. Underneath the rainbow, a gentle trickle of water spouted from a self-contained fountain. From personal experience, Liana had found that the gentle flow of water in the Shrouded Temple of Roots often helped her concentrate and relax into a meditative state. Somehow in this room, the sounds of the crafts elsewhere on the floor could not be heard.

Liana and the Priestess sat down on a pair of orange cushions next to each other, crossed legged, with their toes raised to their thighs in a meditative pose.

Priestess Yi gently released the book she was clasping from her bosom and placed it, open, in her lap. "Let's begin the process," she instructed as both teacher and pupil rested their palms on their knees. "Breathe, feel each breath you take. In and out. In and out. Inhaling deeper and releasing longer each cycle. Notice your breath. Feel the air travel through your body. Focus on nothing but my words and your breathing. Recognise when your thoughts wander and return yourself to the cycle. Feel the muscles in your shoulders and arms relax.

Let your legs become loose with calmness. In. Out. In. Out." The pair sat with stillness for the next fifteen minutes, focussing on their technique. Calming their minds.

The Priestess spoke in the softest of tones to break the silence. "Keep your mind focussed on your breathing and the words I speak. Keep the beating of your heart under control as I read from the book of H'WA - the Histories and Wisdom's of Aurora. This is the only H'WA I believe to still exist. A family heirloom. Many of my ancestors died whilst trying to conceal and protect it from the book burnings that followed the Aura Wars. It is the most important artefact in existence for the Aurora Visendus and up until now, only I know about it. That was, until your mother, Candela, and the other Spectra Children rose from their tombs. But now, it's time you are taught from its writings.

I will read to you now the first attestation from the sacred scripture. This text describes the formation of life on our planet, Mikana."

11
THE MIKANAN ARTEFACTS

"This planet is just one of many, but it is one of a few that is suitable to breed life. Let us call it Mikana - the planet of possibilities. Our lives will not go on forever, so to ensure our continued existence, we must find a path to impart ourselves onto a new world so it thrives in our absence. Yes, living creatures have been around for all eternity alongside us, but they lack our essence. They live only to survive. When they need to eat, they kill. When they are tired, they sleep. When they are thirsty, they find water. Decisions that aren't really decisions. We are the only ones with the essence to seek more. An essence which can laugh. An essence which can create. An essence which seeks the new. But this essence is beginning to fade. For all that we are great at, we suffer with the inability to rebirth ourselves. Plants spread their pollen. Animals take mates. We can do neither, but the latest discovery may change that. A rebirth that will span over millennia. If I can sew myself to the essence of these primates that roam Mikana, there may be hope for our survival. A different form of existing, but still existing.

The primates are a curious animal that seem to have much potential. If we can harness this link, we may stand a chance of survival. We will not be the same essence, but it is survival, nonetheless.

I remember when I said my goodbyes to my siblings before we spread ourselves among the stars and systems to search for suitable worlds. It was of course a dreadfully sad moment, but a necessary one if our species were to survive. We agreed on the portions of the dark sky above that each of us would scout, and we could only hope that just one of them could provide for our future and succeed in carrying on our existence. We knew that moment of farewell would likely be the last we saw of each other.

This is how I came to be here on this planet. I found this world of many living creatures and observed each of its kind for suitability. One of the species in particular stood out. These four-limbed creatures crafted basic tools to aid them instead of relying solely on their own natural form. So, I set about putting into action my plan for bonding my spirits with this world's primitive primates.

I watched these primates evolve over hundreds of years. As they evolved, the bond between their physical being and my spiritual essence grew in strength. The only thing that prevented me from completely integrating my spirits with them was their continued animalistic instincts. They were still so focussed on their basic needs that the growth of their emotional intelligence was painfully slow.

Then came the day when my work was interrupted by Tenebris, one of my more rebellious brothers. The portion of the dark sky he had chosen to experiment with had already succumbed to devastation and extinction, and he wanted a second chance. He of course saw the potential my world had to offer, but I would not simply sit back and watch him ruin my years of careful design.

And so, we fought for power over Mikana. A power struggle which caused a 500-year ice age as Tenebris did all that he could to make me hand over this planet to him. He thought by making it as unsuitable for habitation as possible that I would up and leave, but I had worked too hard. It was an era that almost killed off all of the beings I had helped grow and evolve.

I eventually defeated my brother, if you can call it a victory, for I could not kill my brother. I was simply not strong enough, and neither was he since our essences were slowly dying. Instead, I opted for the next best alternative. I almost completely exhausted my White Spirit - a spirit not gifted to all of my kind - and I created a mirror of this world. A place I called the Morality Realm. A world where Mikanan's could evolve their emotional intelligence from within. But this new realm was also a domain under my control, where I could banish and imprison my brother.

Tenebris possessed the rare opposite of my White Spirit, a Black Spirit. We are the opposites in how we approach our existence, and I know the cage I have created for him won't last forever.

After he was brought under control, I quickly set about thawing this world. To fit in, I took on the appearance of the Mikanan's and imparted the knowledge of each of my spirits onto them.

I witnessed them develop colourful Aura's around their physical selves as they soaked up the learning of each of my spirits.

During my last days of existence, I thought back on my mission, and knew I had done all I could to succeed.

But I knew the threat Tenebris still posed, so I planted the single atom of White Spirit I had left in me into one of the Mikanan's for it to seed and grow so that over time, through their own evolution and experiences, my White Spirit would be truly powerful once again.

When this time comes, the Mikanan who is bearer of my White Spirit at its fullest potential shall be known as the Guardian of Light, and it will be their responsibility to end Tenebris's threat once, and for all.

Should Tenebris break from his cell before the Guardian of Light emerges, I have created six artefacts to help the Miakanan's fight him. These artefacts have been given to each of those who show the most potential in each of my spirits. These artefacts are specially infused with my essence. The Dagger of Red - a blade sharp enough to cut through any substance. The Jewels of Orange - a handpiece that can craft whatever you are holding, into whatever you imagine. The Scriptures of Yellow give the bearer the ability to be the greatest of leaders, one who anyone would follow. The Elixir of Green - when digested can heal the most horrific of injuries. The Quill of Blue - to make even the most stubborn enemy talk the truth. And finally, the Mask of Indigo - the ability to move unnoticed in the shadows, as a shadow.

I instructed these chosen Mikanan's to take their artefacts and scatter around this world to form special places of worship. These Founding Temples served not only to spread the word of my spirits, but to also provide protection in their lands by using these artefacts if they ever needed to fend off the threat of my brother.

Let these words I write now, before I cease to exist, be

countlessly rewritten as verbatim and to be read and known throughout all of my teachings. All Mikanan's should know the threat that still exists from the realm I created - the Realm of Morality."

The Priestess stopped reading from the book of H'WA and closed it delicately. The pair sat and meditated in silence for another hour, allowing Liana to absorb the words of Aurora.

12
THE MERCENARY RETURNS

Waylon slinked toward the meditative chamber; his head bowed as his bare feet padded along the wooden floor silently. He wrapped each of his long, skeletal fingers in succession around the doorknob and gently twisted. He placed the palm of his other hand flat against the door and nudged it open to a crack just wide enough for his lanky body to squeeze through and enter the room.

He observed the priestess and the princess sitting in their restful poses. So restful, that their chests barely rose and fell as they breathed. If this scene was a painting hung on the wall of a gallery, anyone critiquing it would never conclude that the young, blue-haired teenager had the weight (and fate) of the world on her shoulders, or that the woman sitting next to her was leading the resurgence of a forgotten spirituality.

He didn't want to disturb the tranquillity, but as Waylon swallowed in his hesitation, the prominent lump in his skinny throat jumped and he inadvertently made an audible gulp.

Priestess Yi's eyelids flicked open. "What is it, Waylon?" she said curtly. She hadn't turned her head to look at him, instead her eyes stared straight ahead.

"A-apologies, Priestess," he stuttered in his usual nervous manner. "M-miss Amara Langton is here to see you. She's waiting for you in the gardens."

"Thank you, Waylon, you may go. We will be down shortly."

The watchman, bowing his head again, walked backwards out the room.

Priestess Yi placed her right hand gently on top of the left hand of Liana's, who was still deep in meditation. Liana's wrists rested on her knees, leaving her hands dangling over the edge. The Priestess said Liana's name gently to stir her, but she had to say it twice before the words resonated in her mind.

She opened her eyes slowly, like she was awakening early from a deep, dream filled sleep. A feeling usually associated with grogginess, but she did not feel groggy at all. She felt refreshed, calm, and clear-headed.

"I haven't had such an immersive session in a long time," she smiled, almost in relief as much as anything else. The invisible weight pulling down in her mind hadn't disappeared, but had become weightless, like a bowl of water evaporating.

"Sometimes, you need a change in scenery to refocus. Like going away on a trip, then returning home with a desire to rearrange the furniture or refresh your furnishings. You see things from a new perspective or with fresh eyes." Priestess Yi rose effortlessly from her cross-legged position. "Come now, we need to meet with Amara."

"I'm surprised she is here; I wouldn't have put her down

as the religious type," said Liana, also rising effortlessly from her cushion.

The pair exited the meditation chamber and past the muffled noises from the other chambers. They descended the curving, sloping ramp that wound around the circumference of the Tulip Temple until they reached the ground floor and entered a humid, glass greenhouse that was attached to one side of the building. The greenhouse was full of colourful, tropical plants. Many of which Liana had not seen before on the island. She guessed they had been rare imports, but she didn't have a chance to ask as they quickly moved on through into the gardens, where rows of flowerbeds in the six colours of the Inner Core's led the way to a colourful tulip fountain at the head of the garden.

A few couples wandered the gardens, each pair accompanied by a watchman. The watchmen were scribbling notes onto parchments, taking notes. Since the temple had opened, its gardens had become *the* place to get married.

"We want the wedding to be held in the evening, where all our guests can light up the gardens with their Red Aura," said one woman, as they walked past. "We want the celebrations to go on all night, so we can end the wedding by meditating to Aurora and the dawning sun." Drops of sweat formed on the young watchman's forehead as he frantically jotted down the details.

The conversation faded from range as they approached one of the wooden arbours that were stationed at regular intervals along the sandstone walls that enclosed the gardens. Liana could see Amara sitting in one on the far wall, feet up on the bench, devouring an apple whilst she waited.

"Liana!" shouted Amara, swivelling on her behind before jumping up from the wooden seat and throwing her arms around the princess. "Are you okay? I haven't seen you in ages!" Liana was slightly taken aback by the energetic greeting and limply leaned in to reciprocate the hug. Apart from two brief meetings, before and after the Battle of Coryàtès, they didn't exactly know each other. There was also the moment when Amara had seen her as a baby after trailing Sir Tarak on the Day of Darkness, but in Liana's mind that didn't count as a meeting. "What're you looking at?" Amara shouted over Liana's shoulder. "You," she said, pointing at one of the watchmen. "Get everyone inside, will you? We need some privacy."

The watchmen looked at the priestess for confirmation that they should leave. She acknowledged the order with both a roll of the eyes and a nod. Soon, the three of them were alone.

Priestess Yi and Liana sat on the bench whilst Amara leaned against the arbour, still chomping on her apple. *'A Princess, a priestess, and a warrior sat in a garden...'* - it was like the start of a bad Benji joke, Liana thought to herself.

"I sent Amara to Allicalidantè straight after our victory against Zagan," started the Priestess, "I knew the Queen's Table would take an age making decisions on how, why and when to find your Spirits, so I secretly took the initiative and hired your auntie to investigate."

"Auntie?" frowned Amara, throwing her apple core onto the floor. "You make me sound a hundred years old."

"I don't know, Auntie Amara has a certain ring to it," smirked Liana.

"Heh, I suppose it does," chuckled Amara.

"So, Auntie Amara," winked Liana. "What did you find out?"

Amara's expression turned serious as she spoke. "The population of Allicalidantè has been decimated and forced to occupy a crater-like hole in the ground on the outskirts of their land. What was once a thriving city full of fun, theatre and games, is now an impoverished gutter of hunger and despair."

"Son of a sun! What happened?" exclaimed Liana. 'Son of a sun' had become a popular profanity amongst the youth of Swyre. It didn't really make much sense, but it was an insinuation that Aurora had a bastard child. Of course, Priestess Yi didn't look upon the new blasphemous colloquialism with any fondness at all.

"Liana! You of all people should mind your words, especially in the grounds of a temple." Liana, slightly embarrassed by her slip of the tongue, quickly apologised.

Amara continued her divulging of information. "Immorals. They spread like a pandemic through the city. They started by Turning those who either had the greatest influence on the running of the city, or those who could control the supply of basic needs such as food and clean water. As people became desperate, they didn't need the help of an existing Immoral to end up being Turned. The citizens soon started to Turn of their own accord as they scrapped over supplies. I heard stories of neighbours murdering each other, children forced out at night to scavenge in the shadows, elderly relatives being sacrificed to make food last longer…"

"That's awful." Liana thought of the boy in the harbour, Seff, and wondered if he had experienced these horrors. "How quickly did all this happen?"

Amara hesitated, looking to the priestess for approval to respond. The Priestess wasn't a fan of withholding information from Liana and gave the nod for the mercenary to continue. Liana could feel in her gut the answer would be something to do with her. She'd gotten used to it, but the feeling of dread never weakened.

"It appears to have started on your 13th birthday."

And there it was, the inference that the situation in Allicalidantè was because of her, because of who she was, because of who she was supposed to be.

"But how could Immorals spread so quickly? It took Vivek months, if not years, to Turn Zagan's army."

"We have our suspicions, but I'm yet to confirm them."

Liana turned to the Priestess. "Do you think it's Tenebris? That he's broken out of his cell in the Morality Realm? You think that's what my dream was about?"

The Priestess shook her head dismissively. "No, I don't think your dream was a dream of the past. You said he spoke to you, called you the Guardian of Light, so you must have been there at that moment. These Turnings in Allicalidantè have been happening for months, so we can only conclude that there must be someone else behind them. We suspect that it is what is known in the H'WA as a 'Reaper of Morality' has emerged."

"That doesn't sound good."

"And it wouldn't be, but that is only speculation, unless you have seen any substance behind the theory?" she said, directing the question at Amara.

"Still just a theory at the moment," the mercenary confirmed. "But I'm almost certain your next Spirit is still in Allicalidantè." Liana and Priestess Yi listened intently. "There's a huge black, pillar-thing slap bang in the middle of this crater they're now living in. The Dantians, that's what the locals call themselves, call it the Pillar of Sanctuary, but," she leaned in and quietened her voice even though the trio had been alone for some time, "I overheard their prince, Prince Kendrix, call it the Neoteric Temple."

"The Pillar of Sanctuary? Why do the Dantians call it that?" enquired Liana.

"Because they believe it's what's keeping the Immorals from entering the crater and finishing their job, and it's easy to see why the Dantians think that. There's a stream of Orange Aura spouting from the top of it, and everyone I spoke to has said nobody has Turned whilst they started residing in the crater."

"You think my Sacral Spirit is protecting them?"

Amara shrugged. "Seems to be."

"What of this Prince?" asked Priestess Yi. "How would he even know about such a thing as the Neoteric Temple? The Visendus religion is still outlawed everywhere outside of Coryàtès?"

"He's an odd one - that prince. Not sure about him. Definitely hiding something. And the fact he and his father still appear to live in relative comfort - that doesn't do them any favours among their citizens. Maybe it's because of what happened to his mother though," she leaned in toward Liana again, like she was about to tell some secret gossip, even though obtaining information had been her job. "The Dantian's are forbidden from talking about it, but the Priestess put me in touch with a man called Franklin Rozier, who has since decided to live outside the crater."

Amara pulled out a few pieces of crumpled parchment from her pocket. She rather pointlessly tried to flatten out the wrinkles with the palms of her hands.

"The Pillar of Sanctuary. An authentic first-hand tale from a Dantian."

13
TALE FROM A DANTIAN

"The voice of a young woman wailed, clutching a crying baby in her arms.

I'll never forget the look of panic on her face as she ran towards me, trying to escape the massive structure as it towered over us, looming down over our heads in a way, I guess, how we must appear to a spider as we trap it under a cup.

The panicking crowd didn't know which way to run. This made their escape even more fraught, as they criss-crossed in front of each other, bumping and knocking into one another. The kicking-up of dirt under people's feet formed a dust cloud which only intensified the rampage.

Not one person tried to help another, it was simply a matter of self-preservation.

Long shadows stretched out over the cloud of dust and the heads of the onrushing crowd. Shadows of impending death if you were to be caught underneath it. Not to mention the noise. The noise…

It started off with a clunk and a whine, like when an animatronic starts up for the first time and the cogs and levers creak and ache into movement. As it lowered some more, the structure began to cry like a pair of cats fighting over territory. Whines and screeching that only grew louder as the faces of the enormous structure neared the powdery floor.

Out of chance, my eyes met that of the woman clutching her baby. Her upturned eyebrows were a signal of silent begging, a plea to help her. I don't know why, out of everyone, but we became fixated on each other. Maybe it was how her sapphire blue eyes drew my attention, or perhaps it was the innocence of the infant in her arms, who knows how our heart works? All I knew at that moment was that I had no choice but to help her. Against what should have been every natural instinct of survival inside me, I chose to run against the crowd to try and reach her. I may not be the bulkiest man, but I'm no stick either. I pushed and pulled people out of my way. I was knocked back more than once, but I never took my eyes off of hers. It's a particular skill of mine, to be able to block out my surroundings and focus on the task in hand. Our eyes stayed locked onto each other the whole time I fought my way to her.

As soon as I reached her, I grabbed her hand tightly. By now, most of the crowd had dispersed into the unkempt streets of our make-shift city, but the panicked crowd was now the least of our concern.

The face of the structure was nearly upon us. With just three horse-lengths to go until we were outside of its reach, I felt the cold-metallic surface brush my hair and scalp.

Have you ever tried to run whilst crouching? It's not easy. Having already bustled our way through torrents of people both our legs were burning with fatigue, but in a life-or-death situation you find that little extra inside you.

With one-horse-length left, the structure had forced us down onto our hands and knees. I grabbed the young woman beside me with both hands and flung her outside the reach of the structure and in doing so, fell onto my back.

I stared up at the darkness, the cold metal now kissing the tip of my nose. Strangely, I didn't actually feel fear at that moment, even though I knew I was about to have all the bones in my body get crushed beneath the weight of this unfolding pillar. No, I felt warmth, knowing my life was ending having saved an innocent and its mother.

But then I felt a pair of hands clasp around my ankles. I didn't even feel the stones scraping my back as I was dragged and pulled along the floor. I held my breath as the edge of the structure slammed down a finger length away from my head, trapping my ponytail. I might not have felt the scraping of the stones, but I most definitely felt my scalp being pulled from the tautness of my trapped hair. Fortunately, the pain lasted just a few seconds, as the woman I saved cut my ponytail free with a pair of embroidery scissors she kept on her in case of any clothing emergencies. I sat up, thankful to still have my life.

We saved each other that day. I never believed in fate, or a path being set for you, but that day brought us together.

I put my hand on the knee of the woman sitting beside me. We rest our foreheads together, close our eyes and smile contentedly with each other.

Our moment of love is interrupted by the cute chuckle of a 9-month-old baby, who is trying to use a vacant chair as a support to stand up, before his wobbly legs give out and he tumbles back onto its bottom with a delayed giggle.

The event I'm scribing now was months ago, but not

everyone was as fortunate as us. The King's wife being one of the unfortunate ones.

If I were to get up off my wooden chair and walk towards this room's boarded-up window, I'd have to squint through a small slit between two of the wooden planks that act as a barricade. That is the style of life we have right now.

They almost killed us with their curiosity. Why couldn't they just leave it alone? The prince, he had to touch it, didn't he? Killed his own mother, and all those other innocents, just when they thought they were safe from the invisible plague that swept our joyful city. Do you know what they call it, this structure? The Pillar of Sanctuary, A little ironic, don't you think? I understand why, of course. Without the power of the pillar, there would be no Allicalidantè at all. This used to be such a jovial city. Not without its troubles, of course, but nothing on the scale of what happened up here. Good people, people I held in my heart dearly, people I'd known all my life, but they changed. The pillar provided protection, but the conditions down there? Well, there's a reason why we take our chances up here."

14
JEWELS OF ORANGE

Amara folded up the parchment and handed them over to the Priestess.

"That's awful," said Liana.

"I think it really messed the prince up, watching his mother die like that."

"Yes, a truly harrowing story, Amara," interjected the Priestess, in a somewhat insincere tone, like she'd heard it a thousand times before. "But what of the Jewels of Orange - or the cause behind the Turnings?"

"Well, the Jewels of Orange shouldn't be a problem," said Amara, as she proudly pulled a severed hand out from her robes. The lifeless hand adorned a handpiece made of golden chains that linked over each finger, connecting to a central, black plate on the back of the hand. The jewels were not quite dainty enough to be considered fashion wear, like one may wear to a ball, nor was it so glove-like that it could be considered a gauntlet. Within the black back-plate was a sunken circular hole where the Spirit Orb should sit, decorated around its perimeter with sunray patterns.

"It's beautiful," commented Liana, "the jewels, not the dead hand," said Liana, feeling the need to specify what she meant.

"Indeed, they are," said the Priestess, reaching out to take the cold, dead hand. She rotated the dead hand around, carefully observing the intricacies of the jewels, fascinated by the Artefact. "It's exactly as the book of H'WA describes them. The standard Sacral power is to be able to fix broken items using your Orange Aura, like a super strength cement. But when you combine your Spectra Orb with the jewels, you will have the ability to craft anything your hand touches," The Priestess, still in awe at the dismembered body part, carefully passed them over to Liana. "Where did you find them?"

"Some kid. He said he found the hand on the floor after the event with the pillar and figured they didn't belong to anyone anymore. He saw me eating some fruit and offered a trade, since the jewels were no use to him, and good food was more valuable for him and his 'clan'."

"This kid, was his name 'Seff', by any chance?"

"I don't know, I didn't ask. I just saw the jewels and swapped it for all the food I had. We both came away happy."

"Was he wearing a navy-blue shirt and trousers? Ripped, looked like he hadn't changed his clothes in weeks?"

"Yeh, come to think of it, I think he was," said Amara, tossing her apple core to the ground. "You know the kid?"

"Yeh, I think I do."

"The Jewels are still missing your Spectra Orb though. Your Orange Aura must be what is keeping the Immorals at bay, and no doubt is protected within this so-called 'Pillar of Sanctuary'.

It would take an educated guess that this pillar could be the entrance to the Neoteric Temple. Maybe this boy you know may be able to help?" Priestess Yi flicked her hand suggestively.

"Maybe," shrugged Liana.

"Then, Liana, I think you should find this boy and sail for Allicalidantè yourself."

"And go against my mother and the Queen's Table orders?"

"Do you have a problem with that? All I seem to remember hearing from you for the last six months is how obtaining the Artefacts and Orbs is your destiny and you should have sailed to Allicalidantè along with your great uncle and his entourage.

"Well, yes," Liana said hesitantly.

"Then it's settled. You and Amara go and collect this boy. I'll make the arrangements for the journey."

15

CHICKEN

"It's been a long time, Sir Tarak," King Shimon said, before biting into a chicken leg, its juices flowing down the bone into the grey hairs of his beard and onto his hand which held it. The only furniture in the undecorated dining room was a square table, where seven chairs had been squeezed around it for the King, the prince, and their guests.

On their way through the makeshift palace, the group had passed several chicken coops and a small room for growing potatoes.

"The height of the cliffs around the crater cause such vast and dark shadows it means we barely get any sunlight, so I'm afraid our range of cuisine is somewhat lacking." King Shimon said, before stabbing a boiled potato with a wooden fork. "We chose to grow potatoes as they don't need much sunlight, but we had to be careful when burrowing out the holes in the ceiling," he continued as he shovelled the vegetable into his mouth. "The holes had to be small enough to ensure the roof didn't collapse, but still provide enough streaks of light for the potatoes to grow." He spoke with his mouth full before moaning in satisfaction as he swallowed, complimenting the taste of the potato and chicken to everyone in the room. "Since it's so hard to grow anything else here, we have to prioritise using our limited amount of potatoes as feed for the chicken's. Eggs, chicken and fish are the mainstay of our diet nowadays. We reserve eating the potatoes for ourselves unless it's a special occasion." King Shimon then raised a shabby stone cup and toasted to his royal guests. "To the rekindling of old friendships. I only wish I had something other than water to wet your tongues," he said, before sipping disappointedly from the cup.

Saffina pushed the dry-looking food around her wooden plate, and noticed Joel was doing the same. She might not have grown up in riches of prosperity, but at least her family grew their own fresh fruit and vegetables and could afford a pork loin or shoulder once in a while.

Sat opposite, Luci also tentatively prodded the chicken breast on her plate, but her fork failed to pierce the skin. She suspected it was less of a case of a blunt fork, and more the firmness of the meat. Saffina watched as the substitute princess took her knife to the cut of poultry and struggled to cut it into manageable pieces to eat, the meat sliding around her plate as she tried to stake it. No wonder King Shimon had picked his leg up by the bone rather than use cutlery. After finally getting a hold of it and cutting off a slice, she raised a small chunk to her mouth, testing it nervously with the tip of her tongue first. Luci's jaws chewed, and chewed, labouring to break it down. She ended up forcing herself to swallow, although she'd rather have spat out the tasteless shreds of poultry, the texture of which she likened to that of hay on a hot summer's day. Saffina wished inwardly that their stay would be a short one. Get the Jewels of Orange and Spectra Orb out of the Pillar of Sanctuary and go home. That's all they needed to do. How hard could that be?

"Ah, Kendrix, nice of you to join us!" said the King sarcastically as the prince meandered into the room and took the one remaining spare seat next to his father. Luci's longing, puppy-dog eyes didn't go unnoticed by Saffina, and more importantly the prince, who for the first time since having met them managed to curl the corner of his mouth into a shallow, wry smile. "My apologies for not meeting you at the dock, I had some urgent business to tend to."

"It's of no consequence to us," said Sir Tarak, diplomatically. "Thank you for giving us the freedom of your palace."

"Let's be candid about it, it's hardly a palace. It is a big stone building. Not exactly fit for royalty, but such are the times we have found ourselves in."

"And just what times do you find yourselves in?" blurted Saffina, who received a stern glance from Sir Tarak. Since they held no royal standing, she and Joel were under strict orders to say as little as possible and her eagerness to be heard didn't impress Tarak.

"My-my princess, your friend here isn't backwards with coming forward, is she? I guess you and your friends are used to being the centre of attention." The king used his fork to point to Luci's vivid blue hair. Unperturbed by Saffina's manner, the king chose to answer her question anyway. "Why, the disease of course! The pandemic that's sweeping across the mainland! I suppose it may not have found its way to your secluded little island yet," jibed the king, who couldn't help but keep up the appearance of the two lands' chequered history.

"Or maybe we just protect our borders better," replied

Saffina with a swift riposte, to even more disdain of Sir Tarak who mouthed the words *shut up* in her direction.

"Well, if your soldiers are so well skilled, perhaps your royal friend here could have spared some of them before we ended up in this hole," the king's greying eyebrows frowned and the wrinkles on his forehead crinkled, pulling the rest of his bald head tight.

"This pandemic," interrupted Sir Tarak, before Saffina had the opportunity to further worsen the relations that they'd come to repair. "What is it, exactly?"

"It's like poison, but not a physical poison, The poisoning of the mind. It turns loved ones against each other. Makes them do things they would never normally do. First it would cause families to argue and split up, that escalated to stealing to survive, and before long businesses were being ransacked and people were being murdered. It spread so quickly…" His frown turned to one of pity as he remembered the citizen's he'd lost. "Look Sir Tarak, I'll cut to the chase. When Adriya reached out and asked if we'd consider reconciling our differences, it actually came as a relief. We're cut off from everywhere else on the mainland, and we could really use your help, even despite the dishonour your family brought onto mine."

"I can only apologise for the circumstances of the past. If we can put that episode behind us, I'm sure our families can find a way forward."

"I'm in a situation where I cannot let my personal feelings get in the way of what is right for the remainder of me and my people. I must find a way to let go of my resentment towards Adriya and look to the future."

"I appreciate your candidness. Speaking of candidness, I haven't seen Queen Jayne around. Is that because of what happened between our families all those years ago?" Sir Tarak was never one for dodging a difficult question.

"The years after the incident between our families were difficult ones, but sometimes time is a healer."

"So, where is she? Did something happen to her in the pandemic?"

"In a manner of speaking."

He might not avoid a difficult conversation, but Sir Tarak also knew when not to push a subject further. He could see the king was still hurting from a grave loss. The emotional pain of losing a loved one was written across both his and his son's faces.

"Anyway," said King Shimon, breaking the sullen silence, "I'm curious why you reached out to us. In our situation I'd have imagined it would be me having to swallow my pride and approaching the Langton's for allegiance."

"We had little information about your current circumstances," lied Sir Tarak. With his skilled scouts and the knowledge of Candela, he knew the circumstances they were in. He put on his best Chantrah-face, not to give away the fact they'd been scouting the area for some months.

"Well, I don't know if I have what you've come looking for anymore. We don't have much to offer," shrugged King Shimon.

"You have what we need," piped Saffina.

"She's not shy, this one. She has more of a royal attitude than the princess." King Shimon pointed his half-eaten chicken piece in the direction of Luci before moving the bony leg in Saffina's direction. "Why don't you be the one to tell me exactly what it is that you want from me?"

Saffina replied without hesitation before anyone could

interrupt her. "To get inside the Pillar of Sanctuary. It's home to an object we need."

The entire entourage eyeballed Saffina, aghast. This wasn't the plan. Sir Tarak and Luci were supposed to distract the King and his son with diplomatic negotiations whilst Master H, Saffina and Joel found a way into the temple.

'What is she thinking?' thought an angry Sir Tarak.

"I appreciate your honesty, but that is simply out of the question. The Pillar is out of bounds both physically and as part of any negotiation."

"But Swyre can help you. We can transport food, water, goods, materials, whatever you need. All we ask is for access to The Pillar."

"Now look here!" shouted the King as he slammed his palms onto the table and rose from his seat. "I don't know what this object is or why you need it but frankly I don't care. For all that we know The Pillar is the only thing keeping the mind-poison away from my people and it will not be interfered with," he took a deep breath and calmed his voice and sat back down. "I think this meal has come to an end. My guards will show you to your rooms. We'll convene the start of official diplomatic negotiations this time tomorrow."

Two of the guards stationed by the exit moved forward and gestured for the king's guests to follow them. They did so without confrontation and followed the guards through the narrow, burrowed out tunnels of the makeshift palace. Nobody spoke for the entirety of the walk before reaching their destination.

"Room on the left is for the adults," one of the guards pointed out.

"Room on the right is for the children," pointed out the other guard. "There is a bell in each room should you require anything. By order of the king, you are free to roam the palace as you please. It's not like we have anything of worth to steal. However, he asks you to stay within the palace boundary for your safety. You may have noticed, but it's not the best of atmosphere's out on the streets."

"Thank you," said Sir Tarak, confirming to the two guards that they could leave. He waited until they were out of sight before speaking again. "Everyone, in here," he opened the right hand-door. "Now!"

Saffina gulped as they made their way into the room. Three wooden beds lined one wall, blankets folded up on each, and a bell hung on the back of the door. Other than that, the rooms were empty aside from their own trunks that the guards must have brought in whilst they were having dinner.

"What in Aurora's name were you thinking?!" screamed Sir Tarak towards Saffina. A vein on his forehead pulsed. "Did you forget about the past six months of planning and training, or did you purposefully try to sabotage our mission?"

"I..I.." she stuttered, her mind suddenly flashing back to last year when she stood before the Queen in the Tower of Seeds. That feeling of unworthiness and fear, while Liana took the rap for their prank on their school hood nemesis, Yasmin. She eventually found the words she was looking for. "I saw how desperate they were and just thought they would take anything to make their life better. I mean, did you even try the chicken? If you can call it chicken."

"Is that what you're basing this on, the state of their chicken?"

Saffina cowered, avoiding any eye contact with the angry knight.

"You realise the way you acted in there completely undermined mine and Luci's position? How do you think that makes us look?" Sir Tarak let out a long sigh, reflecting inwardly on the consequences of her actions. *'King Shimon will surely keep the temple under an even closer watch now, as well as us.'*

"Sir Tarak," began Luci, slightly hesitant considering his current emotional state, "What did King Shimon mean when he said you dishonoured his family?"

He let out another long sigh before speaking.

"Allicalidantè and Coryàtès were once close allies, full of trade and goodwill. When Mount Indigo erupted and caused the Day of Darkness, King Shimon came to visit as soon as he heard what had happened to pay his condolences and offer their support and aid."

"So, what happened?"

Sir Tarak sat down on the edge of a bed and held his head in his hands. "We needed an excuse for the birth of Liana. Shimon had visited Coryàtès without his wife, Queen Jayne, and his then 2-year-old son Prince Kendrix because he didn't want them to have to witness the devastation.

Clerk Vivek saw this as an opportunity. He suggested at the time, and Queen Adriya reluctantly accepted the advice, that we could use the king's visit to start a rumour that he was primarily visiting to check his unborn child was unhurt following the eruption. That unborn child of course being Liana. Trouble was, with the aid flowing in from Allicalidantè, we couldn't contain the rumours to stay within Swyre and word soon got back to King Shimon, and of course, his wife.

The King obviously knew this was all a lie but when he asked us to quash these rumours, Adriya refused. Having a bastard child isn't a good look for a queen's reputation, but it was softened, almost accepted, if it was born from that of a king.

Naturally, Shimon cut all ties with us as he tried to rectify his marriage and convince his wife he had not been unfaithful.

The only ships we'd receive again from Allicalidantè would be that of smugglers or pirates.

He threatened war, but since our superior navy was unaffected by the Day of Darkness, he decided against it, instead focussing on his trade and strengthening allegiances elsewhere on the mainland. This is the first time we've seen each other in thirteen years."

"Damn, no wonder he hates you," said Joel, who for once had been doing as he had been asked and kept his mouth firmly sealed all evening. "I'm guessing that's one of the reasons why you wanted to keep the actual Liana away from this place. You didn't know how he'd react to seeing the child who almost broke apart his marriage."

Joel sat down on the bed next-door to Sir Tarak. The wooden frame creaked before snapping, leaving Joel sprawled on the floor.

"Jeez, Joel!" the room said, shaking their heads in unison like some sort of dance act.

"Looks like you're sleeping on the floor," giggled Luci.

"Yes, but on the floor of mine and Master H's room," added Sir Tarak. "New rules, males in the left-hand room, female's in the right."

"But-" Joel started to protest, rubbing his bruised leg. He didn't want to be separated from Saffina.

"No arguing, it's time we rested. We have some tough negotiations to begin tomorrow."

16

WHATEVER MEANS NECESSARY

'I feel drawn to staying with her, like I owe her my protection. I don't know how, when or why - but everything in me is telling me I cannot leave her.

I have a lot of strange feelings: the strangeness of my awareness of this Realm, the wholesomeness of my Good Morality, this feeling of need to protect, but I have another odd feeling. A feeling of maturity.

I was entombed at just 10 years old. My body awoke at the same age but immediately began to be Turned. I never really became self-aware; it was like I was a puppet to Vivek and my Bad Morality. But now that I am my natural born self again, at least in terms of Morality. And I feel older. Like my sense of Morality has aged separately from my body whilst I was entombed. If mirrors were able to show my reflection in this Realm, I wonder what I would look like...'

Liana and Amara thumped loudly on the back door of the Swyre's Rest where Seff had been working.

"Go away, we're closed," came a bumbling, female voice echoing somewhere inside.

"We need to speak to Seff," shouted Liana through the thick wooden door.

"He's busy. Come back later," grunted the bumbling voice.

"It's really important."

"I said the boy's busy! Go away!"

"This is ridiculous," said Amara impatiently. "Now listen up!" she screamed. "You're telling the Princess of Swyre and a former Langton army General to get lost. Now let us in!"

"Ugh, Amara, you know I hate using my name to get my way," complained Liana.

"Your mother might teach you how to be a diplomat. Benji might teach you how to play Chantrah. Priestess Yi might teach you how to fight. Master Hayashi might teach you about your inner self, but today, I'm going to teach the art of getting into places you need to be, and there's just one thing to remember: use whatever means necessary whether you like the method or not. And guess what girl, you have more going for you than most. You have the power of a name that's important in both royal and religious circles, as well as physical and supernatural powers. If you add the power of the tongue to your attributes, you'll be able to get anywhere at any time."

"Fine but let me talk to Seff. He hates royals as it is, let alone one like you."

"What do you mean, 'one like me'?"

"You know," Liana waved her hand up and down in front of Amara's body. "An aggressive, warrior type."

Before Amara could protest at Liana's observation, the bumbling voice from inside spoke again from the other side of the door.

"Uh, my apologies, your highness. You should've said right away." They could hear her fumbling with a lock. The door opened in front of them and a petite, rose-cheeked woman looked up at them. Her black bobbed hair was unbrushed and rather dishevelled as it flapped gently in the light breeze. Her attire suggested she was the tavern's chef. "The name's Laurel, I'm the tavern's chef. Don't really do people, like to stay in the back, out the way," explained the chef. "The new boy, you say? Hang on," she drew in a deep breath before calling out back into the building. "Boy! Oi, boy! Get down 'ere, you got a visitor!"

The pacey padding of steps down wooden stairs could be heard echoing through the kitchen before the familiar and scruffy face of Seff appeared, squeezing beside chef's blood-stained chef's whites.

"Oh, it's you," said the boy, whose clothes were also stained in all sorts of colours from spilled food and ingredients. The boy's nonchalant response to seeing a member of royalty prompted the chef to slap the boy on the back of the head and lambast the scrawny child for his disrespect.

"Ow!" Seff held the top of head where the hand had struck. Liana couldn't help but giggle, she got the feeling Seff was never far away from some sort of trouble.

"My apologies, princess, what brings you to the back door of this fine eatery," said Seff sarcastically, putting on a posh accent. The chef raised her hand again ready to punish the boy's insolence, but Liana stopped her.

"It's okay, we're friends. He's only joking."

The chef mumbled and grunted under her breath, rolling her eyes and tutting loudly before reluctantly returning inside.

"Whaddya want?" Seff said, returning to his usual slang.

"We need your help."

"Oh, you do, do ya?"

"We're going to Allicalidantè, but we need some inside knowledge. Somewhere safe to stay, that sort of thing."

"Oh aye. Why would a princess like you wanna be sneaking into a place like that?"

"Just some business I need to take care of, that's not important to you. Probably better you don't know anyway, could be dangerous."

"And what makes you think I'm gonna, or wanna, help you?"

"Because you want to get back and help your 'crew'? We could take them a load of fresh food."

Seff leaned against the doorframe; a pondering look on his face. He exaggerated a long sniff of the air and licked his lips at the smell of a pig being roasted in the kitchen behind him. "And what makes ya think I'll give up my new life here? I have a roof over me head, good food, good drink. Why would I wanna go back to that hell hole?"

Liana hadn't banked on Seff refusing. When she saw the look on his face seeing the Maiden II sail away, she'd banked on him jumping at the chance. "I thought you'd be loyal to your crew," she said, trying to tap into his good morals.

"I am, but if they were in my position, they'd probably be thinking the same."

"What if I said we could bring them all back here with us?" suggested Liana.

"Liana, we can't promise him that!" Amara interjected.

"Who's this broad?" Seff motioned in the warrior's direction.

"She's the person who can get us into Allicalidantè undetected," replied Liana, but the response made Seff hug his stomach as he bent over laughing.

"That's impossible," the boy said, wiping tears from his eyes. "There's only one way in, and one way out, and there ain't no way you're getting that done unnoticed."

"I've already been there and back, boy." Amara moved to barge past the princess, but Liana held her arm up to stop her. The Dantian boy stopped laughing and flinched backwards.

"I thought there'd be some sort of 'honour amongst thieves' philosophy between you and your crew."

"Yeah, well, guess there isn't. I got work to do before chef gets on my back again. Good luck doing what you need to in The Dantè."

"Now listen here you little jerk!" Amara said, grabbing the back of the boy's shirt as he turned away, half strangling him. "She's the princess of this island," she said, pointing with her free hand. "And I'm the queen's sister, trained under the tutorship of the Commanding Knight, Sir Tarak. If you refuse our request, what do you think is going to happen with your little arrangement here, huh? You think we're going to let you off? You think we'll let you carry on with this upturn in your lifestyle? No, we'll have you sent off to the mines. You know what working in the mines is like? Well, it's full of criminals, and not just any criminals. Murderers, psychopaths, you name it. Is that where you want to end up?"

Even with his shirt pulled tight around his neck the boy audibly gulped. "All right, all right. I'll help."

Amara let go, and Seff adjusted his clothing and soothed his throat with a gentle rub.

"Just fer a minute, I thought you might be different," he said, looking at Liana. "I thought there might actually be a royal out there who wasn't a selfish, power-hungry, get-their-own-way thug."

"Watch your tongue," warned Amara.

Liana pursed her lips. It wasn't how she wanted to get the situation resolved, but Amara's way of dealing with it got the result they needed. Afterall, there was more at stake than hurting the feelings of one boy.

"Hey, chef!" shouted Amara into the kitchen.

"Uh, uh... yes!" came the same bumbled response from the chef.

"We're borrowing your little helper here. We'll try and bring him back in one piece," she side-glanced, smirking at the kid.

"Oh, er, of course, of course. I guess I'll have to find someone else for the meantime then," the chef's tone hinted at annoyance, but she wasn't going to outwardly argue.

"Now that's how you treat royalty," said Amara, getting into Seff's face before turning to leave.

'This is going to be a long journey,' Liana thought to herself.

17
HITCHING A RIDE

'You look sad, boy, that you're not going with her. Like you can't do your job to protect her. She looks after you, you look after her, that is how a dog and a human are supposed to work isn't it, Cas?

Well, they are leaving for a place called the Neoteric Temple. I can tell you, I have heard such great stories of that place, and of Allicalidantè. Even despite the Aura War, they always made time for a tournament or two there. In fact, it was a necessary distraction from hunting down Immorals. Even for me, a Spectra Child, those hunts were always such a tiresome business. The tournaments were a time for celebrating Aurora and her gifts to us and just as importantly, a chance to see friends and also make some new ones. I may have personally missed the horrors of the war, but I also missed the best parts of the Aurora Visendus at its grandest. Take care of yourself, boy, it's time I boarded the ship too before I get left behind with you.

Ugh-guh-uh... what is that pulling on me? I can't get any closer to the ship. Am I restricted to staying on Coryàtès? The only thing tying me here would be my body - if I knew where that was.

This is bad. Everything inside of me - which in a nutshell right now is just my thoughts and principles of what is right and wrong, is telling me I must go with the princess and protect her, that this is the right thing to do. How can I do that if I'm unable to leave the island?

I don't have time to go looking for my physical body, much less understand how to merge back with myself.

I must think fast, they are boarding the ship! What can I do? Could I get close enough to the ship and tie myself to it, so it forces me away? If what happened just now was anything to go by, that would be more than painful. And what of the consequences? Would the link with my body be ripped away so I could never return? Would I remain in excruciating pain for the entire time? Would it even work, or would I spring back to shore like a chained animal? An animal... maybe that's the answer.

Hey, boy, since you wanna go with them as well, maybe I could hitch a ride inside of your physical form? I remember Rhonwen telling me before our entombing that it was possible for two moralities to attach themselves to one body.

Well, I think your smile says it all, doesn't it? I wonder if it's as simple as just stepping inside where your physical body is and maybe I can latch onto you somehow. Just a word of warning though, boy, I've heard it makes you a bit chilly...'

Liana knelt down in front of a wooden barrel and placed a shallow-sided, open topped box on top of it. She pushed aside her maroon coloured, Shroud Clan robe and removed a brown, leather pouch from her trouser belt, unwound its flaps string, and carefully tipped the contents of quartz spheres into the box. The sphere's sounded like an extreme game of conkers as they knocked against each other on their way in.

She pulled aside her robe again and unsheathed the Dagger of Red, its red-tinted blade shimmering under the moonlight, and began slicing the spheres in half and hollowing them out. The blade made light work of its task, like a hot knife through butter, as they say.

Once all the sphere's had been hollowed out, she called out her Red Aura. Her kneeling figure now glowed softly like a lamp, except her figure radiated in a crimson red rather than the yellowy orange of a candle.

She picked up two sphere halves and brought them within the boundaries of her aura before snapping them together with her thumb and forefinger, trapping her Red Aura inside. She again picked up the Dagger of Red that was laid down next to the box of quartz spheres and brought that within the boundary of her Red Aura. The tint of red in the blade grew to a more fearsome, fiery glow as it entered her Aura. Using the now hot tip of the dagger, Liana rotated the sphere between her fingers and sealed the two halves. She held the orb up to the moonlight and looked proudly at the dancing red light inside. She had successfully made her first Aura Orb.

It didn't take long for the princess to turn the rest of the plain quartz spheres into Aura Orbs and return them to her leather pouch.

"It's a shame you can't call upon your Morality Aura at the moment, then you could have made the more powerful Spirit Orbs," said Princess Yi, making Liana jump up from the ground, unaware she was being watched.

"I still haven't been able to produce that white light, like I did at the Battle of Coryàtès," she shrugged. "I guess the only person who could teach me is Candela, but only Aurora knows where she is at the moment."

"Waylon and a few of my other watchmen will sail with you," said Priestess Yi changing the subject as the pair stood on a pier at the very far side of the Swyre harbour. Water lapped against the fisher boats and royal vessels that were tethered there as they gently bobbed and swayed like apples hanging on a tree during a breezy autumn day.

"You will have to take a small ship, one which will go unnoticed for a little while. As soon as you reach Allicalidantè, Waylon and the others will return, hopefully before anyone notices the ship has gone missing. You may have to find a way to make your own way home."

"Won't this ship's captain notice it's gone?" asked Liana.

"This ship doesn't have a captain, or a crew, for that matter." explained Amara, who was already aboard the boat and looking down on Priestess Yi and Princess Liana. Her head partially eclipsed the burnt yellow light from one of Mikana's moons giving her a halo effect. "They've all been reassigned to vacant positions in other crews. Until Admiral Remi gets back to sign off a new manifest, this ship is crewless."

"And jus' what experience do these watchmen have o' sailing the seas?" An instantly recognisable pirate-like voice came sounding out from around the corner of a neighbouring ship. "I ain't lettin' no one take this girl out there if they ain't a seasoned seafarer."

Priestess Yi folded her skinny arms defensively, clearly preparing for a confrontation with the city's Merchant Guild Leader. "Do not try and stop her, Benji."

"Stop her? I ain't stoppin' no one. I'm coming along. Gotta make sure she gets there safe and sound. Ain't no good if she ends up drowning at sea now, is it?" he replied, winking at Liana.

"Waylon is perfectly capable," Priestess Yi untucked one of her arms dismissively. "Before joining me in the Tulip Temple, he used to be on a fisherman's crew."

"Ah, I always thought there was something fishy about him!" Benji laughed harder at his own poor joke than it was worthy of.

"Ah, and I always thought you as boar-ing…" Priestess Yi said with a swift come back, making them both chuckle. She'd now unfolded her arms and relaxed a little knowing that Benji was there as a support. Liana rolled her eyes at the poor exchange of jokes.

"Benji, I appreciate your offer, but you were only a ship's cook…"

"Only a ship's cook! Do you know how important feeding a crew of hungry sailors is?!"

"That's not what I mean! It's just, do you even know anything about sailing?"

"I didn't spend the whole of my twenty-five years at sea below deck. There were plenty of times I stepped in."

"But won't my mother notice you're not around?" interjected Liana.

"Ah, I'm sure the priestess here will think of something," he waved a thumb in the priestess's general direction. "Apart from the Queen's Table meetings, we don't see much of each other anyhow. Doubt she'll even realise I'm gone, since the meetings have been postponed while this Jewels of Orange business is happening."

"Fine," sighed the Priestess. "But only Liana, Amara and the boy are to go into Allicalidantè, you will return with the ship. Fewer risks of getting caught."

"Aye, Ma'am!" beamed Benji. Liana could tell how much he was looking forward to getting back out to sea, without the commitment of a long contract under a captain. "Say, where is the boy?"

"He's already on board, sorting out which of his friends gets what rations," Liana answered.

"Ah, that kid's gonna be popular!"

"He's not popular with everyone. I'm guessing Seff's the reason that you happen to know about our little trip?"

"Aye," he grinned.

"Probably wouldn't mention that fact to her," said Liana, looking up at Amara. "Might be an idea to make out it was the barkeep or chef Laurel, otherwise Seff may not make it home to his friends…"

Benji chuckled again, before they made their way up the docking ramp. "Well, what're we waiting for? Let's get going!"

After helping to hoist the sails, Liana moved to the stern of the boat. It was then she realised that she'd never properly been off the island before. Until last year, she'd never really ventured outside of Swyre, yet here she was sailing off with a half-experienced crew to regain the next part of her Spirit, and again save a city from ultimate destruction by a swarm of Immorals.

She raised her hand and waved goodbye to Priestess Yi, and to her trusty companion, Cas. "Look after him for me, won't you?" she shouted to the priestess, who bowed to confirm she would.

As she stood waving while the ship gently pulled away from its mooring, Cas suddenly bounded into a run.

"Cas, what are you doing?" she shouted. "Stay there! Stop, boy! Stop! You can't come, it's too dangerous," she turned and shouted to Benji and Waylon behind her: "Help! It's Cas, he's trying to get onboard!"

Benji and Waylon both looked over the edge of the ship. The stern had already passed the end of the pier.

"Get that net!" Benji instructed Waylon, pointing to a pile

of string on the ground. "Throw it over the side, that pup ain't gonna stop!"

Just as the stern of the ship passed the end of the pier, Cas leaped into the water and wrapped his paws through the holes of the net.

Liana, Benji and Waylon slipped backwards onto their backsides as they made the effort to pull the net up and over the side. A fluffy looking-pleased-with-himself grin greeted them, before Cas wildly shook off his wet fur. The combination of smells of sea water and dog splattered over them.

Liana wrapped her arms around Cas "Guess you are coming along afterall."

18

MUSICAL INTERLUDE

'*Sorry, Cas, I don't know how this works either. Don't bark at me, I'm here so I can protect her too, you know. Just accept that we're stuck with each other for the time being. If we're going to get along, you're gonna have to let me take the lead, since I'm the one who can understand everything. Yes, I can feel your canine instincts, but those instincts might not be enough to protect her. It's just a feeling I have, okay? Good, I'm glad you understand me. Now, let's practise some prowling and jumps so I can get used to the motion of your body.*'

Liana looked down on the beachy cove below as Benji and Waylon pushed their rowboats back out to sea towards the borrowed ship anchored in the bay.

"Ya can't come wearing that!" said the squeal of Seff, tugging at Liana's maroon robe from behind. "I thought you were leaving that behind!" he said, flinging his arms in the air in disbelief. "You forgotten that ya gonna be joining me in the streets where we can't even get food. Only King Shimon and Prince Kendrix would wear something so well made."

Liana rolled her eyes. She had been thankful for a short break from Seff as they had come to shore on separate row boats. She realised he was now really getting under her skin with his high-pitched voice and incessant rambling of how bad his life had been.

"I need to hide my dagger and pouch somewhere. I don't have anything else," shrugged Liana.

"Of course you don't," said Seff, this time rolling his eyes. "What's the inside look like? Maybe ya can turn it inside out?"

Liana pulled her robe open. The hexagonal, honeycomb material was the same inside as out.

"Well, there's only one thing for it," Seff said, as he lunged forward and grabbed the Dagger of Red and its sheath from Liana's waist.

"Hey! Give that back!" Liana threw an arm out to grab the dagger back but only caught a fistful of air as Seff jumped backwards.

"Not 'til we sort this out," he said, and began randomly cutting and shredding at the princess's robe.

"What are you doing?! Master H will kill me if he sees me like this!"

"Ya won't even get a chance to see him again if someone on the streets sees you dressed all properly. Trust me."

After hacking and ripping away a number of holes and gashes in the robes, the Dantian boy picked up a nearby tree branch with several sharp thorns and started thrashing at Liana's black top and clay-coloured trousers, the clothing she often wore out and about for day-to-day activities in Swyre. She wasn't one for always looking cute and pretty in typical princess-like dresses and preferred the mischief and mayhem of being with Saffina and Joel out and about in the city, but even that was being overdressed from Seff's point of view.

"You're lucky I've got more of these back home," frowned Liana.

"You have to look the part, Princess. I can't be bringing back a swanky girl in fancy clothing like you to me crew can I?"

"I'd hardly call myself swanky," protested Liana, who had never thought of herself as being a particularly aristocratic person. In fact, she wasn't, since she'd recently found out she had no royal blood in her and was adopted in the Langton monarchy.

Seff stood back to admire his handiwork. "Great! Now, just one more thing ought to finish off ya new look…" he said, reaching down and grabbing a fistful of mud and dust from the ground before launching it at Liana, hitting her square in the face. "Oops! Guess my aim was a bit off."

Liana stood momentarily frozen to the spot, arms outstretched, mouth agape in surprise as mud drooped down her chin and plopped onto the ground between her feet.

"I can't believe you just did that! You did that on purpose didn't you?" she said eventually. "I'm gonna get you, you little wort!" and she took off, running toward her anti-royal tour guide.

"I promise I didn't! I meant to get your shirt! Promise!"

Liana chased Seff in circles, picking up her own fistfuls of mud and dirt and slinging them at his back as he tried to run away. Every now and then he'd manage to return with his own mud ball, most of them missing. Being older, taller and more athletic than the short and stick-thin boy, it didn't take Liana long to hunt him down and tackle him to the ground. The pair rolled around in the dirt slinging more mud balls at each from close range. Soon, they were each covered from head to toe and panting heavily, sprawled out on their backs giggling as they looked up at the colourful dawning of the Mikanan sky.

They might not have known it, but at that moment they were both thinking the same thing. That was fun. Fun - something neither of these two children had experienced as much as their peers in their lifetime. Both, for very different reasons, but it felt good to let go, albeit briefly.

"C'mon you two, no time for larking about," said Amara, sternly, as she strode past them.

"What took you so long?" Liana asked as she brushed off whatever dirt she could from her now suitably grubby clothes.

"Sorting out a disagreement between Benji and Waylon," sighed Amara.

"About what?"

"Everything," she said. It was her turn to give a laboured roll of the eyes, before something caught her attention and stopped her in her tracks. "Hey, do you hear that?"

A light breeze carried the tuneful sound of a metallic plucking and an airy whistling from a nearby wooded area. Amara gripped the handle of her whip. Liana that of her dagger. The pair were cautious about what approached them in this foreign land. Seff cowered behind them.

Amara and Liana readied themselves into their battle stances and drew their weapons. The warrior's knees slightly bent, feet one in front of another and shoulder width apart, with her whip drawn behind her. The princess stood straight with her legs together, one arm held out in readiness to call upon her Red Aura, the other bent and clutching the Dagger of Red.

Twigs snapped. Branches rustled. The music grew louder, and from the edge of the wooden area through a yellowing bush, out popped two young men. One was playing a wooden flute. The other was playing a guitar-like instrument, except in place of strings were long metal tines, like a cross between a guitar and a kalimba.

The man playing the guitar-cross-kalimba (Liana chose to call this a Kalimtar) was short and round with long dark hair and an equally long beard. He bounced between his feet as he plucked the metal tines on his instrument whilst the flute playing man was tall, slender, and had a long face and chin. As he played, his eyes danced along with the music he was playing.

"A princess!" announced the short man.

"A warrior!" announced the tall man.

"And a boy!" they announced together, peering their heads around Liana and Amara at Seff. "This must be who we must serenade!"

Ooh...
The lady Princess so vibrant and bright,
The female Warrior so full of fight,
The boy who's not always so polite,
Listen to what we were told to write!

Near 6 months ago we saw her,
A woman with a fabulous Aura,
She told us to wait by these woods and flora,
For a Princess, a boy, and a Warrior!

And she said...
You must tell them my quest is not cast aside,
Nor have I been captured and tied,

Assure them I've have not fallen and died,
I remain unturned and still on their side.
Beware the king and his tribe,
There's something that they all do hide,
To everyone they have surely lied,
But one among them has defied.

Seek out the shopkeeper, she'll help you,
For there's bigger issues I must pursue,
Liana your Spirit you must accrue,
Save The Dantè, they need you.

And that Monty,
And that Mack,
Is that!

The trio watched bewildered as the musicians danced their way joyfully back toward the woods from where they'd come. Curiously, Liana enjoyed the song. The tune was catchy, and for a brief moment, she thought she saw herself glow a faint orange aura, but immediately shook this from her mind knowing it was impossible, since her Sacral Spirit was in an orb in Allicalidantè.

Seff stepped out from behind the aunt and niece. "What was that all about?"

"A message from Candela," replied Liana. "'*Beware the king and his tribe... seek out the shopkeeper... bigger issues to pursue*'?"

"She could have just written a note," Seff said sarcastically.

"Or sent a Jackdaw," suggested Amara.

"Jackdaw's can only fly so far. She must be far away from here. '*Near 6 months ago...*' she must have come here shortly after the Battle of Coryàtès but didn't stay to take the Jewels of Orange back home. What could be bigger than helping me regain my next Spirit?"

"I don't know, Princess," Amara said, cautiously still holding her whip. "We should get going."

19

A CITY ABANDONED

After a short hike through dusty, heath-like land, the misfit trio (and dog) came to the edge of the old city of Allicalidantè. Liana's mouth hung open in a mixture of awe and disbelief as they walked through the city's abandoned suburbs.

The city's once colourful stone buildings still stood tall and proud, but the paint and decorative features were peeling and falling off. A few smashed bricks lay on the road, but had it not been for the lack of people, the city showed no sign of other dilapidation. Holey banners flapped loosely on flag poles that were placed on the odd important building showing the city's symbol - 'Bandera de las Artes'. Seff explained this translated as 'Flag of the Arts' and it showed a dancing figure holding a paintbrush and a flute, set upon a square diamond-shaped games board. The atmosphere was eerie, but Liana felt there was something else, or rather, lack of something else, which gave the city its creepy edge.

"There's nothing alive here," she said, kicking a cloud of

dust into the air. "No people, no dogs, no cats, no birds. Not even a plant or a tree."

"It happened so fast," said Seff, who was looking through the bars of a fence to a long, single storey building with a bell-tower rising from the middle of it. "This was my school," he said with a solemn, reflective tone (which, to Liana, sounded strange in his squeaky voice). "One week we were all enjoying ourselves an' playin' games, then week by week more and more children and teachers started to get nastier and nastier. Kids were cheatin' whilst playing games, excluding their life-long mates, beatin' them up for no reason. Teachers started to turn up late to class, punishing kids for whatever reason they could. Worst of all, it looked like they enjoyed it."

"That's awful," said Liana, putting a sympathetic hand on Seff's shoulder.

"What made you run and hide for the crater?" asked Amara.

"The king," Seffs hands tightened in anger around the bars as he said the two words.

"If King Shimon saved you, why do you hate him so much?"

"He didn't save us!" shouted Seff angrily, spittle's of saliva spraying over Liana's face, much to her disgust. "I was hiding with some other unaffected children on the school roof, avoiding everyone else until it was time to go home to my parents who were also still unaffected. That's when I saw the king, the prince, and some of their staff ridin' by thinkin' their disguises would fool anyone that saw 'em. Well, they didn't fool me. They took the back roads towards the cliffs - or what I'd always known to be cliffs. Turns out, this giant, square crater with this huge pillar slap bang in the middle of it had appeared outta nowhere, and that's where the king and the prince headed. I could tell they knew summin' they didn't wanna tell the rest of us, the same thing they're still hidin' from us."

"But how did all the people end up in the crater if only the king knew about it?"

"Told me new crew to spread the word, didn't I? Tell anyone they thought were still good that they'd be safe in this new crater. Of course, some of the wrong kind were told. That was gonna happen, but I thought if we could get enough good people there we'd be okay."

"But it wasn't okay?"

Seff shook his head, "Ended up with skirmishes all over town. Me parents got caught up in one. I dunno if they became bad, or if they got killed. Either way, they ain't here no more." A single tear streamed down from each of his eyes as he thought of his parents.

"I'm so sorry, Josef," said Liana, moving her whole arm around his shoulder to comfort him.

"Fortunately, after most of us got into the crater, the pillar made this weird beam of orange light which somehow stopped 'em getting in. The bad ones who did get in were weeded out, and the only way in or out now is through a narrow gorge leadin' out to sea which is always guarded," he sniffed and wiped his nose on the arm of his sleeve as he finished his account.

"Sounds like you're a hero to me," said Liana, nudging the boy with approval.

"Yeh, I guess so," he smiled back.

"I wonder what the king knows…" said Liana, thinking out loud.

"Now you see why I don't trust 'em. Any of 'em."

"Come on, let's keep going," said Amara, keen to get back on track.

The number of decaying bodies grew as the trio moved through the city centre and closer to the cliffs. Corpses strewn sporadically in the dusty streets. They had to cover their faces to try and stop the rotten, vomit inducing smell into their noses.

Around the next corner, the pavements were lined with upturned and broken tables. Chantrah boards, game pieces, puzzle boxes and a host of other gaming equipment lay idly on the ground.

"This used to be Amusement Avenue," Seff said, bending down to pick up a Chantrah game piece. "Every shop on this street was dedicated to some form of fun. This shop here," he said, pointing to a wooden sign above the door which read 'The Wingman'.

"This place had the reputation of sellin' the finest Chantrah gear on this side of Mikana, and that shop there," he said, now pointing across the street. "They sold anythin' that could be played with a ball. Bats, gloves, leather balls, hoops - they had it all."

Cas padded over and with his snout, nudged a deflated ball that sat crumpled on the shop doorstep, before raising an eyebrow that suggested he'd have preferred to stay at home after all.

They continued down Amusement Avenue and Seff continued to point out what each shop specialised in. Wooden plinths were randomly spaced on the pavements that were, according to Seff, used by street performers such as mime artists, painters, musicians, dancers, monologists and many more.

Liana imagined how enthralling this street would be in its

prime. The fun, the creativity, the happiness and the inspiration. Right now, though, it was the depiction of a cowardly, deceptive king who stood by and did nothing as his people were Turned.

"Over here," whispered Amara, signalling for the trio to duck behind the corner of a building. "The next street is the last. We've got to stay low, and quiet."

"Why do we have to be quiet, don't we just need to get to the edge of this crater place?" asked Liana.

"Not exactly."

Liana and Seff gave each other a quizzical look before following in Amara's silent footsteps. They soon realised why she had issued the instruction as they poked their heads up over a garden wall.

"Who're they, and where's the crater?" asked Seff, looking out at a large campsite scattered amongst a field of orange tulips.

"They, child, are the Dantian Immorals who were Turned from your city, amongst others who have gathered here," replied Amara, allowing them a moment to take in the huge number of people in front of them.

"And the crater?" asked Liana.

Amara paused before answering: "They're standing on it."

20
ENEMIES OF THE PAST

'Darkness. A huge mass of darkness. To think I was once like this. Then she saved me, returned me to the light. I can only hope she can repeat the miracle of the Battle of Coryàtès here too.'

Liana's eyes glazed into a glossy white and she began to convulse, not violently, but enough for Amara to have to sit her against the wall of the building behind them.

"What's going on?" asked Seff, who despite his despise for royalty, had an edge of fear in his tone of voice.

"She must have entered the Morality Realm," Amara put her palm on Liana's forehead, checking her temperature.

"The Realm of what now?"

"The Morality Realm," repeated Amara, with a tone of annoyance as she tried to concentrate on checking Liana rather than answer the boy's questions. She gently tapped her cheeks and pinched her ear lobes for a response, but the princess did not react. "Liana," she whispered, "Liana, can you hear me? What's happening? Please, give me a sign you're okay."

Liana slowly turned her head to the left and opened her mouth as if she were about to speak, but no words came out. A few moments later, the sound of muffled voices echoed around the street corner.

"Quick, boy, help me move her out of sight," Seff picked up the princess's ankles, whilst Amara hooked her arms under Liana's armpits, and they hastily hoisted her around the corner of the building. Amara peered around the corner but ducked back as soon as she saw who the voices belonged to and cursed under her breath.

"Summin' wrong with you now too?"

"Those voices belong to Yasmin, Eugene, and…" she stopped herself before saying anymore.

"Am I supposed to know who they are?"

"No, but you sure need to know who they are now," Amara shook Liana's shoulders gently, trying to return her from the Morality Realm. "Come on, come back, come back to us," she urged as she shook. To her relief, Liana's white-glazed eyes faded back into their usual vibrant blue colour. It took her a moment to compose herself and adjust to her surroundings.

Liana's breathing was deep. "Ugh, my head," she winced in pain, feeling her temples, which throbbed like a bass drum beating along to a marching song.

"Princess, you ok?" asked the boy, actually showing genuine concern for his travelling companion.

"I-I think so," she placed her hands on Amara as she came round for balance.

"Yasmin, Eugene and Vivek, they're here, Liana. They're all here. They passed by just as you left our realm."

"I know, I saw them," Liana continued to hold her temples in pain. "I saw them from the Morality Realm. But me going there wasn't intentional, I didn't make it happen. It was the same experience as what happened on my birthday with Agatha and Nalan. I wasn't in control. I thought I'd learned to control it, but I've not been to the other realm since the day of the battle with Vivek." Liana rambled; panic stricken at her inability to control her power of Sight. "It just took over me, again. I was trying to come back, fighting with myself to return here, but it's like someone else wanted me there. Wanted me to see something in the Morality Realm,"

"It's okay, it's okay, calm down. Focus, do that meditation stuff Master H. or Priestess Yi teaches you," Amara did her best to reassure Liana, although empathy wasn't her strongest characteristic.

Liana closed her eyes and focussed on her breathing, blocking out her surroundings, observing herself inwardly, observing her beating heart, observing the ins and outs of her lungs, observing the tension in her muscles. Soon, she began to find control again.

"Vivek. He's different, in the Morality Realm, he looks different. His hunched over, old body is gone. He no longer needs a stick to walk, but he also has no features. No face, no creases, no contours to his body. He's just a black silhouette. A matte black plain silhouette with a Black Aura."

"I can't believe he's still alive," said a shocked Amara. "After that blast from your aura, I was sure those birds carried him away to his final resting place."

Liana shook her head, remembering how he was carried off by a mass of Jackdaws after she cured the Zaganite Immorals of their Bad Morality in the Battle of Coryàtès. "They were heading to the gathering of Immorals, we have to see what they're up to," she jumped up and raced back over to the low-standing wall, peaking above it like a lion watching its prey.

"So, she's here then?" Vivek tapped the top of his walking stick impatiently.

"My contacts in Swyre say she is part of a royal entourage visiting King Shimon and his son, Prince Kendrix," replied Yasmin.

"Excellent! If Plan A doesn't work out, we will find a way to make her our Plan B. Once we have unsealed the Neoteric Temple and this fake ground beneath us disappears, our latest Army of Immorals will descend upon her, the temple and the remnants of this city. All we have to do is wait for our puppet to see through his task. Of course, if he fails, she will do the work for us instead."

"I can't wait to see the look on her face when we take the jewels and her precious dagger from under her nose," Yasmin grinned, evilly. "Isn't that right, Gene?"

Gene said nothing, and just grunted in response.

"Not sure I like Immoral Gene, he's not much of a talker."

"Ignore him, he's just another Turned, no different to the others. Not like you, I need more of your naturally born Bad Morality, Yasmin. If I am to defeat Liana this time, I need to stay topped up at all times."

"Of course," said Yasmin, bowing her head, before pulling aside the neck of her brown shirt and exposing the skin just under her left collar bone.

Vivek raised his hand, a black mark covered his palm like a spider's web, stretching up his wrist through his veins. He touched Yasmin's skin, and blasts of misty black wisps pulsed up his arm. His Black Aura grew stronger and thicker.

"This isn't good," said a concerned Amara.

"Not good at all," agreed Liana, shaking her head in disbelief at the sight before her.

"Kinda cool though," an awe-struck Seff said, before

getting elbowed on both sides from his companions. "I-I mean, it's kind of cool how those tulips are just regrowing after they get trampled on," he said, trying to recover.

"I know that's not what you meant, but you're right about the tulips," Liana agreed.

A large, circular field of orange tulips lay below the feet of the Immorals, but as one of the delicate flowers was stepped on, another would sprout up next to it. The Immorals, clearly bored and with nothing else to occupy their minds, were playing whack-a-mole with their feet - and losing.

"I reckon that field of tulips is right above the pillar," said the boy.

"Your Sacral Spirit must be keeping them alive," suggested Amara.

"That's totally amazing, but if it's powering these tulips and this false floor, won't my Spirit eventually run out?" Liana said, concerned if they didn't get to their goal in time, that she would not attain her Orange Aura. "We need to find the Sacral Orb and figure out how we can take it without letting in the Immorals. First thing's first, where's your secret entrance to the crater below?"

"About a hundred metres over there," said Amara, pointing easterly in the direction of a small pile of rocks. "We'll have to stay low and go around, the Immorals have grown in numbers since I was last here."

They moved stealthily, crouched low behind walls and shrubbery around the gathering of Immorals. A few skirmishes broke out among the group, before being ordered to fall in line by Vivek.

'I guess that's what happens if you have no morality. No sense of order and being free to take what you want, at the expense of others. Perhaps we could use this against them,' thought Liana as they

neared the rock pile, their avoidance of being detected helped by the distractions within the Immorals.

"Between these rocks is a narrow entrance that leads into the crater below. Have either of you been caving before?" Seff shook his head in response to Amara's question.

"Only through the old mines, from the Tomb of the Transcended," answered Liana. "But they were purpose built mine shafts, not small and tight like this."

Amara could see the trepidation in both the children's faces. She again had to put on a reassuring manner. "There are tight spots and damp areas, so don't be afraid of your clothes getting wet or torn."

"Can't I just protect us with my Red Aura Screen?" suggested Liana.

"Can you be sure it won't affect the rocks, won't cut any away or dislodge them?"

"No, probably not, you've seen how powerful it is."

"Then it's best you don't use it, we don't want it to cave in on ourselves. Just follow me, watch where I put my hands and my feet and copy me exactly. And mind your heads. Here, take these," Amara handed out a leather headband, with notches in like a belt, but smaller in circumference. Attached to the headband was a Quartaltium casing with wood-bound rags inside, saturated in fat, the same formula that's found in traditional torches. "Put these on. We'll light them just inside the entrance, we don't want to draw attention to ourselves out here."

"This thing's heavy," complained Seff as he buckled the belt around his head.

"You want to be able to see down there, don't you?" Liana retorted as she tightened her own band as tight as she could make it. "Wait, what about Cas? Will he be able to make it through?"

"I doubt it, it definitely requires fingers and thumbs."

"But we can't leave him here. There's nothing to eat or drink, and what about the Immorals? I couldn't live with myself if he got Turned."

"We'll take him," said a voice from behind. "Looks like he could keep the other scavenging hounds at bay."

"Franklin!" Amara announced excitedly, like when you see a good friend you haven't seen in a long time.

"Miss Amara, I see you brought friends with you this time."

"Liana, this is Franklin, the man who told me about the Pillar of Sanctuary."

"Pleasure," said Franklin, tipping his dusty bicorne hat.

"Franklin, this is Princess Liana Langton. Otherwise known within the Aurora Visendus as the Light from the Dark or Restorer of the Spectrum," said Amara, slightly sarcastically. All these titles made Liana blush hearing them out loud.

"You can also add 'Guardian of Light' to that, apparently," added Liana, reluctantly, but for some reason thought it was a necessary addition to the conversation.

"Those are some impressive titles you hold, but I can tell you first-hand, a title isn't what makes you who you are. For our sake though, I certainly hope you live up to them. I can relate. I'm a doctor, you see."

"And one of the best Chantrah players in the whole of Mikana," added Amara.

"Supposedly," Franklin gently chuckled. "But when I tell people I'm a doctor, they assume I'm a Doctor of Medicine. After I've let them tell me about all their ailments, they do get quite mad when I tell them I'm a Doctor of Engineering and suggest they seek out a medical professional," Franklin chuckled again to himself.

"As a Doctor of Engineering, I'd think you'd want to be around the Pillar of Sanctuary as much as possible. Sounds like a piece of engineering you'd want to study," said Liana.

"Well, that is why I was there that day, despite the warnings given to me by Priestess Yi."

"Priestess Yi?"

"Last year, at the city's prestigious Tournament of Tournaments, where I was finally hoping to become the Chantrah Champion, a figure grabbed me and whispered in my ear words I have not forgotten. It was an eerily accurate foreshadowing of what was to come." Franklin paused before recounting the words. Liana wasn't sure if it was just for dramatic effect or if just saying the words aloud was in some way painful for him to hear. He spoke softly. "When this city is turned into a joyless casket, be sure to stay away. There will come a time when we need your skills." He paused again and looked Liana in the eyes. "I didn't listen. I stayed and I almost died. If it wasn't for her," he said, averting his gaze toward an unlit lighthouse. "I wouldn't be here talking to you." Liana could just about make out the outline of a woman standing in the gallery. The group stood in silence for a moment as Franklin stared at the lighthouse with longing eyes. Even the ineptest reader of emotions could tell he was deep in love.

"He's a good dog," said Liana, changing the subject whilst stroking Cas's head. For some reason, she felt Franklin could use the comfort of a furry friend. "He'll do anything to protect you, but please don't let anything happen to him," Liana pleaded.

"I promise," said Franklin, who kneeled and ruffed up Cas's white fur. Cas's canines showed through his huge grin.

"We decided to take up residence in the lighthouse to keep an eye on this entrance, and it's a pretty good defence when the only way to reach us is at the top of a spiral staircase. Little chance of being overrun."

"Clever," Amara said with respect for the decision.

"I'm Seff, by the way, not that I'm important enough to be introduced," Seff poked his head up out of the darkness of the opening to the small cave.

"It had nothing to do with importance," argued Amara.

"Then what?"

"It's 'cause you're annoying!" said Amara as she pushed Seff back into the hole with the sole of her boot.

"Yeh, you keep telling yourself that!" echoed Seff's voice from the darkness.

~

Amara struck a match and lit each of the mini torches attached to their heads. The yellowly glow of the flames mixed with the translucent-blue of Quartaltium glass emitted a green light around them.

They continued to traverse down the slippery cave, sliding, jumping, side-stepping and clutching as they carefully followed Amara's lead.

After approximately twenty minutes, the three emerged from a dry, dead bush whose roots still clung to the side of the crater's inner cliff face. Their clothes and skin even more muddied and even more shredded than when they had entered.

"Well, you definitely fit in now," joked Seff as patted himself down, wiping as much sludge off himself as possible.

"Ugh," is all Liana could muster as she hung her arms out

like a scarecrow. She may not have been a traditionally pristinely kept royal, but even she hadn't gotten this grimy before. After brushing herself down, she eventually looked up and took in her surroundings. The night sky, which should have been filled with stars, was just a mass of black. A shadowy mass of black feet walking about on a fake surface of orange energy created by her Sacral Spirit, which was flowing out the top of the massive, black metallic-like pillar protruding above the tops of the dishevelled rooftops. Whatever berries that had once grown on the cliff face walls had long been stripped and the flora left to die, leaving behind dried and browned clumps of bush to hang limp like a decade old unwashed hairbrush might look.

"Hush," said Amara, putting a finger to her lips. The sudden gesture from Amara made Liana jump. "I think there's someone coming, quick over here, we don't want them to know about our little exit here," she hurriedly ushered them into a large trunk-like crate, big enough for them all to fit, and closed the lid. The slits between the wood enabled them to just about see out to see who was passing by.

"Hey, that's Prince Kendrix! I'd know that ring anywhere," said Seff, as the prince's hands parted the sticks of the dead bush. "The ring was his mother's. King Shimon must've given it to him after she died."

"Prince Kendrix? What's he doing sneaking out? And how does he know about this route out of the crater?"

"Something else for us to investigate," Amara contemplated out loud as he disappeared out of sight.

"Well, at least the princess 'ere *definitely* won't have any issues fittin' in now," the boy clenched his nose. "Not only does she look a mess, this crate's had dead fish in it. Now she'll smell like we do too!" Seff found this hilarious as he leapt out from the crate and made off down a make-shift wooden walkway between two buildings.

"Oi, come back here!" shouted Liana, who wore a face like thunder as she and Amara watched the annoying brat flee, but she also knew his jibe was completely accurate. She did indeed smell horridly of fish.

21
THEORY OF MORALITY

Queen Adriya's tall, slender figure stood stern-faced on the docks at the mines. Her soft-faced complexion formed a natural-born front for her direct personality. Her straight, jet-black hair rested elegantly down the front of her shoulders, meeting her folded arms. She was not happy. Priestess Yi stood nearby, fiddling with the bracelet that kept her orbs together. Marginally smaller in height, had it not been for Priestess Yi's slightly squarer cheekbones, one may be forgiven for mistaking the queen and the priestess for sisters without knowing them in advance. Of course, everyone on the island knew who they both were so that mistake had never been made. If it ever were made, that person would be in a cul-de-sac of castigation from both parties for even suggesting such a possibility, such was their fiery relationship with one another.

Priestess Yi released a small giggle as the ship in front of them struggled with the task of docking close enough to the pier. Three times it had attempted, and finally, on the fourth try, it was close enough for its crew to disembark down the gangway.

"See, I told ya, if ya just listened to me in the first place," the unmistakable accent of Benji, Swyre's Merchant Guild Leader, berated the skinny bald man walking next to him. Waylon pushed his spectacles up the ridge of his nose as he tried to argue back, but the stuttering of his speech only hampered his effort to debate. By the time he'd finished his sentence, the pair were already on the pier and stood before the Queen.

"Do you purposefully seek out to put my daughter in harm's way, *Benjamin*?" The Queen wasted little time in getting to the point.

"Now 'ang on, only my mother ever called me…"

"I will call you whatever I want, *Benjamin*," the Queen said, with an emphasis on saying his name in full. "Did I make a mistake in making you the Merchant Guild Leader? It seems like a bit of extra responsibility has gone to your head, *Benjamin*."

"Ya don't learn how to be a master of Chantrah by readin' the play books, yer Majesty. Sure, they give ya the rules, but ya gotta be in the game, to know the game. Ain't no good havin' someone else play it for ya whilst you sit on the side-lines. Lianas got to learn, make her own mistakes, find her own way of winning."

"I'm not interested in your philosophies, *Benjamin*. The Queen's Table was in agreement. At least, I thought we were," the Queen shot a glance towards the priestess.

"Aye, but what happened to ye thinking of an excuse, eh priestess?"

"What can I say? The Queen's too clever, saw right through my cover story."

"Oh, come now, priestess. As if Liana would have gone fishing with Benji to the northern waters - she can barely stand the sight of dead fish. She hates the 'flip-flopping, boggle eyed things,' as she calls them. Especially when they're out of water, they creep her out."

"Yes, I guess I should get to know Liana a little better before I try creating cover stories for her in the future," reflected the priestess.

"Let's hope for your sake there won't be a need for creating them in the future," jousted the Queen.

The three members of the Queen's Table walked off towards the mines, still arguing amongst each other. Waylon lagged behind them in tow. They neared rows of warehouses that lined the mines harbour port. The warehouses kept stock of the island's main exports of Quartz, Cobalt, and the refined amalgamation of the two - Quartaltium, the island's trademark translucent blue glass.

The Queen gazed south, past the harbour and warehouses, towards the mining entrance and reflected on the sight of the four large walls that formed two triangles against the cliff face. Thankfully, the deconstruction of them was nearing completion.

She avoided coming back to the mines whenever possible, in an attempt to put the battle with Vivek and Zagan out of her mind. She'll never forget the feeling of being dropped off the top of the battlements by her former clerk and aide, Vivek, and then being buried under the rubble with Liana. She'd also never forget the feeling of relief and awe as she looked up into her daughter's eyes at that moment, the red glow of Liana's Red Aura preventing them from being crushed. The memories of her near-death experience made her shudder and she hugged herself as the salty sea breeze also caught her bare arms.

"Mr Ellwood, I trust you are well?"

"I most certainly am, your majesty," said the beaming face of a slightly plump man in braces, with curly blonde hair whose cheeks dimpled deep as he smiled. A small tuft of blonde hair sat on his chin and quivered in the wind. He joined the group in ambling down the harbourside past the large warehouse.

"I hope you were able to see your son before he set sail?"

"Absolutely, I did. Very proud of him, I am. As is his mother, she is. Both proud of him, we are."

"Liana is lucky to have friends like Joel and Saffina," replied the Queen, sincerely.

"Why are you here, I ask?" said Mr Ellwood, in his usual strange manner.

"Imagine watching a conversation between these two," Benji whispered to Priestess Yi, signalling with his thumb between Mr Ellwood and Waylon. The priestess couldn't help but giggle.

"Priestess Yi and Benjamin here decided it would be a good idea to sail my daughter to Allicalidantè," the Queen's answer to Mr Ellwood's question quickly silenced the pair's hushed laughter.

"They don't trust Joel and the others, I think," responded Joel's father.

"Apparently not," agreed the Queen. "But the priestess did mention to me, whilst I was interrogating her about my daughter's whereabouts, that she is concerned about the effect releasing her Good Morality had on the Zaganites."

"Concerned, she is?" Mr Ellwood raised a quizzical eyebrow.

"You are not concerned?"

"No, I am not. Everything is great here, I think. There is no trouble, in fact. They all help each other and accept why they are here, they do."

The noisy sounds of the refineries began to come within earshot. To their right, a middle-aged woman carrying pails of water turned her ankle on a loose stone. A man with a long, unkempt beard rushed out to help the woman, and asked if she was ok.

"No trouble, see."

"What do you make of it, priestess? Seven months and no trouble. Output has barely dropped off either."

"From a purely governance and industrial perspective, it is obviously good news, but from a Visendi and Liana perspective, I can only draw one conclusion.

When your uncle, Sir Tarak, first found Liana he mentioned seeing a burned figure in the shape of a foetus in the grass next to her. I have deliberated over this ever since and I have settled upon a theory about Liana's ability of Sight and her extraordinary power of Good Morality.

Every living creature should be able to be Turned. From Good to Bad, Bad to Good, whether intentionally or unintentionally, guided or unguided, everything has both Good and Bad within them, it just depends on any number of variables and factors which way you sway.

But despite their past experiences and the conditions they are working in, these miners remain of Good Morality and have done so ever since they were Turned back by Liana following the Battle of Coryàtès. It's as if they are not even capable of a relapse."

"That's good, isn't it? We don't want those of Bad Morality causing chaos and disruption."

"For us and for them it seems like a positive narrative, but we need to ask ourselves: what if Liana's Good Morality is not limitless? Candela already alluded to this fact after the battle.

So now we consider this: What if the burned figure in the grass was Liana's Bad Morality? What if, on the Day of Darkness, her Moralities became separated, and her Bad Morality escaped or somehow found its way into another?"

"You mean, find its way into someone like Vivek? It would explain a lot. He was once trusted by not just me, but my father also. Served in our family for years before the events with Zagan without a hint of doubt about his loyalty. And it is true, Liana was born from the joining of a Spectra and an Immoral. It does not seem too far-fetched of a theory," nodded the Queen.

"If my theory is right, it means there could be someone out there with the same power of Morality as Liana, but for the Bad. And as Liana uses up her own Good, the less she will have left for the inevitable fight with her opposite self."

The questions and theories of morality that Priestess Yi proposed concerned Queen Adriya. They concerned her deeply. Even if Liana regained her Spirits and fought off those opposed to her, what state would this war leave her in?

22
THE SHOPKEEPER

"Ugh, I hate these flip-flopping, boggle eyed things," complained Liana as she stared at the fish cooking above the open fire that Amara had made in the dead-end of a vacated alleyway. "I can't believe that little twerp ran off," she complained some more.

"Took off with all our food too. How'd he even do that without us noticing?" wandered Amara.

"Stupid little thief. Boasting to his crew right now I expect," Liana pouted.

Amara sliced open the fish and the pair picked at the white meat reluctantly. *'If Benji was with us he could at least make it edible,'* thought Liana.

"Well, that was terrible," Liana wiped her hands on her filthy robes.

"I've had worse," said Amara, a clear reference to her time in the mines. "Shh, I hear voices. Quick, put the fire out," Amara hurriedly stamped out the flames.

A female voice whispered through the otherwise quiet

street. "Tell me again why we're roaming the streets when everyone else is asleep?"

"The boy said there was a way out."

"But Dimitra, we're breaking curfew."

"It's not like there's going to be any guards this far away from the palace."

"You don't know that."

"Look, Myra, do you want to get out of this dump or not?"

"What I want is to get my ring fixed after that brute of a woman back on Coryàtès smashed it up. It's all I have left from my precious father, before he was crushed by that thing," the woman glanced up over the tops of the makeshift dwelling toward the towering pillar.

"Will you stop going on about that damn ring?"

"It's one-of-a-kind! Or at least it was. If I could find the woman who made it then maybe she could fix it!"

"She probably died in the abandoning of the city, like most others. Our best bet is getting out of this place and I'm fancying our chances somewhere else."

The woman with the broken ring sighed. "Yeh, you're probably right."

"Besides, I can't bear to eat another stinking fish."

"I know how she feels, and I've only had one," quipped Liana to Amara, receiving an elbow to the ribs for her wit.

"Dimitra, I hear guards! What did I tell you?"

"Quick, Myra, down this alley!"

The two women bolted down the alleyway towards Liana and Amara, who were now crouched in a sunken doorway.

"There's nowhere to hide!"

"We'll be fed to the king himself if we're caught outside this late at night!"

"Quick Dimitra, what do we - wahhh!" The two women

were whisked out of the middle of the alleyway by Liana and Amara, who held their mouths closed with the palms of their hands, shushing them until the guards had passed and only releasing the women once they were sure the guards had passed on by.

"Thank you!" said the woman called Myra, with a sigh of relief. "I'm glad you didn't hand us in for being out after curfew!"

"And risk all of us ending up on the king's plate? I'm pretty sure this body tastes better than that fish." Amara patted her chest.

"You certainly picked a good hiding spot," Dimitra observed. "We were standing right next to you and never even saw you."

"I'm good in the shadows," replied Amara.

"Well, we best be off," said Dimitra, somewhat nervously.

"Hold on," Amara grabbed her by the arm, "I heard you mention something about a boy. Was he wearing a navy-blue shirt and trousers, with a filthy robe? Kind of annoying…"

"Oh, erm, yes, he was, actually," Dimitra confirmed.

"Where was he heading?"

"He was hanging around near that shop about an hour ago, you know, the one which sells puzzles and games, down on the main street that runs between The Pillar and the harbour. Said he'd tell me of a way out of this hole, all I had to do was handover this bag he was holding to some shopkeeper and promise not to look inside. I agreed and he told me how to get out of this place. That's where we are heading now, you're welcome to come along if you like."

"Let me guess, he told you you have to climb through a cave in the cliff, through a bush, at the top of that dead-end alleyway up there," Amara said, pointing.

"Yes, how'd you know that?"

"Because he sold us the same lie," lied Amara.

"What? But, what about the bag?"

"Illegal delivery. Didn't want to get caught. Guards are probably on to him. How'd you think those puzzles get made? Not out of this driftwood that's for sure," said Amara, knocking her knuckles on the wooden frame of the doorway they were standing in. "Probably been stealing off that ship from Coryàtès too. Reckon you handed over a bag of nice fresh fruit and veg."

Myra gasped. "That would explain why that shop owner still looks so well fed! I knew this was a waste of time, Dimitra!"

Dimitra clenched her fists and stamped her foot. "Ugh, I just want to get out of here."

"Why don't you take us to this shop, and we'll see if we can help you get out of here?" suggested Amara.

Myra and Dimitra looked at one and mutually shrugged in agreement.

The four set off. Myra and Dimitra led the way, with Amara and Liana ten paces back, ready to dip into the shadows at any sign of trouble, fully prepared to hang their guides out to dry if the situation required it.

"Why'd you lie to them about the cave?" asked Liana.

"Well let's face it, for starters they'd probably get stuck in there,"

'Fair point.'

"Secondly, you know what's waiting for them up there, and we can't have our only way in and out exposed to any random eejit."

'Another good point.'

"So, this shop, what are your thoughts?"

"It must be where his crew hide-out."

"But why get someone else to deliver the food? It'd be more like Seff to charge down the door and announce himself their saviour and revel in all the glory."

"That does sound just like something the annoying twerp would do, so I honestly have no idea why he'd get someone else to hand it over."

The newly formed foursome set off down the alleyway, a mix of cobblestone and dirt beneath their feet.

Myra looked over her shoulder and whispered to Dimitra. "You know, there's something familiar about that woman, I just can't put my finger on why."

∽

"Well, here we are," announced Dimitra. "The only fun place left in The Dantè. What are you gonna do, hang around until the kid shows up and rough him up? You look like the sort, with that scar of yours."

Amara touched her face where the long, trench-like scar cut down past her eye and down her cheek. She didn't need reminding of it. "Something like that."

"So, you gonna get us out of here now?"

"What am I, a magician as well? I said, '*We'll see* if we can help you get out of here'. I'll look into it, okay? Maybe that kid does have a way out, and if he does, I'll beat it out of him. You can join in, if you want." Amara teased the slightly dim women knowing violence wouldn't be in their repertoire of skills. Come to think of it, Amara wasn't sure what would be in their repertoire of skills.

"Oh, erm, that's not really our thing."

"Yes, we prefer other people to do the beating."

"We've been known to watch a fight or two."

"Well, preferably not child beating though, we have morals you know."

Amara leaned into Liana and whispered: "You wanna check that?"

"Nah, I think we're good," Liana chuckled.

"Shame, might've given me an excuse to beat them and all," Amara said sarcastically.

The two women prattled on until Amara interrupted assertively. "Myra, Dimitra, are you staying or are you going?"

"Staying."

"Going."

"What do you mean going?" said Dimitra.

"What do you mean staying?" said Myra.

Amara sunk her head into her hands as the young women squabbled with each other, before the shop door opened with a squeak and a large, frowning woman stood imposingly in the doorway. She wore a dirtied headscarf, which matched the dirt stains on her cheeks, and a grey dress which fell to just above her ankles with a brown canvas apron over the top. The bickering pair stopped their argument.

"Sorry to bother you, Miss…" Liana waited for a response, but the only reply she got was a sniff from the large woman's nose, followed by the wiping of snot on her sleeve, causing Dimitra to gag.

"Do you know a boy called Josef, or Seff as he likes to be called? Is the little twerp here? I have words for him…" piped Amara. The large woman's mouth curled up slightly in amusement. Liana couldn't tell if this was because she also thought Seff was a little twerp, or if she simply liked Amara's directness.

After a few awkward seconds of silence, the large woman

turned sideways with a grunt and held her arm out inviting the foursome inside. Due to the size of her belly, none of them could help but brush up against the large woman as they squeezed on through into the shop entrance. Not even the slight, teenage figure of Liana could avoid it. Dimitra gagged again as she was sure she felt some sweaty wetness touch her arm as she sidestepped past.

Once inside, Liana's eyes widened as she looked around her new surroundings. Sitting on floor-to-ceiling shelving on all four walls was a huge variety of wooden and stone objects. She slowly walked around the room inspecting them. One bay of shelving housed 3D shapes of all varieties. Cubes, spheres and pyramids seemed to be the most common. Liana picked up one of the sphere's and turned it over in her hands. She heard something rattle inside and noticed the faint outline of a joint running around the sphere's equator. She instinctively twisted the two halves and gently shook the object. She heard a clunk inside, which allowed the sphere to come apart in her hands. Inside was a small, silver coin, a reward for completing the puzzle.

She continued to peruse the shop's offerings. There were card games, board games, standard picture puzzles, and brain-teaser puzzles which required assembly through lateral thinking, such as one puzzle that consisted of just 7 strangely cut puzzle pieces that you had to fit into a rectangular receptacle. Try as she might, Liana could not get the pieces to fit.

One bay lay almost completely empty. A small place card read 'outdoor games'. A few wooden bats were lying lonesome on the bottom shelf.

"This is where the ball games used to be kept, but there's no livestock to make any new balls out of," said Myra, who was standing next to Liana holding one of the bats, practising a rather weak swing.

In the centre of the room sat three hexagonal tables, each with a pair of chairs. The shape of the tables themselves were a giveaway for what was to be played on them, it was the trademark shape of a Chantrah game table. Two of the tables were empty and not setup, but one table had a tablecloth over the top of it, covering the pieces underneath.

"Is this a special board?" Liana asked, as she moved her hand towards the cloth, wanting a peek inside. Her hand was slapped away aggressively, with another grunt, by the large woman. Liana raised her hands defensively. "Okay, okay, I won't touch it," she said, somewhat annoyed. *'It's only a game board,'* she thought to herself.

"What's your name?" Liana asked, trying to build some rapport, but the woman simply turned her back on the princess and waved her question away. Liana rolled her eyes at the rudeness as the large woman took a seat in a rocking chair that wasn't quite wide enough for all of her to fit in between the armrests. The rocking chair rolled back and forth, creaking under the strain in the corner beside a square desk. On the desk lay various cutting and measuring instruments; vice's, clamps, and rolled up parchments of drawings and scribbles. It was clear this was where the shopkeeper designed and built her goods.

"Do you know a boy called Seff?" Liana asked the shopkeeper a question for the third time but wasn't expecting any sort of useful response by now, so it was a surprise when the woman half-grunted, half-spoke the words: "In there," with a half-hearted wave of an arm towards a door behind the workstation desk, under a sign which read 'Private - Keep Out'.

"Thank you," replied Liana in one of her official royal

tones of pleasantry. *'Kill them with kindness, as my mother says,'* she thought to herself regarding the woman's bad manners. *'Has to be through a door which says 'Keep Out' though. Nothing alarming about that at all...'*

Liana and Amara made their way through the doorway. Dimitra and Myra decided to stay and browse the shop - the sign probably put them off, Liana thought.

Through the doorway was a dark corridor which acted as a stockroom, of sorts. Piles of wood and stone lay against one wall, while cabinets and paperwork lay against the other. Another doorway greeted them directly ahead and the pair had to tread carefully over the debris covering the floor.

They entered the second doorway and came across a floor full of blankets, clothes, and pillows. Amongst the heap of cloth, eight children were sound asleep, snoring. A staircase to the left led up to the first floor, where Liana assumed the shopkeeper lived.

One of the boys stirred and jumped up in surprise at the sight of Liana and Amara standing over him, and in doing so, trod on one of the other children, and like wildfire the children all awoke in a frenzy.

"Who are you?" shouted the eldest child, a girl about the same age as Liana, with the same slang accent as Seff. "How'd you get in 'ere?"

"It's okay," Liana said reassuringly. "The shopkeeper let us in, we're looking for your crew leader, Seff."

23
STUBBORN OLD MEN

King Shimon, Prince Kendrix, Sir Tarak, and Luci once again conversed at the table where the entourage had first sat down for their meal of bland chicken. It had now been a week since they'd first landed in Allicalidantè and negotiations between the two monarchies had still not progressed. The restricted menu of egg or oily fish was only hindering the discussions as Sir Tarak and Liana's doppelgänger were becoming more and more temperamental without a decent meal inside them.

It had also become apparent, that despite the palace's grand exterior of carved pillars and stairways along the crater's rear cliff face, that the inside didn't consist of anything more than what the entourage had already seen, with the exception of individual quarters for King Shimon and Prince Kendrix.

There was no grand throne room, no hall, no games rooms, not even a laundry room. Clothes were packed up in bags by the king's servants and taken to be washed down in the harbour where a few of the Dantian women and children had made small businesses from providing laundry services.

Money was of no use in this new Allicalidantè and trades for services were made in payments of the best-looking food or clothing. If the weather and tides were just right, then the fishing vessels may venture out a little further and return with mussels and crabs, but due to the condition of the ships, it was risky to venture too far out of the canyon and often it was safer to stay inland.

The fishermen also required King Shimon's authorisation to travel outside the confines of the crater and canyon, for he did not want to risk losing any equipment that was used to source food. So much so, that the curfew put in place in the crater was partly in place to deter the fishermen from attempting to make it across the Eastern Sea to Swyre at nightfall. The promise of a better life on Coryàtès, even if it had been to be smuggled into Zagan's army, was appealing to a Dantian in their situation. King Shimon realised this and put an end to unauthorised travel after two vessels didn't return. Archers were positioned and camouflaged along the canyon cliff faces to enforce his ruling. The difference in the manner of how the King ruled was stark in comparison to his own family, thought Sir Tarak.

"I still can't believe you won't accept our offer," said a frustrated Sir Tarak as he slapped his hand down on the cold stone table.

"For the last time, we will not leave the last of what we call home," King Shimon's cheeks shook under his full-grey beard angrily.

"But how much longer can you really think you and your people will last here? We're offering all of your people asylum in Swyre in exchange that we can remain here and research the

Pillar of Sanctuary," explained Sir Tarak, for what felt like the hundredth time.

"When we sent you aid on your Day of Darkness, did we suggest you up and leave your homes and come and live in The Dantè? No! We shipped over whatever you needed to rebuild."

"That was different. We hadn't been forced into a cul-de-sac of no return," argued Sir Tarak.

"To leave would be to admit defeat."

"Even if it means all of your people perish?"

"I would rather be known as the Last King of Allicalidantè than the cowardly king who fled."

"Then you would rather be known as a fool."

"Do I need to remind you that you are here as our guest!"

"Do I need to remind you that I have a ship roaming nearby stocked full of fresh fruit, vegetables, lamb, beef, venison and wine that will all be turning bad if these talks don't progress swiftly?"

"If you were truly an honourable monarchy, you would be distributing to those in need regardless of our talks."

"If you had any intelligence, these talks would already be over with, and your people would be feasting. I am no fool, I will not show you my cards before making a call."

"Ha! Are you trying to speak in the tongue of The Dantè with metaphors of games? You are more skilled with your tongue than I give you credit for, especially for a warrior," King Shimon waggled a finger in Sir Tarak's direction with a sarcastic snicker. "Tell me," He started, straightening his face back to a serious frown. "Why is our pillar so important to you?"

Sir Tarak drew a deep breath, before answering: "I'm not at liberty to say. It's a curiosity to us. We are a land known for its research and innovations. Progress excites us. Clerk Vivek has advanced our technologies in many ways. You of course know of our Quartaltium trade."

"Ah yes, Clerk Vivek. I'm surprised the old man wasn't chosen as one of your aides for these negotiations," King Shimon stated provocatively.

"He's more interested in applying theories and research than discussing the terms for them," Sir Tarak fidgeted nervously in his seat.

"Ah-ha!" shouted King Shimon, bolting up from his seat. "Liar!"

"Excuse me? How dare you!" responded Sir Tarak, rather unconvincingly.

"We might be living a sheltered life here, but I am not completely sheltered from news of other lands. I heard that whilst we were retreating into this damned crater, you had a civil war of your own, led by that clerk, nonetheless. And you take me to be a fool? Ha! From what I understand, there was more than just wood, metal and stone used as ammunition. Tell me, have you harnessed your own new power, and now you simply seek to take ours whilst we are too weak in order to make your monarchy even stronger?" King Shimon's insinuation and knowledge of the events on Swyre caught Sir Tarak off guard. His scouts had only ever reported that the Dantian's only ever heard of unrest on Coryàtes, nothing more. *'How did the king know so much detail?'* Sir Tarak wracked his brain for an answer to his own question, the only answer being that someone had talked since they docked, but with the limited crew he had brought, he found that theory hard to believe. The Queen's Table had been clear that they did not want other lands to know about the powers of the Visendi. They did not want other lands being targeted by the Immoral enemies of

Liana for their own gain, for their numbers would surely grow. The Queen's Table also did not want the additional threat of other lands possessing these abilities. Priestess Yi informed her subjects that if they should spread word to other lands of their powers, they would be banished from the religion and risk losing their Aura's. This proved too much of a deterrent to most citizens who enjoyed having their Red Root Aura for show. Although not keen on lying to her followers, the priestess was not averse to bending the truths of the religion, having been forced to preach it underground for many years before the Day of Darkness.

"If your theory were true, why would we bother to set up these negotiations? We could have easily taken this sunken hamlet for ourselves," jibed Sir Tarak in response.

"Hamlet? Pah! Petty insult, I might have expected more from you. Then again, I might not.

I will give you three more days to adjust your terms. I may agree to let you venture into the boundaries of the pillar for a small period of time, so long as you provide us with food, drink, ships and weaponry for the duration of your stay. With that support, we may be able to stand on our own two feet again."

"You can't stay here, and you know it. You simply can't afford to turn down any deal of ours, you must see sense,"

"I do have ways of ensuring you can't leave, Sir Tarak. I just hope it won't come to that."

"Is that a threat?"

"Only if you make it one."

The king and knight stared each other down. The day's negotiations had soured even more, and neither were prepared to back down. Luci broke the silence. Her and Prince Kendrix had been largely spectators throughout the entire discussions. "Well, why don't we go back and discuss our options with the other's, Great Uncle?"

"Yes, we should do the same, father," suggested Prince Kendrix.

"Later," the King and Knight said in unison, before each stormed off in opposite directions, leaving just the prince and fake princess in the room. They waited until the pairs of footsteps had faded out of earshot, before Luci threw herself into the arms of the prince.

"Kendrix, isn't there anything you can do to persuade your father to let us be alone with this pillar? If your people are around whilst we conduct our research, there's no telling how much danger they may be in," Luci put on her widest puppy-dog eyes and rested her palms on his chest plate.

"I've tried. He's a stubborn old man. My mother was the only one who could influence him," Prince Kendrix said as held Luci's hands. "I want to help you find the secret of the pillar, this thing which both protects us and kills us, but it is not so easy, princess. I do know that when this is over, I want us to be together."

The teenagers gazed into each other's eyes and slowly moved their lips together into a soft kiss.

24

PLAY AGAIN TOMORROW

"Seff ain't our leader!" announced the older girl, as the group of children burst out in laughter. "Sure, he tipped us off and kinda saved us when he saw the king was retreating to this pillar place, but he's used that to hold over us ever since."

"Yeh, 'I saved you all so I should get the best pick of the food,'" a younger girl mimicked.

"And cheating to win in games, thinking we wouldn't complain," piped up one of the young boys in the group.

"Would always sleep furthest away from the door, the safest place in case of danger," said the first teenage girl. "He's no leader of ours. Why'd you think we kicked him out?"

"Kicked him out?" Liana repeated. "He told me he snuck onto the Maiden II to smuggle back food and clothes from Swyre for you all because he was your crew leader."

"Ha! That'd be him just tryin' to make up for screwin' us over all the time. Worm his way back in, like."

"Yeh, but we ain't interested," squeaked another younger girl, who was probably no older than 6 or 7 years old.

"Heh, I knew that kid was as annoying to everyone else as he is to me," said Amara, who'd taken a seat on the staircase.

"If he wanted back in, then why'd he get Dimitra and Myra to deliver the supplies he stole from us?"

"That food was yours?" said another boy. "Now I feel bad," he added, hanging his head like he was ashamed.

"It's fine, you need it more than us."

"Not what you were saying ten minutes ago," Amara said under her breath, loud enough so only Liana could hear her clearly, jibing at the princesses' complaints about her cooking of the fish.

"So, how'd you all end up here, in the game shop?"

"Miss Rothkofsky found us sheltering on a small stretch of shingle under the pier whilst she was out searching for driftwood and invited us to live with her."

"Rothkofsky? Is that the name of the shopkeeper?"

"Yeh, she's really kind," said the tiniest girl.

"She does her best to keep us warm and fed. Aside from the fishermen, and the king, obviously, she's probably the most well-off person here. No one comes close to her craft for making toys and games."

"Fishermen often offer her the best produce in exchange for a puzzle or game to take back to their families. There's not much else to do for fun around here."

"But she needs materials to make new stuff, so we'll go out and forage for decent pieces of wood or help prepare meals like seaweed soup so that she has the time to make them."

Liana raised a perplexed eyebrow. Were they really talking about the same woman who grunted at every question she asked?

"So you don't know why Seff had someone else drop off the supplies he stole from us and then disappear?" asked Liana, bringing the conversation back onto the boy.

"No idea, don't sound like him. Surprised he ain't dancin' around and singing how great he is for gettin' it," said the older girl, folding her arms. "You ask me, he's up to summin'. Definitely smells fishy." Liana smiled at the girl's obvious pun.

"Who're you, anyway? Walkin' in 'ere askin' all these questions."

"Oh, right, sorry," apologised Liana. She went around always assuming everyone knew who she was, but since they weren't on Coryàtès and she had been hooded the whole time to hide her vibrant indigo-blue hair, she'd forgotten the need for introductions. However, she couldn't introduce herself as the Liana Langton, the Princess of Coryàtès, for she was already supposed to be here visiting King Shimon.

"My name is Luci," she lied. "And this is my Auntie Amara."

"And what're you doin' here? Your skin looks too smooth to be from The Dantè."

Liana hesitated, thinking of an excuse. One sprang to mind quicker than she thought it would. "We were servants of the Langton's in Swyre. They didn't treat us well. We were leashed. No freedom. Our only life was to serve night and day, so we ran and hid aboard the first foreign ship we could find, and found ourselves here."

"That is bad luck, ending up here. I thought the royals there were supposed to be fair."

"Not to those close to them, who they can control," replied Liana. Amara could see the truth behind the lies that her niece spoke. How Liana felt squeezed and suffocated by her mother and the Queen's Table, and the warrior knew too well how that felt. You had to behave in a certain way to be truly accepted by the Langton family and its ancestry. "How about you, what are your names?"

"I'm Wyn," said the eldest girl, who'd done most of the speaking. "This is Kali, Brent, Zach, Xabi, Taylor, Roberto, and Savannah," she said, pointing around the room from smallest to tallest. "Four boys, four girls, perfectly balanced," she said, smiling at her orphaned friends.

"It's nice to meet you all, although I probably won't remember all those names," admitted Liana.

"It's okay, we won't be offended, so long as you're not as annoying as that other little twerp," said Wyn.

Amara jumped up and put her arm around Wyn's shoulder. "I like this one, she thinks he's an annoying twerp too!"

Wyn giggled. "You're more than welcome to stay. It's not much, but you won't find much better in The Dantè, unless you're secret royalty of course and actually live in the stone palace," joked Wyn. Liana laughed awkwardly.

"We are a little tired after the journey, perhaps we should rest, Luci," said Amara, doing her best to back up Liana's lie.

Roberto and Savannah, the next eldest of the children, gave up their spots on the blanket pile on the floor, and headed out into the shop. It wasn't comfortable. Liana was used to the best fabrics and pillow fillings. Amara on the other hand, who was used to living without usual comforts, started snoring almost as soon as her head hit the pillow, mouth wide open. Not a Langton look at all, thought Liana to herself, but to her it made her aunt seem more endearing. Eventually though, the princess drifted off into a deep sleep.

∼

Liana woke in a sweat. The image of Vivek syphoning Yasmin's Bad Morality still lingered in her mind as she woke from her nightmare recalling the events of yesterday, but the nightmare didn't end with their descent into Allicalidantè. It ended with the featureless, matte black face of Vivek disintegrating. Specks of black rushed towards her like a colony of bats disturbed from their slumbers. Her instinct was to protect herself with her Red Aura, but she was auraless, and could only cover her face to stop the impending infection before the nightmare ended.

Amara and the Dantian orphans were still sound asleep. Roberto and Savannah had returned and lay squeezed in between the other children, blanketless. Liana took the opportunity to finally lower her hood and wipe the sweat from her forehead and neck, the first time she'd lowered it since arriving on the mainland. The hood was her only option. She'd tried dying her hair before she'd even discovered the secrets of the Visendi, but no matter what colour or dye formula she used, it would just run straight through and never hold.

The princess picked up the blankets she'd borrowed and covered up their original owners. A bucket of clean water lay at the bottom of the staircase. She bent down and wet her hands, dabbing the back of her neck. The evaporation of cool water would cool her down following her night terror, a trick her great uncle had taught her on the eastern Coryàtès beach many years ago.

She proceeded to tiptoe out the room, through the storage corridor, and make her way onto the shop floor. The one Chantrah table was still covered. Liana was too curious not to have a look underneath.

Grabbing the corner of the sheet, she slowly lifted it up and over, unfolding the cloth to be sure she didn't disturb the contents beneath it. A thin layer of dust floated up and found new places to settle. Liana crocked her head to the side as she looked at the contents of the table.

Under the cloth lay a standard 8x8 Chantrah board, with Shooters, Jumpers, Wingmen and Infantry in various positions around the board - as if the game was half-way through. What was different about this board was the replica Pillar of Sanctuary sitting in the centre, taking up the middle four squares. Liana marvelled at the build quality. It was completely wooden, but beautifully finished off both sanded and varnished. She reached out to touch the replica pillar, but a large hand grabbed her wrist.

It was Miss Rothkofsky, the shopkeeper. She was still wearing the same, dirt-stained headscarf, but at least she'd washed her face. Liana noted her surprisingly soft skin, however when the shopkeeper frowned, her forehead wrinkled and several lines of crows' feet formed around her eyes, turning the soft skin harsh.

Since gaining her Red Aura and experiencing the Battle of Coryàtès, Liana hadn't experienced fear. She remembered the feeling of fear; how she felt being taken at knife point by Nalan, hiding from the White Robes in the Swyre forest, or seeing her mother hanging in mid-air helpless under the power of Vivek. But now that she had the power of the Aurora Visendus inside her, it made her feel safer. It may have been a complacent way of thinking, but it was clear that only an incredible power could hurt her. Yet for some reason, the touch of Miss Rothkofsky made her feel wary, like she could hurt Liana if she really wanted to. It was a strange intuition.

She sensed something imperious about the shopkeeper that she couldn't quite work out.

"Do you know what I hate about most puzzle makers?" The shopkeeper lifted the lid of an oblong box sitting on one of the shelves on the shop floor revealing a rather strange image of a dragonfly with bat wings. It was also the first time Liana had really heard the shopkeeper speak a full sentence, and she was surprised at how fluid her voice sounded, with no hint of the prickly grunt she'd heard before. The princess shook her head in response to the shopkeeper's question.

"The thing about most other puzzle makers is they draw and paint a design but then use the same cutting press, which means the puzzle pieces can be interchanged between different designs." The bat-winged dragonfly suddenly made sense; they were two different puzzles interchanged with each other. "I prefer to custom make every one of mine," she opened another box on the shelf. The picture on this puzzle was an orange tulip set upon a pitch-black background. "This one, for example, is easier to start in the centre than at the corners,"

Liana realised looking at the puzzle that the usual tactic of starting with the corner pieces wouldn't give the solver much chance as they're all solid black. "Yes, I see. You'd have a better chance starting in the middle and working your way outwards," she observed.

The shopkeeper confirmed the observation with a nod and strange grunt. "Come," she said, and led Liana by the wrist around to the otherside of the Chantrah table. She pulled out a seat and sat down. Miss Rothkofsky then took the chair opposite. "You can win in five moves. See if you can beat me."

Liana studied the board. She recalled being in a similar position against Benji the week before in the tavern and losing terribly. She racked her brains trying to recall the moves Banji made in response to hers, but she'd played so many games against him that day it was all a blur. The game was evenly matched. Three Infantry, two Jumper's and one Wingman down each. Both players had both their Shooter's still on the board.

Liana moved up a Wingman three squares up on a right diagonal, attacking one of the shopkeepers' Jumpers. The pillar in the middle of the board added a strange dimension, as it hindered cross-board moves, forcing players into making trades and sacrifices.

The shopkeeper moved her Jumper back one square into a more defensive position, and with her piece on the retreat, Liana moved up a second Wingman. Liana now had almost full control of the right-hand side of the board.

The shopkeeper moved out a Shooter from its home-square into the home-square of her middle Infantry piece, which had succumbed to being taken before the pair sat down. This move was a common defensive strategy, as the Shooter acted like a watchtower, covering several positions at once. Liana had to force it out of position, even if that meant sacrificing a higher-ranked piece of her own. She moved her own Shooter in behind her two Wingman, attacking the shopkeeper's Shooter, but also completely covering the right side of the board. Liana's Wingmen and Shooter each covered each other. The Shopkeeper pushed her apex Shooter to attack Liana's left flank. Liana's second Shooter was covered by an Infantry, so if she were to take Liana's left-hand Shooter, the shopkeeper would lose a Shooter of her own.

Liana paused to think ahead. She had already made three moves, could she reach the Target in just two more? Then Liana saw it. With the moving of the shopkeeper's apex

Shooter, she could draw out the second Shooter, which was still in its home square. Liana moved her home-square Shooter and took her opponent's Shooter down the left-flank. Of course, it was protected, and the Shopkeeper took Liana's Shooter with the Wingman that was covering the square. This gave an opening down the right, and enabled Liana to sweep up the board with one Wingman into a square only covered by an Infantry piece. The Shopkeeper knew she was beaten, as there were only two outcomes now. Either she took the Wingman and gave Liana's outermost piece clear access to the Target, or she allowed the Infantry piece to be taken, again giving clear access to the Target. Miss Rothkofsky played out the end and Liana punched the air with delight.

The game was over, but it was the sudden movement of the game pieces that halted Liana's celebrations. They somehow began to move themselves off the board and file into their respective formations on each side of the table. The board itself began to fold up on itself and into the sides of the replica pillar, just like the real Pillar of Sanctuary.

"I'd like to play again," Liana said. She didn't feel like risking another nightmare by heading back to her makeshift cot.

"I'm happy to play again," the shopkeeper replied. Liana waited for the shopkeeper to reset the board, but she just sat there, staring at her.

"So... how do we go about doing that?" asked Liana, who'd never seen a Chantrah board like it before.

"Why don't you give it a try first?"

Liana was mildly irked at the shopkeeper's response. She was still a bit groggy from the lack of proper sleep and just wanted a straight answer. This wasn't one of Master H's mentoring sessions, she just wanted to play a game of Chantrah.

However, she also wasn't in the mood for arguing, so she leaned over the game board and tried to see if there wasn't anything immediately obvious to get the game going again, which of course, there wasn't. She reached out and felt the pillar to see if there were any buttons or latches, but felt no ridges or indents, but she did notice the pillar move slightly.

Liana grabbed the replica pillar and twisted it. Multiple clicking sounds came from within as she turned it around and around, like a wind-up toy until it would turn no further. She gently released the pillar and watched it slowly unwind itself whilst playing a familiar sounding tune.

"It's like a music box, and it's playing the same song that Monty and Mack played." Liana observed aloud. The shopkeeper made no comment as the sides of the pillar began to unfold whilst the metallic tune still played until the music stopped and the gameboard was revealed.

"Well, that was unbelievably easy," she said rather surprised as she looked at the unravelled board, laying flat and ready for the game pieces to be placed. Liana reached for the white set closest to her, but they seemed to be stuck. She tried lifting and sliding them, but they would not budge. After a few moments, the board began folding up on itself. "Wait, stop! Damn thing!" Liana saw the corner of the shopkeeper's mouth rise with a *'I knew that was going to happen'* expression, which just irritated the princess even more.

Then, a thought struck her. The sound of the tune had the metallic tone of Monty's Kalimtar, but not the whistling of Mack's flute. She reached out and grabbed Miss Rothkofsky's wrist and placed it on top of the pillar. "It's a game for two people, so maybe two people need to start it," and she instructed the shopkeeper to turn the pillar. The tune of Mack's flute sounded out and the gameboard flattened out except this time, the game pieces moved into place ready for the game to start.

Liana smiled inside as Miss Rothkofsky's grin turned to mild surprise. She obviously hadn't expected Liana to solve this first-time around. "Is this a true replica?" she asked the shopkeeper. "Does the real Pillar behave this way?"

"We will play again tomorrow," repeated the shopkeeper.

"I need to know, I have to know, what happens if you beat the real pillar at Chantrah?"

"We will play again tomorrow," the shopkeeper repeated again.

"Argh, please, Miss Rothkofsky, answer my question. It could make a difference between life and death!"

"We will play again tomorrow," she repeated again. "Now, go back to bed. Don't forget to cover up that hair of yours, or people will talk."

Liana had forgotten she was unhooded. Did the shopkeeper know who she was? If she did, she hadn't let on, nor did she seem bothered.

Liana followed the shopkeeper through the storage corridor and watched as her large frame plodded up the stairs to her own room. She lifted her robe's hood back over her indigo-blue hair and lay back down to her spot amongst the blankets. With questions spinning in her head, she found it impossible to settle back to sleep.

25
BUMPS IN THE NIGHT

"You're hiding something from me." The frustration was clear in Prince Kendrix's voice as he addressed Luci. His chambers in the stone palace were considerably bigger than the dorms that the Swyre entourage had been given, and much more homely too. The chambers' entrance door was lockable, so there was no need for guards to be posted outside meaning he could have his own privacy. Inside, banners hung on the wall above a green, fabric sofa that stood next to a round table with two chairs. A second door led to a bedroom with a four-poster bed and en-suite bathroom. The only thing that Luci thought was missing were windows, but she didn't mind since the flickering candlelight gave the prince's abode a romantic ambience.

"I'm not hiding anything from you. I just want to get what we came here for so we can be together," lied Liana's doppelgänger. Luci had continued to keep her true identity from Kendrix despite their secret relationship, and his sixth sense could tell she was not being completely truthful with him.

"Why is the pillar so important to the Langton's?" questioned Kendrix. "Or do you not care enough for me to tell me yet?"

"I do care for you, but if I told you, you wouldn't want to be with me."

"How do you know that if you don't at least try and explain?"

"I just do."

Kendrix slammed down his scabbard onto the lounge table in exasperation. "I can't help but feel like you're using me. Using whatever we have to get whatever it is you want from the pillar. Is what we have even real?"

"Of course it's real, it's just really, *really* complicated," she rested a palm on the small of the prince's back.

"You already know what power the pillar has, don't you? You don't want to research it, you want the source of its light. That's what you're hiding." The prince dug his fingernails into the wood. Rarely did he get so emotional, but the turmoil between his head and his heart was difficult to control. The lack of response from Luci told him all he needed to know. "I want to know what it is."

"I can't tell you."

"You have to tell me," Kendrix replied, spinning around to eyeball Luci.

"You wouldn't believe me," she swallowed, and her eyes became watery, not out of fear of confrontation, but out of fear of losing the prince forever.

"If you want these negotiations to end, I have to know what you know," the prince glared nose-to-nose at Luci, longing for an answer.

"The only thing you need to know is we can save your people. We can save you all."

"That's not enough! I can't take an unsubstantiated promise to my father, he'd laugh in my face!"

"I can't give you anymore."

Kendrix grabbed her by the shoulders. "You have to tell me what you know!" he screamed, unloading his anger. "I need to know everything about the pillar and its power," he said in a calmer voice, releasing his grasp.

Luci wasn't mad at his outburst. She couldn't imagine what it must have been like hiding in the crater for as long as he had.

"I think I should go," she said, tamely shaking her head before giving the prince a gentle peck on the cheek.

The prince nodded in agreement and unlatched the door. "Same time tomorrow night?"

"Same time," Luci confirmed as she left the room, her dyed indigo hair flowing behind her as she moved swiftly into the corridor so as not to be seen.

As she turned the corner, she bumped head-first into Saffina.

"Ouch!" they cried in unison, both grabbing the centre of their foreheads.

"Jeez, usually this stuff only happens with Joel," said Saffina, still clutching her head.

"What are you doing?" they both said again at the same time. Luci shifted her weight from one foot to the other, clearly uneasy with the question.

Saffina folded her arms. "You first."

"I was er-" Luci desperately tried to find the right fake excuse, but as much as she looked like Liana, she didn't quite have her quick-thinking skills for getting out of trouble.

Saffina looked down the corridor at the prince's door. "You

were with him, weren't you? I knew you'd been sneaking out."

"Please, don't tell Sir Tarak," pleaded Luci.

"Why shouldn't I? For all I know you've been feeding him information. No wonder our negotiations aren't going anywhere. Tell me, what are you getting in exchange?"

"No, it's not like that."

"Then what is it like, *Liana*?"

"Looks to me like you were going to see him too, *Saffina*."

"I was just following you, seeing what you were up to!"

"Well it'd be your word against mine. Probably best if neither of us rats the other one out, wouldn't you agree?"

Saffina unfolded her arms. "Fine, but I think the prince is bad news. Something doesn't seem right about him."

Luci lowered her palm from her still throbbing forehead. "You're just jealous because I get to spend time with him and you don't."

"Am not!" protested Saffina. "There's nothing strange about the prince, believe me." Saffina scowled suspiciously at the doppelganger.

"I'm heading back to our chambers now. I need to be awake for another round of important negotiations in the morning, unlike someone who managed to get themselves uninvited."

After Saffina's interference in their first discussions with the king, Sir Tarak had banned her from being anywhere near the negotiation table and restricted the attendance to himself, Master H and Luci. It had made for a very boring couple of weeks for both Saffina and Joel.

Luci scurried down the hallway. Saffina waited until the doppelganger was out of sight before making her way to the prince's door.

Knock. Knock-knock-knock. She hammered on the door like a secret code. She heard the scrape and click of the iron bolt unlocking from the other side.

"Saffina, what're you doing here?"

She hesitated, flustered. The prince's baggy white shirt was three-quarters of the way unbuttoned and his hair dishevelled. "Um, just checking what time everyone needed to meet in the morning?" she replied, rather than confronting the prince like she had planned.

"Usual time."

"Oh, okay, one of the guards told us something different so we thought someone had better come check," she said nervously, twiddling a strand of hair.

"You bump your head?" said the prince, pointing to a small red lump on her forehead.

"Oh, yeh, it's nothing."

"Looks fresh. You want to come in and put a cold flannel on it?" offered the prince.

"Oh, naw, it's fine, really."

"Ok then. Well, see you in the morning."

"See you in the morning." The prince closed the door and Saffina waited until the sound of the scrape and click of the locking of the door and flung her head back in self-annoyance. "I'm such an *idiot*."

She walked away from the prince's chambers and turned the corner, this time bumping into Joel, although this time luckily only shoulder-to-shoulder.

"Joel!" she exclaimed in surprise, realising he'd probably seen her at the prince's door.

"Saff? What were you doing at Kendrix's..."

"Got to go!" she announced and ran away down the corridor.

Joel tried to stop her but could only watch as she bolted, his stomach churning with jealousy.

26
ESSENCE OF TENEBRIS

"I'm so bored," Yasmin puffed stroppily as she poked the campfire with a stick. The embers crackled louder as they took the angsty prodding. She looked at Gene and rolled her eyes as he lay emotionless on his back, his hands linked together resting on his stomach. "Still not speaking, huh?"

Gene stared into the starry night sky. If he was listening to Yasmin, his body language gave no indication that he cared or understood what his friend was talking about.

"Of all the things Vivek is capable of, and he still can't get you speaking." She lobbed the stick into the fire and looked around at the other clusters of campfires amongst the field of orange tulips, before pushing herself up to meander around between the tents. Many of the Immorals were drowning in drink, drunkenly moaning about how unfair life was. Some could not speak after being Turned, like Eugene, but most could still communicate. Some of them complained about the riches of royalty, some grumbled about never having a day off of work in their life, others sounded off about their wives or husbands. No matter what their protests were though, they all agreed about one thing - the promise of power and freedom.

"*Imagine a life where no one tells you what to do, where your choices are really your choices. No unwritten rules of society on how to 'behave'. No laws or legislation preventing you from taking your own justice. Work the jobs you want to work. There will be plenty of Visendi to be our servants. This is the life awaiting for you, a life that Tenebris can provide. Live your life for you, not for others. Help us take down the Visendi, take down their chosen one, and you can be free.*" Yasmin recalled Vivek's speech to his latest Army of Immorals incarnation when they'd first set up camp directly above the Pillar of Sanctuary.

In the months after the Zaganite defeat at the Battle of Coryàtès, Vivek had taken Yasmin under his wing as her mentor. One of the many things he had imparted onto her was how easy people could be persuaded under the guise of promises around love, money, power or freedom. "*Appeal to one or more of these motives, and the Turning process of a non-Immoral will begin. Convince an Immoral that one or more of these motives are within their grasp and they will follow for the cause. If you can do this articulately and with a particular eloquence, then you are on your way to becoming a leader who many will follow.*"

As Yasmin wandered between the groups of Immorals, she recalled how easy Vivek had made it seem to turn a whole city against itself.

∽

A fter the chattering of Jackdaw's had carried a limp Vivek away from the island's battlefield to the mainland, he managed to muster up the strength to send a message in one of the birds to Yasmin. Counting on Yasmin's hatred for Liana, it was not much of a gamble that she would come to his aid. A short message containing the location of one of her father's smuggling vessels was all the message required, and then the Jackdaw would take her straight to him.

It had taken Vivek a couple of weeks to recover from Liana's blast of Red Aura at the Battle of Coryàtès, but Yasmin had cared and nursed his recovery. It was probably the first time she'd ever really helped someone.

Back on his feet, Vivek set about his task of rebuilding his forces. The mainland offered the perfect mix of population density. With exception of the northern fishing villages and the convicts of the mines, Coryàtès population wholly resided in the city of Swyre. However, out in the mainland, many smaller villages and communities occupied the lands between major towns making the Turning process easier. One Turned village quickly became two, two became three and the more people Vivek Turned, the quicker the next community would be taken. The more followers in his charge, the easier it was for people to be swayed by the promise of a better life.

Yasmin couldn't help but be impressed with how Vivek would garner and inspire each new community they happened across. He'd find the central commune, set up a makeshift pulpit, and preach of the hardships he could see before him and how he could see a better future for them. Should anyone doubt him, speak up against him whilst he was preaching, he would demonstrate his Visendi abilities. Whether he chose to show his Red Aura Screen or send a message in a Jackdaw, the demonstration of this power always convinced even the most sceptical of the audience. Of course, he never told them that they would never be able to achieve these powers. Attaining these powers meant praying to Aurora and long, hard days practising the necessary skills in each Inner Core.

"I don't understand one thing," Yasmin asked Vivek when they were alone whilst wandering a dirt path between villages. "If you're Immoral yourself and choose to follow Tenebris, how come you have the powers of a Visendi? Even if you once learned them, you don't practise the Visendi ways now, so surely, they should have faded away?"

Vivek contemplated the question for a few seconds before choosing to respond to his student. "What I tell you now, you tell no one else, understand?"

Yasmin nodded.

"This staff I carry with me is much more than just a walking aid." To Yasmin's surprise, Vivek lifted the waist-high staff off the ground, straightened himself up from his hunch-back gate, and strode like a man thirty years his youth. "I have never needed a stick to walk. As you attain the Inner Cores of the Visendi you live longer and your body's cells ageing process slows. Whilst I was under the employment of the Langton's, and since the religion was outlawed, I had to keep up appearances and age as a person is meant to. I grew this scraggly, grey facial hair and started walking with a stick. But there's more to the stick than meets the eye." Vivek handed his metallic walking stick to Yasmin to inspect.

"Looks like a normal stick to me," said Yasmin, spinning it around every way she could. "It's just a bit fancier than the usual wooden ones you'd find in a carpenters shop back in Swyre." The silver stick had no carvings or engravings on with the exception of its grip, which was made of quartz and had simple ribbed bands etched out of it.

"You see the bands etched in the handle? They turn. Each band has a notch across it. Line up the notches and pull the handle up."

Yasmin followed Vivek's instruction and the quartz handle flicked up on a hinge. Bored into the silver section of the stick were six tubular cylinders, each glowing with the rainbow of Aura's.

"The handle keeps the Aura's from escaping. Quartz is known for being resistant to both chemical and physical weathering. Turns out it's also resistant to Aura weathering too. The stick is the mobile stockpile of my aura from when I attained my Inner Core's. It wasn't difficult to borrow Liana's dagger back in Swyre to Peel my aura's and store them when I decided to change allegiance. I also keep a few small bottles of each on myself just in case anything happens to the stick." Vivek showed the inside lining of his robe and unbutton a flap to reveal eighteen small potion bottles with the familiar dancing aura's darting about inside them. "I can't regenerate my own Auras anymore, so if my Aura's become weak, I consume a bottle and refill it from the stick."

Yasmin pushed the stick handle down until it clicked back in a closed position and randomly spun the ribbed bands to lock it in place, before handing it back to her mentor.

"What happens when you run out?"

"Then I shall be auraless, but this is a plentiful supply for our mission. I have two secret stashes back on Coryàtes. One in Castle Langton and one in your father's old residence. Only trouble is getting to either unseen, but that's a problem for another day." The pair continued onwards, Vivek's stick returning to its usual rhythmic, clinking sound.

"So, what is our mission? We've been consuming villages for months now. What are we building up to?"

"After we take the next village, we will be onto Allicalidantè."

"Allicalidantè? We can't surely take a city of that size, even with the amount of Immorals we've built up."

"Yasmin, what does a city like The Dantè have that these smaller villages don't?"

"I don't know... trained soldiers for one."

"Ah, but why do they have trained soldiers?"

"Well, to protect whosevers royal butts are sitting on this land's throne."

"Exactly. Royalty. If we can get into the heads and Turn one of the members of aristocracy, and with our Immorals throwing the proverbial cat amongst the pigeons amongst the regular plebs, then the city will soon fall." Vivek lifted the other side of his robe and unbuttoned another flap. This time revealing a small, singular vial of thrashing black aura.

"What's that?" Yasmin gawped, getting in for a closer look.

"This vile of Bad Morality is the Essence of Tenebris himself."

"That's incredible, where did you get it?"

"That is a story for another day."

"Well, can I hold it?"

"Of course you can't!" an offended Vivek heaved his robe shut hastily. "Do you have any idea how invaluable this vial is to us?"

"Not hard to guess," Yasmin glared back, annoyed at the sudden change in tone of her mentor.

"This vial can make an Immoral into a Reaper."

"A Reaper?" One of Yasmin's frowning eyebrows raised into a now quizzical look.

"A Morality Reaper. You'll see their power when we're in The Dantè. With the right person as a Reaper under our control, this war will soon sway in our favour."

"I'm your most loyal supporter, shouldn't I be first pick for this role?"

"One day you may well be the right person, but for this mission, you are not."

Yasmin sighed inwardly, annoyed. She wanted to be the one to destroy Liana and get her revenge and if this Essence of Tenebris could help her, she wanted it. But she also wasn't stupid and knew how intelligent Vivek was, or how vengeful he could be, and she wasn't prepared to risk being hunted by both Liana and Vivek by doing something stupid like stealing the vial. "So," she said, "tell me why we want this particular city?"

"Because, my faithful student, that's where Liana's next Spectra Orb is. Either we take it before she does, or we get rid of her before she becomes more powerful."

"You sound like you're afraid of her? I grew up with her, she's really not all that special."

"If the predictions Aurora makes in the Visendi's Book of H'WA are true, then she is incredibly special. But, they are predictions and not prophecies. We can still make this world our own."

~

As Yasmin recalled their journey to this moment, she became twitchy at the thought of Liana gaining her next Aura. She bent down and plucked a tulip stem from the ground. The plant grew back immediately and flowered its orange petals. She tossed the plucked stem into a nearby fire where the surrounding Immorals had all fallen asleep, each slumped in uncomfortable looking positions following a night on the bottle.

'This Reaper better hurry up and finish the job quickly. I want to see Liana's face when she realises we have her next precious orb.'

27
NARROW ESCAPE

'I know boy, but we can't follow them into the crater, as much as we want to be near Liana to protect her. Just trust me, will you? There's not a lot we can do about it. We can still be useful up here. Ugh, this whole sharing-a-body thing is exhausting.

Finally, Franklin is asleep. Now's our time to do some more investigating. Just… try and keep quiet in my head, will you Cas? I need to concentrate and having your primitive thoughts in my head is incredibly distracting.

Didn't you hear what I said? Keep quiet! Do you realise how difficult unlocking a door is when you have paws instead of fingers and thumbs? Damned dog…

Finally, outside. Better make sure we close the lighthouse door behind us. Now, let's see, I think it was this way. I recognise the smells… the unique smells of each dead person's decaying scent… this is so weird. The stones feel rough on my paws as we walk. Whatever plant life that grew here before has long gone and what were once living fields full of long grass and wildflowers are just dirt *plains full of stones and boulders. Everything looks so dark and grey, not like the swaying, swishing, brightness of the white glows of fauna and flora in the Swyre forest.*

I can see a bright glow of orange up ahead, that must be the field of tulips. It seems so strange to see colour in this realm, but a welcome sight for sore eyes.

The Immorals are still camped amongst the tulips. There seems to be even more tents than yesterday. Seems like a few of them are wandering around, but most are asleep. Above, only one of the moons of Mikana is even partially visible through the clouds above, the other two are completely obscured. Its colour gives the orange glow such a beautiful contrast.

"I don't trust him to get the job done," *I hear the sound of Yasmin's voice from inside one of the tents. She appears to wait for a response, but none comes.* "If we're to infect and Turn the entire crater below, it all depends on him getting close to Liana. How can Vivek trust him with such an important task? And what motive does he have to see the task through? Surely, I am better placed to do his bidding. I can be disguised. I'm the one motivated by revenge. I don't even know where they banished my father to, or if he's even alive. I hate the Langton's so much. They've done nothing but make my life worse. Even if you hadn't been Turned, you'd see it too, Gene. You're the only one who's been with me the whole time, and I need you with me still, even if you can't talk back."

Yasmin's rambling doesn't reveal much, but enough to know Vivek is plotting something. What is it and who is doing his bidding this time?'

The stone cracked and fell away under Liana's feet as she walked up the steps of the make-shift palace.

"Watch yourself, Princess," said Amara, catching her by the bicep.

"Thanks. Good job taking out the guards, I doubt I could have done it as stealthily."

"Heh, maybe auras are overrated. Can't exactly be stealthy if you're lighting up the whole street. We can't be too long though, I only knocked them out, they could wake up at any time. So, what are we doing here anyway? Hang on, don't tell me, you want to get inside and torture Prince Kendrix until he tells us what he was doing sneaking out the hidden tunnel, right? I'm game for that."

"No, Amara, that's not why we're here," Liana eyerolled at her aunt, with a smile. "I've been playing Miss Rothkofsky at Chantrah every night for the last five days and the only time I won was on the very first night. The board we play on has a replica of the pillar, but I haven't gotten near beating her since."

"So?"

"So, I figure the board in the game shop must be some sort of replica, but if I'm to find out how to get inside and retrieve my next spirit, then I need to do some research on the real thing." Liana took out a spyglass from her robe that she'd 'borrowed' from the drawer of Miss Rothkofsly's desk and held it to her right eye.

"Pretty sure stealing isn't very moral."

"I'm not stealing, I'm borrowing."

"Without permission."

"I'll put it back."

Amara spun a pocket knife between her fingers as she sat down on the stone steps, clearly disappointed that the plan didn't involve any violence. "See anything?"

Liana didn't answer whilst she focussed on twisting the barrels of the spyglass to get the perfect focus. She looked at the enlarged pillar in her spyglass up and down, before lowering the spyglass in frustration.

"Nothing. I can't see anything. There's nothing to indicate any sort of entrance. I can't see any markings, joins, or discolouration." She huffed and dropped her arm which held the spyglass. "This was pointless."

"Why don't you just ask the shopkeeper?" said Amara, jumping up eagerly, ready to head back.

"I've tried, but she's weird with me."

"Like she knows you're hiding something. Something like your true identity?"

"Hmm, maybe," Liana dropped down to sit at the same level as her aunt. "Sometimes she behaves like she's teaching me something, and other times she just completely blanks me and just grunts at me. I'm convinced she knows more about this place than she's telling me but won't tell me what it is, like she's not sure if she should."

Liana put the spyglass away and the pair descended the steps. Before they reached the bottom, they heard a commotion. Hurrying down the rest of the steps, they turned a corner onto a street that ran parallel to the pillar's boundary wall and saw a group of people gathered. Someone was standing on a pile of wooden boxes, shouting to the crowd, but they couldn't get close enough to properly see the person's face and it was mostly covered with a hood that created a shadow across their features, but by the sound of their shouting voice they were a young male.

"I saw it, in my dream! I was standing right here, speaking to a crowd, just like we are now. A voice urged me over the wall, urging me to touch the Pillar of Sanctuary. This is my calling! This is my destiny! I am the one to save you all!"

Before Liana, Amara, or anyone in the crowd could do

anything, the man vaulted over the wall and started running toward the cubed structure. The crowd gasped, stunned. The wall was not built to keep people out, it wasn't high enough for that as this man had proven by stacking just a few crates, it merely acted as a perimeter marker. It didn't need to be built much higher. Since the day their queen had been squashed by it, no one dared go near the structure.

Instinctively, Liana sprang into action. She eventually managed to push past the crowd, and jumped onto the stack of boxes and leapfrogged the wall.

"Someone do something!" shouted a woman from the gathering, as the man, chased by Liana, sprinted toward the pillar.

"No, wait!" Amara tried to shout after her niece, but she had been caught out by Liana's quick reactions. She moved to chase after her, but the sound of King Shimon's voice behind her prevented her from doing so. She couldn't risk being recognised.

Damned scar,' she thought to herself. Although the King's last visit to Swyre had come after she'd been sent to the mines, her scar was a giveaway. Plus, she didn't want any of the Queen's Table entourage to know she was also in Allicalidantè. She slinked away into the shadows and, quite feline-like, jumped up into the boardwalks of the street's first-floor housing. A good vantage point to watch things unfold from.

"What's going on here?" the voice of King Shimon boomed.

"That man jumped the wall and is heading to the pillar, your highness!" Someone shouted from the crowd.

"And a girl's chasing after him!" Screamed another voice.

The King stood part-way up the palace steps. "Nobody move," he ordered. "Do nothing. Their fate is their own."

"Stop!" Liana shouted at the running man. "Wait, please, wait!"

The man slowed and came to halt next to the pillar. He gazed up in awe at the massiveness of it. Liana eventually caught him up.

"I heard the prophet," he turned to Liana with a brainwashed glint in his eye. "The prophet told me I had to do this. That I could save our people!"

"There's no such thing as prophecy, only prediction." Liana thought of her own supposed destiny as she replied, a destiny her real mother had bestowed upon her when she entombed her and the other Spectra Children to put a halt to the reformation of the Immorals of their time. Her future wasn't a prophecy, it was a prediction of hope, based simply on how different she was. The fact that she was the first Seventh Spectra Child, breaking all previously held beliefs that there could only be six Spectra Children. "I know you've never met me, nor I you, but please hear me when I say, don't do this," she begged the man.

"I have to," he said, and reached out to the pillar. The moment his palm touched the glossy, smooth, black surface, the pillar clunked and whirred into action. The four large sides began to unfold ominously down above their heads.

"We have to go!" screamed Liana, pulling the arm of the man.

"I-I don't understand. I-I thought something else would happen. I don't know what I expected, but this isn't what my dream told me."

"Come on!" Liana urged.

"Am I... Am I not the chosen one?" The man stood firmly rooted to the ground despite Liana's arm tugging.

"Why, what else was in your dream?" Liana checked above. she'd have to start running soon.

"Nothing. The voice just said I had to show the way. What have I done? We're going to die! Oh, I'm as bad as the ones who drove us here, aren't I?" The man said in a panic, his eyes began watering as the realisation of his mistake hit him, but Liana couldn't help but think there was something else strange about the man. Something deceptive.

Liana wished at that moment she could check the man's Morality, but she neither had the time or capability. "We have to go!"

"I'm sorry!" the man sobbed.

"You don't need to be sorry; we just need to get out of here!"

The man fell to his knees and cried into his hands in despair. The walls of the pillar creaked and groaned as they slowly unfolded their way to the ground.

'These walls will soon be on top of us! I know I shouldn't, but I might not have a choice. I'm going to have to use my Red Aura.'

Liana formed a red dome around herself and the man, and dragged him to his feet, a look of shock on his face as he watched the dancing glow of red light around him. The pair ran towards the boundary wall. They made it past the first encroachment of the pillar side, which slammed into the ground kicking up a sandstorm of dust. The structure now formed a cross in the dirt. Looking back over their shoulders, the flattened side behind them began to unfold again to finish creating the square shape of a Chantrah board.

The pair ran as fast as they could, still under the protection of Liana's Red Aura. The unfolding surface above them was almost upon them as they neared the barrier wall.

"Hang on!" Liana shouted, as she jumped into the wall.

The strength of her Red Aura broke through it, sending stone and brick flying into the street. Liana and the man lay face-down and covered in dust on the ground. "You okay?"

"I-I'm alive!" The man said with surprise and joy.

Liana looked up through the hole she'd made in the boundary wall. The gameboard had almost hit the ground, but a glint caught her eye. She hastily rolled over and felt her sheath. She'd dropped the Dagger of Red! Liana jumped back up and sprinted toward the opening in the wall, calling upon her Red Aura again.

"Wait - what are you doing!" she heard the man behind her shout. She didn't listen, she couldn't let the dagger get crushed.

She slid on her stomach through the newly formed opening in the boundary wall and grabbed the dagger. The gameboard jolted to a stop above her. It creaked and moaned as it tried to push downwards, Liana's Red Aura Screen fighting with the pressure of the huge structure. Her aura held firm and allowed her just enough time to roll back out the way. The side came crashing down once her Aura dissipated, creating another cloud of dust, filling the princesses' lungs. She coughed and sputtered as she tried to catch her breath. The crowd that had gathered came running towards her. Liana was expecting the usual wave of compliment, awe and adjudication for saving someone's life with her powers, but to her surprise, she wasn't greeted with any sort of thanks or congratulations.

"I'm going to catch her and get a reward from the king!" shouted one man.

"I want to know what else she can do! Maybe she has other powers!" shouted a woman.

"I'm going to use her as protection from everyone else,

who knows who'll Turn next?" shouted an elderly sounding man.

'Time to go!' Liana said to herself and ran off in search of safety down a nearby side-street.

∽

Liana skidded to a halt. This alley was a dead-end and she hadn't shaken off the crowd - or rather mob - that was chasing her. Other citizens had joined in the chase, and picked up pitchforks, axe's, knives and other make-shift weaponry along the way.

She flattened herself in the shadows of a doorway, hoping the mob hadn't seen her duck down the alleyway. Peering around the door frame, she watched as the mob raced past, with shouts of "where did she go?" and "I think she went that way!"

Liana breathed a sigh of relief and slid down the door in exhaustion onto her behind.

"I never got a chance to thank you," the voice of a man said just a few deep breaths later. Liana looked up to see the man she rescued standing over her.

"I couldn't let you get crushed now, could I?" she said with a smile, glad it wasn't a member of the mob. "Say, now I can see you clearly and I'm not running for my life, you're actually a lot younger than I thought."

He stroked his chin with a hint of arrogance. "And you're exactly who I thought you were, Princess Liana." With a swift movement of his hand, he knocked down Liana's hood revealing her indigo-blue hair.

Before she had a chance to respond to the revelation that this man knew who she was all along, a blur fell from above and knocked the man unconscious in front of her. Amara dusted off her shoulders with pride.

"Guess you're wondering who that was, eh?"

Liana, speechless, could only muster a nod.

"That was Prince Kendrix. Didn't you recognise the ring?" Amara held up his floppy hand. "The real question is, what was he doing?"

"And," added Liana, "what do we do with him now?"

28

RHONWEN

'We need to get down into the crater, Cas. No, I know we can't do it tonight, we have to get back to Franklin and his wife, we don't want them suspecting anything. Maybe we can give that cave entrance a go tomorrow? Good, I like your attitude, you really are a good pup.'

"That was totally awesome!" Kali, the smallest of the Dantian game store orphans, came bursting in through the shop entrance. Miss Rothkofsky raised a quizzical and annoyed eyebrow behind her magnifying monocle. Kali's outburst had interrupted some intricate work she was doing on a game piece at her workshop desk.

"She, like, lit up all red and went full on bad-ass and stopped the pillar from squashing her like an ant, and saved some other guy as well!" Kali panted heavily. "You think she's the one? You think she can get us outta this hole?"

Before Miss Rothkofsky or any of the other orphans had time to reply to Kali, Liana and Amara walked in. Prince Kendrix's body lay limp between them, as they each had an arm around one of his shoulders, his legs dragging on the ground. Liana let out a cry of relief as they let him fall to the floor.

"Seriously, I can't believe how heavy an unconscious body is. I'm aching all over!"

"Well, I wasn't going to do it on my own." Amara rolled her head and stretched out her back, like it was the end of one of her training sessions. "And I certainly wasn't going to let you use your aura."

"No, you just let me break all the bones in my back instead," Liana muttered under her breath. Amara didn't hear her, fortunately.

Kali came running up to Liana and excitedly jumped up and down on the spot in front of her. "Do it again! Do it again! Show them what you can do!"

Despite being used to receiving attention in the streets of Swyre, the shouts from Kali made the princess feel like a circus act being begged to perform a magic trick.

"Quieten down, Kali," Miss Rothkofsky said as she pulled the orphan aside by the shoulder. It didn't stop Kali from bouncing. "We don't want to upset the Princess of Coryàtès now, do we?" the corner of her mouth rising in a wry smile.

"You-you know who I am?" Liana lowered her hood and revealed her vivid indigo-blue hair. Kali stopped bouncing and froze, her jaw dropping in a gawk. Meeting a princess and seeing the powers of the Aurora Visendus was no doubt the most exciting thing to have ever happened in her life, Liana thought. She chastised herself inwardly for feeling annoyed at being asked to 'perform' by the girl. It can't have been easy living in this pit for months or having witnessed the destruction of the abandoned city above.

"I had my suspicions. The stand-in you have in your place

at the palace is a poor double. I could tell simply by how she held herself when they came parading through the streets. She doesn't exhibit the same gravitas that you do. Right now, though, we need to decide how we're going to handle the prince here."

"The *who*?" Kali picked her jaw up off the floor. "Is that Prince Kendrix?!"

"Yep, sure is, kid." Amara had sat herself down at the shopkeeper's workstation. She leaned back, the chair balancing on two legs, and rested her feet on the work table.

"Off!" Miss Rothkofsky shouted and scowled. To Liana's surprise, Amara didn't argue and lowered her feet off the desk. Even she didn't dare cross the shopkeeper's wrath.

"Why is he asleep? Why do you have him? Why have you brought him here? Are we in danger? I have to get the others!" Kali's mind went into overdrive.

"It's okay, kid, slow down. We'll sort this all out." Liana lowered herself to the eye-level of the pre-teen child, whose brown, scraggly hair had been cut unevenly to shoulder length, probably by Wyn, thought Liana. "Can you do me a favour? Can you find me some rope?" Kali nodded and ran off eagerly to carry out her task.

"So, are you two going to tell me what happened?" Miss Rothkofsky had stopped speaking in grubs and groans, instead speaking in a more eloquent tone.

"Liana got baited," said Amara, partially distracted as she twirled one of the shopkeeper's carving knives between her fingers.

"The prince pretended to be a deluded citizen and made a run for the pillar as a self-proclaimed 'chosen-one'," Liana explained. "Naturally I chased after him, I didn't want to watch someone get squished, especially since I have the power to stop that happening. We heard about the incident involving the queen."

"And that man you rescued turned out to be Prince Kendrix?" said the shopkeeper.

"After being chased by the onlookers," began Liana.

"For their own selfish causes," interrupted Amara, stabbing the carving knife into the desk in anger.

"I darted down an alley to hide, but the prince found me. He knew my name, who I really am."

"So I took care of it, temporarily," chortled Amara. The shopkeeper stood with her hands on hips - or rather, one hand, one wrist, and stared disgruntled at Amara. That's the look Liana remembered from previous nights. "What's that look for? He's working for some nasty people upstairs. We caught him sneaking out of the crater not long after we arrived. We could've just saved all your asses down here!"

"I wouldn't be so sure. Take him and tie him up to a chair," ordered Miss Rothkofsky to Amara. "Don't take your eyes off him. We can't let him get back to his stone palace and report to his father, or we'll all be in trouble, and I'm sure you don't want the pain or death of a bunch of orphans hanging over your head."

Amara stomped her feet onto the ground and let the chair fall backwards onto the floor as she stood up. She didn't like taking orders, especially from a mere shopkeeper, but the job needed doing. She dragged Prince Kendrix by the hood along the floor and disappeared into a back room. Miss Rothkofsky waited until Amara had left the room before speaking again.

"You're probably wondering how I know who you are? Well, I didn't for sure. It's just a feeling. Maybe it's a connection we share inside us."

'Connection? What connection? I couldn't feel more confused and disconnected with a person.'

"You're also probably wondering how I know so much about the Pillar of Sanctuary, as they call it around here, and how I managed to make an exact replica of it? All valid questions, but first let me ask you, why didn't you take on the pillar just now? Why didn't you attempt to play it?"

"I'm not very good at Chantrah," Liana replied matter-of-factly.

"You didn't know how to walk when you were a baby, yet here you are walking about my store. No one helped you solve that puzzle; you did that all on your own when you weren't even conscious of what you were trying to do."

"That's completely different!"

"Why?"

"Because that's a natural instinct."

"So does that mean running away from a challenge is also a natural instinct?"

"I didn't run away."

"Then why aren't you out there right now?"

"I had to save the prince from being crushed and I had a better chance of us surviving by running."

"So, you did run away."

"Yes, but, wait, that's not what I…" Liana crossed her arms in frustration. "Just what's the point of this conversation?"

"I know the ways of the Visendi have not been taught for centuries, but I was hopeful there may have still been someone to guide you in the ways of the Inner Core's as you've clearly never heard of the Five F's."

"You know about the Aurora Visendus?" said a shocked Liana.

"I do. Seems like you don't though."

"Hey, I know about the Five F's; Fight, Flight, Freeze, Friend, Flop." Liana reeled them off the top of her, Master H's training still fresh in her mind.

"Ah, very good," said the shopkeeper, with a slightly patronising tone. "You may be able to list them, but you don't *know* them. You haven't lived them, haven't practised them consciously."

"Fine, you got me, I only just found out about them from my teacher, Master H."

"Master H, as in Hayashi, of the Shrouded Temple?" asked the shopkeeper. Liana nodded to confirm. Miss Rothkofsky smiled; a surprisingly endearing smile compared to the frowns she was used to seeing. "So, we were right to hide the tomb there. The Hayashi's have earned their place in Visendi legend, that's for sure."

"Hang on, if you know about Master H, and the Tomb of Transcended, and the Aurora Visendus, and who I am, then that must mean you're a…"

"Spectra Child," Miss Rothkofsky finished Liana's sentence. She pulled off her headscarf and revealed short curls of bright orange hair. "You can call me Rhonwen, and the Neoteric Temple is my home."

29
VANISHING ACT

Saffina and Joel peered around the corner; their cheeks pressed against the cold stone wall.

"Told you I heard someone," whispered Joel to Saffina below him, his taller, skinny figure towering above his friend.

"Strange place for King Shimon to have a conversation," Saffina whispered back.

Dust could be seen floating lazily through the arrows of dim light from the ceiling of the potato growing room, creating a striped, strobing effect on the king. The king's grossly enlarged shadow cut across the columns of light so only his head and crown cast against the wall. Another smaller shadow of a head cut across the columns of light next to him. The distorted shadows appeared to show him reaching out to a boy.

"Thank you for coming to me with this information," said the king. "You could have saved myself and my son from a very embarrassing situation." Head gently bowed; his deep voice softened almost to a whisper. "I assume you would like to be rewarded somehow?"

"If ya could spare any potatoes," the smaller of the shadowy heads answered. "Or a couple of those chicken's I saw earlier, that'd be grand, yer Majesty."

"That shouldn't be a problem. Grab one of those sacks and fill it up. Do you want the chickens dead or alive?"

The movement of a thoughtful hand to mouth in the shadow on the wall hesitated a few seconds as they considered their answer.

"Er, alive, I guess. Get a good load of eggs outta them first I reckon. Ha! My crew are gonna love me!"

"Let's head down to the coops now. It's best if you get on your way quickly."

"Ok, whatever ya say, yer Majesty."

A block of cold covered Saffina and Joel's backs as they flattened themselves against the wall to hide from the two figures as they made their way out of the room.

"It's just a kid," Joel whispered as they watched them leave the room and turn down the corridor toward the chicken coops.

"Yeh, I wonder what information he had for the king that would see him rewarded like that?" replied Saffina. "We should follow them, and when the kid is alone, we jump him."

"Jump him? Like, ambush him? Shake him down? Not really our style, Saff. I mean, he's just a kid."

"A kid who's being rewarded with one of the most precious products in this damned crater. We need to know what he knows."

"I don't like it, doesn't sound very Visendi-like."

"You've seen how long talking can take. We've been here two weeks trying to strike a deal and it's not exactly picking up pace. I can't take it here anymore so if this kid knows something that can get us inside that pillar, we have to seize the opportunity."

Joel sighed a deep breath and reluctantly followed Saffina's lead down the stoney corridors after King Shimon and the boy. It wasn't a long walk to the room of chicken coops.

The makeshift wooden coops contained several varieties of chicken; Orpington's of all colours, silkie's with pom-pom like feathered hats, Maran's whose shadowy black feathers blended into its surrounding and speckled Barnevelders, to name just a few.

The constant clucking and crowing of the cockerels created a veil of noise that prevented Saffina and Joel from hearing the king and the boy's conversation, but their body language suggested the only words they had was centred around the choosing of the chickens. It seemed the boy somehow managed to convince the king to let him take two hens, one Barnevelder and an Orpington, and an Orpington cockerel. Choosing was the easy part, though.

Lifting the lid to one of the coops, both the king and the boy stepped in and proceeded to attempt to catch the chosen birds.

Saffina and Joel could not hold back their giggles as they watched King Shimon bent over, hands outstretched, being run in circles by the hen's. Wings flapped and slapped him in the face and his cheeks reddened as he became flustered and out of breath. Even as non-lip-readers they could understand the unfavourable words King Shimon was shouting as he and the boy tripped over each other's legs, and both ended up sprawled head-down in chicken excrement. A firm finger-point later and the king got up and stomped off, leaving the boy to catch his reward for himself.

"Hey, now's our chance." Saffina grabbed Joel's wrist and dragged him toward the coops before he had a chance to respond.

"Hey, boy!" Saffina had to shout over the now screeching chicken's, who had all become greatly disturbed at the failed catching attempt. The boy, still sitting frustrated on the ground, looked up, startled.

"Who're you?" he asked.

"Want to ask you the same thing," responded Joel. The boy looked Saffina and Joel up and down, studying them.

Saffina grabbed the boy by the scruff of his shirt and lifted him to his feet. "We don't have time for smart-ass answers, kid, just tell us what you told King Shimon."

"Hey, hey, put me down!" yelled the boy, grabbing the wrist of Saffina's hand that clutched his collar.

"C'mon, take it easy. You'll tell us, won't ya kid?" intervened Joel, gently placing a hand on Saffina's forearm. She hesitated at his physical touch, and slowly released the boy from her grasp.

"Help me catch this chicken and I'll tell ya."

"Fine," said Saffina. "I can tell you how to catch it, but I'm not doing it for you." She held out her hand, palm up, with her fingers slightly bent - like an upside-down spider. "You gotta approach it slowly but be ready to move quickly to scoop it up. With your other hand, be ready to smother its wings from above."

The boy lowered himself again and slinked toward his reward. He got himself within arm's reach and followed the instructions he'd just been given. It was a bit clumsy, and he didn't completely smother the wings as a practised poulterer would, but he succeeded and stood up with his prize.

"So?" Saffina asked.

"So what?" replied the boy.

"What's your name and what did you tell King Shimon?"

"Oh right, yeh." replied the boy, pretending he'd forgotten already. "Easier if I show you."

"Show us?" said both Joel and Saffina, who also both raised a doubting eyebrow.

"Yeh, I'll show you...here!" The boy launched the chicken he was holding into the faces of Joel and Saffina and took off out of the room and down the corridor, his quick footsteps echoing back through the chambers. The squawking chicken flapped to the floor and after a tangle of wafting arms the friends were able to compose themselves again.

"So much for the talking route!" Saffina reprimanded Joel. "I told you we should have just forced it out of him."

"Come on, there's no time for arguing, he's getting away!" Joel said, bursting down the corridor. In his mind he was having conflicted thoughts if he'd done the right thing, or whether Saffina's approach would actually have been better and more efficient. *'Surely the moral choice must always be non-violent, even if it's less effective?'* The question played on his mind as they ran after the boy's echoes through the twists and turns of the carved-out palace.

The makeshift palace was not large, and the chase through the corridors soon burst out through the main entrance. The boy was already at the foot of the steps and running around the pillar's walled boundary.

"He's quick for someone carrying a sack of potatoes," puffed Joel. He'd decided long ago that his lanky figure wasn't built for sprinting. They turned the corner of the boundary wall, but what they saw shocked and confused them. "How did he get that far ahead?"

Seff had already run the length of the boundary wall and was headed towards the main street leading to the harbour.

"That's not possible," Saffina said in disbelief. The pair continued on as fast as they could run. They reached the end of the boundary wall and looked around for any sighting of the boy. "He's gone," Saffina bent over, hands on her knees, wheezing.

Joel, hands on hips, spotted two young women nearby who looked to be deep in a disagreement. "Hey!" he shouted. "Hey, you two!"

The women abruptly stopped their verbal jousting. "Those kids look familiar, Dimitra," whispered one of the women.

"I agree, Myra, but where do we know them from?" Dimitra whispered back. The two women hesitated and cautiously began to walk over. "How can we help you, children?"

"Did you see a boy... with a sack... run this way?" Joel mustered between deep inhales of air.

"Yes."

"No."

Saffina raised a judgemental eyebrow at the conflicted response. The two women looked at each other.

"No."

"Yes."

Saffina crossed her arms and scowled. The two women looked at each other again, nervously. If there's one thing Saffina does well, it's to say everything without saying anything.

"Well, we're not sure," shrugged Myra.

"How can you not be sure?"

"I saw the boy you described, over there, running by that wooden cart," said Dimitra pointing behind Joel. "I turned and said to Myra 'he must be worried about making it home before curfew', but when I turned back, he was already gone. It's like he vanished."

"All I saw was a whirlwind of black dust," said Myra.

"Maybe you'd pay more attention if you looked up from that ring once in a while," Dimitra folded her arms and pouted.

"You're just jealous!" said Myra, shoving her friend.

"Am not, why would I be jealous?" Dimitra shoved back.

"Because you don't have anything nice."

"Yeh, I don't even have a nice friend!"

"Says you!

"Yeh, I do!"

Joel and Saffina slinked away and left the friends to their argument. They headed toward the cart to look for any clues. They both kneeled down and touched the rough, gravelly ground. "There's some scuffed footprints here, but they just stop. Can you see any black dust they were on about?"

Joel shook his head. "Something strange about that kid."

Then, from their crouching position, a pair of hands on each of their backs pushed the pair over into the dusty stone.

"Hey! That was rude!" chastised Dimitra. "We haven't finished talking to you!"

Dimitra and Myra's anger now channelled from each other to Joel and Saffina. They loomed over the teenagers with arms folded.

"I recognised the boy," said Dimitra. "I think I know where he might have been heading."

"You do?!" Saffina and Joel said in unison. They would

never admit it to each other, but they both loved it when that happened.

"Yep, and we'll take you there, but only if you apologise first!"

"Apologise? What for?" they said again in unison.

"We've just remembered where we recognise you from."

30
VINES

Saffina and Joel swallowed with a gulp. All of a sudden, the pair of bickering, slightly dim women appeared strangely intimidating in the lowly dusk light. Did they recognise them as Saffina Greymore and Joel Ellwood, best friends of Princess Liana Langton who should be being closely guarded as part of the Coryàtès entourage?

"You jumped us back on Coryàtès and stole our horses, that's how my ring got smashed!" Myra exclaimed angrily, shoving her ringed finger in each of the teenagers faces.

Saffina and Joel weren't sure whether to be relieved that they hadn't been recognised as Liana's friends, or worried that this woman would want her revenge for knocking her off a horse and breaking her ring. As it turned out, they didn't need to worry at all.

"Fortunately for you, we want to catch up with this boy too," said Myra.

"We've been hanging out at this shop where some of his friends are," continued Dimitra.

"Not that they'd say they were his friends."

"Nope."

"Definitely not."

Joel stood up and brushed himself off, before offering a gentlemanly hand to help up Saffina, who smiled and accepted. "So, what do you want with the boy?"

"He promised to get us out of this hole, but as you can see, we're still here!" sighed Dimitra.

"And we're not the only ones who want words with him. Some woman and a girl were looking for him too. They're waiting out at the shop too."

"Kid sounds real popular," joked Joel.

"Oh, I'm Myra by the way, and this is Dimitra."

"I'm Saffina, this is Joel."

"Well, now we're all introduced, guess we'd best get going since it sounds like we're already third in line. Show us the way, ladies." Joel flung out his long, lanky arms to allow Dimitra and Myra to lead the way, but in doing so, slapped Saffina square on the nose with the back of his right hand.

"Jeez, Joel!" Saffina clenched her face. She checked for blood, fortunately there was none. Just a pounding throb of pain. The women giggled like little children.

"Just so you know, *Myra* and *Dimitra*," Saffina shot them a death stare, shutting down the pair's laughter immediately. "Back on Coryàtès, you were riding our horses. We just took them back. Now get on with it and lead the way."

~

Myra knocked on the shopkeeper's door. It opened with a creak and Rhonwen's figure filled the doorway. Her curls of bright orange hair bounced like springs; her headscarf unusually absent.

"Oh, I haven't seen you without your headscarf before. I love your hair! It looks just like mine." Rhonwen acknowledged the compliment from Myra with a shallow nod.

"Who're they," Rhonwen said bluntly, obviously referring to Safifna and Joel.

"They're looking for the boy."

"Isn't everybody?" Rhonwen said dryly. "Well, you're all in luck, he arrived not long ago."

"I knew it!" shouted Dimitra, before shoving her way inside, seemingly no longer bothered about her bare arms brushing up against the sweat of the shopkeeper. Myra followed hastily behind. Saffina and Joel entered with more caution, not sure what to make of the shopkeeper.

"Where is he then?" demanded Dimitra.

"Sharing his spoils with the children," Rhonwen answered, whilst lowering herself into her desk chair. Myra and Dimitra headed through the stockroom door towards the sleeping quarters of the orphans. Saffina and Joel moved to follow, but Rhonwen stopped them. "I think you two may be more interested in that door," she said, pointing to the only other door in the room, directly opposite the store's entrance.

"It's really important we speak with the boy," said Saffina stubbornly.

"I expect it is, but you're in my shop and that door is the one you want to go through first."

"We might be in your shop, but that doesn't mean you can tell what to do and where to go. We need to speak with the boy, he has information that may affect the lives of everyone in this wretched hole."

Rhonwen bolted up from her sitting position. "Do you think I don't know what you're doing here? Go through that door, and I'll make sure the boy doesn't leave before you've spoken to him," she said sternly.

Saffina's death stare returned, but for some reason, despite their aura powers, Joel got the feeling this woman shouldn't be messed with. He also sensed the boredom and hunger of being in the crater was making both him and Saffina even more cranky than usual. He decided to drag his friend towards the door. "C'mon, Saff, let it go." Saffina huffed and sighed whilst shaking Joel's hands off of her.

The door opened out into a wide room. A locked cabinet was the only object other than a long, slender table which ran the length of the room, chairs neatly tucked under, except for one. The chair to the far right of the table was occupied by the tied-up Prince Kendrix. Sat on the table either side of him were the two familiar faces of Amara and Liana.

"Liana!" Joel and Saffina again shouted in unison.

"What're you doing here?" the three friends all said at the same time, making them laugh. The upbeat greetings suggested they had all forgotten about the manner in which they had departed Coryàtes. "Long story," they all said together again. The unity of their words demonstrated an unbroken bond that wrapped them together like a trio of vines entwined with one another. Sometimes the stems of the vines become damaged, grow in the wrong direction, or are weak, but with a bit of pruning new stems grow to create an even stronger plant. This is how Liana thought of their relationship, they remove the bad bits and move on to become stronger.

"What's he doing here?" asked Saffina, stirring Liana from

her metaphoric thoughts, pointing towards the tied-up Prince Kendrix.

"He baited Liana into rescuing him from the pillar," said Amara, wiping the juices of an apple from her mouth who was literally enjoying the fruits of her labour having regained the supply bag Seff had stolen from them. "Liana being Liana took the bait. Liana again being Liana, saved both of them like the badass she is," smirked Amara.

"Except, loads of Dantian's saw me use my Aura."

"Yeh, so we're hiding out here, trying to get him to talk," Amara punched the prince hard in the arm. He muffled a cry of pain through his gag. "We think the prince has got something to do with the Turnings in the abandoned city, and why our old friend Clerk Vivek and his new Army of Immorals are standing right above us as we speak."

"Clerk Vivek is here?" gasped Joel.

Amara nodded. "So is Yasmin, and your brother," she said looking at Saffina, whose eyes began to glaze over with water. She quickly wiped them with her sleeve and straightened herself. 'At *least he's alive*', she thought. '*He can still be saved.*' "So, has our prince said anything yet?"

"Not yet. Although I'm yet to try my more, shall we say, unique techniques," Amara drew a knife from her right boot and pressed it threateningly against the prince's neck. Her scarred face up in his, eyeballing him.

"We're not torturing him. It's not how my mother handles these matters," Liana said with authority to her aunt. Regardless of age and relation, she could, and would, command where necessary. It was the moral thing to do. Amara twirled the blade between her fingers before suggestively putting it back into her boot. Prince Kendrix breathed a sigh of relief. "How come you two aren't in the stone palace?"

"We saw a kid making some sort of deal with King Shimon. We chased him back here, but he was quick. Too quick," Joel said, rubbing his chin.

"This kid, was he in all navy blue clothes and kind of annoying?" asked Liana.

"That's him! We met two women who figured he'd come here," replied Joel.

"His name's Seff, and he's not *kind of* annoying. He *is* annoying," piped Amara. "Is he here?! Little traitor's gonna find this apple core shoved down his throat."

"Hold on!" Saffina held out an arm to stop Amara barging through. "We need to know what information was so valuable he got rewarded by King Shimon, and how he managed to get away from us so quickly. We think King Shimon is up to something, and it looks like it involves his son too."

"Any idea what that something might be?"

"No clue, but if Vivek is here too, it can't be good."

~

After a brief catchup of how they had all ended up in this small shop, the doors to the room flung open. Dimitra and Myra breezed in.

"The shopkeeper would like to see you all," announced Dimitra.

"We still haven't interrogated the boy yet!" Saffina replied, angrily. "Why is she keeping him from us?"

"How are we supposed to know?" replied Myra. "She wants to see you on the shopfloor. Now."

"I'd better stay here and watch our guest," suggested Amara. The trio all gave the warrior a sceptical glare. "Don't worry, I'll follow my orders, no torturing," she sighed. "You know, I still can't get out of my head that I've seen Dimitra and Myra somewhere before." Saffina and Joel shared a knowing glance and chuckle with each other. Amara had been with them when they took their horses back on Coryàtès.

"What's so funny, you two?" asked Liana.

"We'll tell you later," they laughed.

31
THE NEOTERIC TEMPLE

"Liana," began the shopkeeper, this time in her gruff toned voice. "You trust these two?"

"With my life."

Rhonwen moved to the windows and closed both a set of curtains and a set of blinds in each. The room would have become pitch black, had it not been for a single candle flickering gently on her work desk. The shopkeeper removed her headscarf and even in the dim light, the trio of friends could see her blazing orange, curly hair bounce like tiny springs. In an instant, her posture, her demeanour, her aura, seemingly changed. She stood tall, her eyes sparkled, her skin glowed. She smiled a gentle smile. Saffina and Joel stood open mouthed with confusion.

"My name is Rhonwen Rothkofsky, and I am the Spectra Child tasked with looking after the Jewels of Orange and the Neoteric Temple."

"Nice to meet you, ma'am," Joel bowed respectfully. The act made Liana laugh inside. She'd never seen Joel bow to someone before, not even when first meeting her or her mother. He wasn't a disrespectful person; he just innocently saw everyone in the same light. She liked that about him, how everyone through his eyes were simply people and not positions in layers of authority and bureaucracy.

"So, why are you here running this shop, not in the temple preparing to take on Vivek and the Army of Immorals? You don't seem to be doing your job very well," said Saffina, straight to the point as always.

"I'm doing more than you realise, child," Rhonwen turned to Liana. "I thought you said the Visendi teachings had returned to your land? Seems like someone in this room doesn't understand the basic principles of respect."

"Seems to me like you're hiding out in this shop rather than fighting for the poor people who've lost their Morality," Saffina argued back. Liana had noticed how much more argumentative Saffina had become since becoming a Visendi, like she had a new found confidence compared to a year ago. She pondered this for a few moments, and the more she spun these thoughts around in her mind, the more she realised that her friends were developing their own identity with their own clear traits. She wasn't sure if the shift was simply due to them growing up, or if the Visendi way was nudging them down a particular route.

She moved her ponderings to herself. What was her persona? She wasn't sure she could answer that. Perhaps it's easier to see what others' disposition is, than to be able to accurately analyse your own?

Liana shook herself from her own distracting thoughts. She had to focus on what Rhonwen wanted to tell them.

"I'm doing more than you realise," Rhonwen's tone was

sharp and unwavering. *"We're* doing more than you realise," she put a hand on Liana's shoulder.

"We are?" questioned the princess.

"Liana and her aunt arrived here with the Jewels of Orange; the Mikanan Artefact designed to give strength to the chosen one's Sacral Spirit. An Orange Aura gives Visendi the ability to grab and move objects. Let me show you."

Rhonwen's frame began to glow, a shimmering and dancing orange light, thick like a translucent marmalade. It was the same intense and vibrant colour that was being emitted from the peak of the Pillar of Sanctuary. The same type of whirling and seemingly living light of Red Aura's of the Inner Root Core's that the three friends had attained on the battlefield against the Zaganites less than a year ago.

Even with the curtains and blinds closed, the three friends shared a nervous look between themselves. They weren't convinced that the shop wouldn't be lighting up like a beacon to anyone walking down the cobblestone street outside. The shopkeeper pushed her right hand out in front of her, and a stream of her Orange Aura broke out from the shape of her glowing figure and wrapped itself like a lasso around the tiniest Chantrah playing piece, an infantry unit, on one of the game boards in front of them. The small game piece floated its way gracefully to Rhonwen, carried by the rope-like aura stream of light. She reached out and took the piece from her Aura in her hand.

"A strong Sacral Aura can move tiny objects with the grace of a dancer, or ones of enormous size with the strength of a wrestler."

The shopkeeper walked to the Chantrah board from where the piece was taken and placed it back on the square she had lifted it from.

"Awesome," said Saffina and Joel together.

"Liana, your Sacral Spirit Orb, in unison with the Jewels, will give you an even more impressive ability. You will be able to craft whatever you need, out of whatever you have. There are a couple of limitations. There must be enough of the element, and you will not be able to change the element's properties, but the ability to craft items without hours of hammering or smelting will make many a blacksmith jealous."

"Double awesome!" Liana said aloud excitedly.

"You'll be pleased to hear I managed to get the Jewels off my real hand, princess," Rhonwen opened the drawer to her desk and handed the intricate handpiece back to Liana, who had given the Artefact to the shopkeeper after she had disclosed who she really was to her.

"What do you mean, *'managed to get the Jewels off your real hand'?*" asked Joel tentatively.

Rhonwen removed a surprisingly lifelike animatronic hand from the stump of her left wrist. Saffina and Joel gasped in shock. The hand was so lifelike they hadn't even noticed it wasn't her real hand, and she worked her carpentry with it so well. "I woke up in the Neoteric Temple just over thirteen years ago," she squeezed herself into a rocking chair and softly swayed backwards and forwards. "I felt a bit groggy, and very, very hungry…"

"Sounds like you in the morning," Liana nudged Joel, whose stomach gurgled right on cue.

"Before we were entombed," Rhonwen carried on, ignoring the interruption, "the Spectra Children all agreed the best way to keep the Spectra Orbs safe was to keep them far away from one another, to prevent them all falling into the wrong hands all at once. We of course had no idea the state of the world we would wake up in, especially considering the state we were leaving it after the Aura Wars.

We found an invocation to Aurora in the Scriptures of Yellow which specifically related to the act of fast travelling to a founding temple. We had no idea if it would work. Turns out it did. We all were transported to our founding temple's after being awoken from our long slumber."

"That's what the rainbow out of Mount Indigo on the Day of Darkness was that my mother talks about," said Liana.

Rhonwen confirmed with a nod. "The fact that the invocation worked gives me faith that Aurora is alive and listening, even if she cannot always act or answer."

"So, what happened here? Why are you fronting as a shopkeeper?" questioned Saffina.

"I had been happily living out of sight in the Neoteric Temple for 12 years, patiently waiting to see if Candela's daughter would ever realise her aura powers, which I must admit, I had my doubts if she ever would, considering the ban on the Visendi. I'd heard of small factions being forced to operate underground in small clusters across Mikana, but I never really had much hope that the Visendi way would ever resurface." The single flicker of candlelight on Rhonwen's desk created a long shadow on the wall behind her and turned the contours of her face dark like she was about to tell a horror story.

"Then just under a year ago, things here in The Dantè took a dark turn."

"Let me guess, around the time of Liana's thirteenth birthday, when she started having Morality visions?" Saffina surmised.

"Yes, the timeline appears that way. Her coming of age into teen hood must have triggered something inside of her and her power of Sight must have acted like a beacon to those who follow the path of darkness, the ones who are determined to rise to power by the process of Turning and manipulating, commanding those of Bad Morality. They tug on loose strings of doubt and empty promises in order to control them. Those who follow this path call their religion Sentio Tenebris, which translates as 'Feel the God of Darkness'. They call themselves Sentians.

Whilst you were facing your battle on Coryàtès, I was facing my own battle here. The usual sunshine of personality and joy in the citizens of Allicalidantè was slowly dimming, like one of the eclipses of our moons over the sun. Someone was Turning them, and a few months ago, there came a tipping point. A point where those with Bad Morality had become so disruptive that the Turning sped up exponentially, as those unturned could feel no joy and reacted as they were being treated. This created a day of violence and riots. Allicalidantè's own Day of Darkness you could say." Rhonwen sighed in disappointment. Disappointment that she could not prevent the riots and the Turning tipping point. "I had built up my reputation among the citizens with a shop on the high street," she continued. "I thought it would be the perfect place where I could observe and get to know people. I used my network to offer sanctuary to anyone running from the riots."

"How did you do that? Aren't the Founding Temple's all hidden from non-Visendi?" questioned Saffina.

"Believe it or not, this whole crater is what was the Neoteric Temple. Back in my day, 200-years ago," she held up two fingers of her right-hand to emphasise the timeframe. "This temple thrived with the creativity and joy of Visendi worshippers. We had no need to hide the Founding Temple's back then, for the religion wasn't outlawed."

"So this whole crater was actually the Founding Temple for studying the Sacral Core. What was taught here?" Saffina's barriers had lowered from defensiveness to curiosity.

"Joy. Creativity. Games. Events. Arts. Crafts. Once you have learned and mastered the toughness to basic survival in the Root Core, the Sacral Core teachings provide a new type of energy. An energy that sets Mikanan's aside from many other creatures. The energies of fun, humour, pleasure and entertainment," Rhonwen remembered nostalgically.

"However, for preservation and security, we had to conceal each temple before our long slumber under Mount Indigo.

The Orange Aura you see streaming out of The Pillar is what makes this temple hidden by creating a fake floor, or ceiling, depending on how you look at it, and layering it with a field of orange tulips. I had to persuade as many Visendi as I could to part with a great deal of their Orange Aura's. Gilroy came with his Dagger of Red and Peeled them, whilst I crafted the largest orb you will ever see. We had to have enough Aura for the temple to remain hidden for thousands of years if needed, as we had no idea how long we would remain in the Tomb of the Transcended." Rhonwen gestured with her arms the size of the orb, holding her hand and wrist about two feet apart.

"But in order for me to provide sanctuary to the desperate people of this city and allow them access to the temple as non-Visendi, I had to disrupt the pillar so the crater would become visible.

So, I removed the orb that I had created two centuries earlier and stopped the stream of Orange Aura. The fake ceiling above dissolved and as a rain of tulips fell, the orb I had created two centuries ago went dark. Once the crater had filled with the fleeing Dantians, I had to find a way to conceal the temple again, so I used the strongest aura available to me, Liana's Sacral Spirit.

I separated her Spectra Orb from the Jewels. The light inside the Spectra Orb came alive, like it was reacting to the situation around us. I played with it between my fingers for a few moments. The glass-like orb clinked against the metal of the Jewels. I placed it where the large orb that I created had been, but when I did, a surge of power erupted. That's how I lost my hand and the Jewels of Orange," she looked longingly at the stump where her left hand used to be. "Ever since then, we've been trapped down here, and the Immorals above have been trying to get into the temple."

"But now that Liana is here with the Jewels, you can let her into the pillar so she can just take back her Spectra Orb and then she can Turn the Immorals back, like she did on Coryàtès," said Joel.

"One problem there Joel, I still don't have my ability of Sight back. I haven't been able to use it since that day, remember?" sighed Liana.

"There is another problem. Since I disrupted the orb I created and replaced it with Liana's Spectra Orb, the pillar went into lockdown. The lockdown was a failsafe in case it was a Sentian trying to take the orb," replied Rhonwen.

"Ok, so how do we unlock it?" asked Joel.

Rhonwen paused, the candlelight flickered with a sudden draft that made her shadow and dark contours on her face dance a wild dance."The Three Trials."

32
THE THREE TRIALS

"The Three Trials?" the trio of friends said together.

"Did I suddenly start speaking a foreign language?" Rhonwen said sarcastically. "That's what I said."

"Go on," a resigned Joel sighed. "What are they? What are we going to have to do?"

Rhonwen, her face still dimly lit by the single flicker of candlelight, motioned a hand towards the hexagonal tables on the shop floor. "You must first activate the pillar, then beat it at a game of Chantrah."

"Hence the giant folding out game board," said Saffina.

"And then?" asked Liana.

Rhonwen paused briefly with short and almost unnoticeable flinch. The flinch didn't pass by Liana.

"The third trial is one that only seven of us can pass. It requires the sacrifice of a Spectra Child's Morality Aura."

"Well, that's okay, there's two in this room. I'm sure either of you could spare some," Joel said innocently.

"Joel, I don't think she means sacrificing a little bit, I think she means all of it," Liana swallowed nervously.

"But won't that mean whoever is sacrificed will end up like Gilroy? Lifeless, their body an empty vessel." Joel shook his head. "But that can't be Liana if she's supposed to be the Guardian of Light, which means we'd have to sacrifice your Morality Aura?" Joel pointed at Rhonwen who nodded to confirm. Before she could reply, Joel's cheeks reddened, his blonde curls bounced, as he entered a rare fit of rage. "That's ridiculous Rhonwen! We lost one Spectra Child already, and now we're going to lose you too?! After all you've done for the people of Allicalidantè and for the Visendi, for Aurora, you're just going to give yourself up? You're going to leave Liana, leave us, so we have to continue on without your help?" Joel kicked over a chair as he turned his back on the group.

"There are only seven of us, Joel. Gilroy and Liana are clearly not an option."

"What about Candela? She's a Spectra Child."

"We have no idea where she is," replied Saffina.

"She's also Liana's mother," said Rhonwen.

"She already has a mother, Queen Adriya, she doesn't need another one," Joel's words came out rather more heartless than he intended to, which got him on the receiving end of a cold glare from both Liana and Saffina.

Rhonwen, wanting to avoid a confrontation, stepped in and placed a reassuring hand on his shoulder. "Why does this matter so much to you? We barely know each other, child."

"I just can't stand seeing people get hurt. It makes me angry; it makes me sad, it makes me frustrated all at the same time. Why can't people just get on with each other? Why do we even fight for power? Fight for money? Fight for objects, things which don't even matter. Why should you have to sacrifice yourself so we can move on?"

"It was designed to make it as difficult as possible for a Sentian to break. An Aura can only be cut with the Dagger of Red. The chances of a Sentian capturing a Spectra Child and obtaining the Dagger of Red would be incredibly unlikely. We all knew the importance of sacrifice if the time came when we entered the Tomb of Transcendence," Rhonwen answered on behalf of her other five siblings.

"But this is stupid, there must be another way,"

"Joel…" Saffina placed a hand on his other shoulder.

"No, don't console me or try to make me feel better. Don't you ever stop to think about what we've witnessed in the last year? The murders of Evelyn and the residents at the Shrouded Temple of Roots. The people we buried from the beaches at the Battle of Coryàtès. Gilroy's empty body, the hungry Dantians who've lost their homes. Do you ever think about it at all?"

"Of course I do, Joel."

"And this is just the beginning," he interrupted "There's still four more Spirits and Artefacts to get after the Jewels of Orange. I mean, we're just kids," Joel wiped his nose with a sniff and cleared the drops of tears that had formed under his eyelids.

"I think about the same things every day," a tear now rolled down Saffina's cheek. "And you know how I get through it? You. Your jokes. Your clumsiness. Your optimism. You get me through it, Joel. You."

Rhonwen stepped away as the friends pressed their foreheads together and closed their eyes. "Are you not joining your friends?" she said to Liana who was looking on, somewhat emotionless.

"I'm the reason for what they are feeling right now. If I wasn't here, if I didn't exist, if I wasn't their friend, they'd be happier, wouldn't they?"

"Happier? Happiness is too difficult to quantify. You can't hypothesise about 'what ifs', it's a pointless thought process, a distraction. Focus on the truth, and the truth is those two friends of yours wouldn't be here if they didn't love you."

The room stood silent for a short while and the air hung heavy as everyone reflected on the recent past of death and discovery, the less recent past of friendships forming and joyful play, and the near future of the Three Trials, and the further future and darkness that may be yet to come.

Rhonwen softly broke the silence and whispered to Liana, "Your male friend here has a clear potency towards a Green Aura."

"What do you mean?"

"Everyone has a natural preference in their Aura, one that is stronger than the rest. It's obviously clearer among us Spectra Children what our preferences are, but in fact everyone has an inclination. His Green Aura will be particularly strong, I can tell. That will come in useful later on in your journey."

"What about Saffina's? What's her preference?"

"Difficult to tell, but she is not afraid to speak her mind, which usually goes for those with a strong Yellow Aura."

"And me?"

"Do you really need to ask?"

"Right. Restorer of the Spectrum. Guardian of Light. I don't have one, do I? Equally strong in all auras as I'm 'the one'." Rhonwen smiled a friendly smile at the princesses' correct deduction.

Joel broke off his connection with Saffina and asked

another question. "So, the trials, does the same person have to do all three?"

"That's up to the temple."

"What do you mean, up to the temple?"

"I've found these Founding Temples have their own sort of consciousness, almost like they have traces of Aurora running through them. I cannot say for certain what will be and what won't be allowed."

Joel got to his feet, wiped his eyes dry again, and drew a deep breath. "It's time we came up with a plan then. We only have one shot, so we have to give Liana the best possible chance of getting to the third trial and getting back her Sacral Spirit." His friends nodded in agreement with solid determination, it was time to get Liana's Spirit.

33
BREAKING CURFEW

Liana wrapped her dirtied robes tightly around her as she stepped outside. Flakes of dirt fell from the garment and were carried off by a chilling breeze that whistled through the dusty street where the games shop was situated. The cracked patches of mud that remained created a tortoise-shell-like pattern on the fabric. She looked to the sky, longing to see the trio of Mikana's moons, but of course she didn't. Just a starless blackest-of-black ceiling above her. The two-way flow of glowing Orange Aura dancing out the top of The Pillar to her right caught her eye. Fragments of the aura would spark off and then regroup again. She found the effect mesmerising. The contrast against the darkness was enchanting. She suddenly felt the same awe she had felt when she first saw a Red Aura. A magical wonder of intrigue and curiosity.

"Remind me why he's coming again?" said a perturbed Saffina, pointing ahead, disrupting Liana's thoughts. Seff walked laboriously in front of them, huffing and puffing with every step and complaining about being tired.

"So, we can keep an eye on him," replied Liana.

"Can't Amara do that?" Saffina suggested.

"That'd be the equivalent of a death sentence," Liana joked. "Besides, we still haven't got out of him how he outran you both."

The group of five; Liana, Saffina, Joel, Rhonwen and Seff, made their way cautiously towards the boundary walls of the pillar, being careful to stick to the shadows. It was past curfew.

The trio of best friends neared the edge of the street and stooped behind an upturned table, where Rhonwen and Seff were already crouched behind. Liana realised that despite Rhonwen's larger frame, she could scarcely remember seeing her movements in front of her, like she had disappeared into the shadows themselves.

"Guards, over there," Rhonwen said, pointing to her left to four guards talking with one another on the corner of the boundary wall. "Best wait it out to see where they begin their patrols." After a few minutes of talking, the guards broke away one at a time in the direction of the group, passing them by. As one guard turned the corner of the boundary wall, the next guard would break off and follow. The pattern of patrol meant at any one time there'd always a guard walking each section of the boundary wall.

"How're we going to sneak past them?" asked Joel. "We've no chance of getting by unseen."

"I have an idea, but I'm not sure if it'll work," Rhonwen replied. "Follow me."

The shopkeeper led the children out from the upturned table towards the walled boundary and immediately caught the eye of the patrolling guard. "Let me do the talking," she whispered.

"Halt!" shouted the guard, before making his way authoritatively over to the group. A worn and torn navy-blue cape flapped in the breeze behind him. "Curfew has passed, shopkeeper. What are you and these kids doing out in the streets?"

"Darwin! Why haven't you picked up that order yet? It's taking up room in my shop," Rhonwen put on her acting skills as the grumpy shopkeeper.

"That wasn't me, ma'am, I haven't ordered nowt." said the guard, slightly taken aback by Rhonwen's abruptness.

"You sure? Ugh, that's the trouble with not having any paper to write orders and receipts on. When am I going to get some, eh? The king's been promising me some since we arrived in the damned hole."

"I've no idea about that, ma'am. But that doesn't explain why you and these kids..."

"Me and my shop are the only reason the people stuck down here haven't all gone mad and started killing each other, you know!"

"Yes ma'am, but..."

"Do you realise how much work goes into my products, just for them not to be picked up? I only charge a few fresh fish for each order, how hard is it to drop by and pick up your stuff?"

"Enough!" shouted the guard, losing his patience. Liana was beginning to doubt Rhonwen's plan. Winding up the guard didn't seem a good idea.

"Oh, come on now Darwin, don't you recognise these children? They're from the Coryàtès entourage."

The guard looked at them one-by-one. "This one isn't," he

said, pointing to Seff. "Definitely seen him around here before, causing trouble."

"Well, it seems the other three have taken to him."

Liana, Saffina and Joel all had to use their own acting skills to avoid the truth showing on their faces from that statement. They weren't sure anyone had taken to liking Seff.

"They got lost exploring and wandered into my shop. I couldn't have Sir Tarak Langton thinking something had happened to his niece and her friends in The Dantè now, could I? What hope would we have of escaping this damned place then?"

He considered the shopkeeper's words. "Fine," said the guard, finally. "I've *never* let anyone off from breaking curfew before. The king is strict on the rule. If I'm found out, he'll have my head."

"I don't have many kind words to say to people, but I am truly grateful for your understanding, Darwin." Rhonwen faked a seductive smile, which looked more like a hyena's grimace.

"Go, before one of my comrades appears round the corner." Darwin waved the group by. They all inwardly breathed a sigh of relief as they cowered past the towering guard. They rounded the corner, out of sight.

"So, how're we gonna get over the wall?" Seff asked the group. Liana reached into her robes and pulled out the handle grip of the staff Master H had given her when she stayed with him in the Shrouded Temple of Roots. She flicked her hands in a see-saw motion and the poles extended forming the full length. It felt like forever since she'd seen Master H, since she'd heard his words of wisdom. He was only a stone's throw away in the stone palace but seemed so far away. *'What would he be saying to me right now?'* she thought. A shimmer of red lit up the area as the princess called upon her Red Aura. She held the pole out horizontal at shoulder height. "I'll give you a boost," she answered in response to Seff's question.

"Cool! But what about you?"

"She can get over herself," Saffina answered on Liana's behalf with a smirk.

The Red Aura didn't quiver under any strain as the group used it to climb over the wall. Not even when the larger framed figure of Rhonwen made use of the temporary, supernatural step. Liana then used the trick with her Red Aura and staff that Master H had shown her as they descended to the Tomb of Transcendence, creating small aura platforms to vault on as she ascended herself over the wall with minimal effort. She landed on the other side gracefully onto one knee.

Now inside the perimeter, the group made their way to the pillar. The last time Liana had gotten so close, she hadn't had the chance to take in the sheer enormity of it, or the beauty of the smooth, black gloss finish. Somehow it shimmered and reflected their faces despite the blackness of the night. Out of the corner of her eye she caught Saffina and Joel gawking at it too. Rhonwen's neutral expression didn't surprise her, since she was involved in its creation, but she was surprised at the nonplussed look on Seff's face. Her suspicion got the better of her. "What's the matter, doesn't impress you?" she asked him.

"Oh-oh, y-yes," Seff stuttered. "It's incredible up close, isn't it."

Worst. Liar. Ever.

"Someone's coming!" Rhonwen announced, as two figures slowly emerged from the direction of the stone palace out of the shadowy darkness. Two large gates in the boundary wall which stood at the foot of the steps to the stone palace closed shut behind the approaching pair. The group hid, peering around the corner in the pillar's shadow. Their gasps almost gave them away once they saw the faces of who had approached the monument.

"You were supposed to be the final piece of the puzzle," announced the instantly recognisable voice of King Shimon. In his right-hand he tightly held the dyed-blue hair of Luci, who was struggling as hard as she could against his grasp, but to no avail. Her hands were bound behind her back and her voice muffled with a dirty rag gagging her. "I just needed the last sacrifice. One more, the last sacrifice of the most powerful spirit, then I could have gotten out of this hellhole." He pushed her to the floor, scraping her knees and elbows in the process. Tears formed in Luci's eyes. Liana may not have liked her doppelgänger, but she was in real trouble, and she knew exactly what it was like to be taken against your will. The fright of not being in control, not knowing your capture's intention, not knowing if you'll ever see your loved ones again.

King Shimon removed a black glove from his left-hand. Saffina and Joel had never seen him take off his gloves throughout the whole of the negotiation process, and now they could see why. In the palm of his hand, a black darkness, blacker than the blackest black any of the group had ever seen, swirled and danced.

"He's a Reaper," Rhonwen half-whispered, half-gasped, ominously.

"A what?"

"I haven't seen one since the Battle of Grimstone. A Morality Reaper bears the mark of Tenebris. The mark enables a Reaper to Turn someone instantly, as opposed to traditional methods that can take weeks or even months of careful interaction."

"That doesn't sound good," Joel said, stating the obvious.

"That's not the only problem."

"It isn't?!"

"There's only one way to get the mark of Tenebris, from Tenebris himself."

"So does that mean Tenebris is alive?"

"It would appear that way. If Tenebris has broken free from his prison in the Morality Realm, then I'm afraid there's only one thing he'll be wanting." Rhonwen looked over her shoulder at Liana. "You."

Liana didn't have time to react before King Shimon moved his marked hand to Luci's chest where her heart was located. A Black Aura wafted over the doppelgänger like an early morning fog. Once the dark matter had fully encased itself around her, a white shockwave jolted out from inside her and was absorbed by the pillar. Luci's body fell limp. King Shimon stood with his arms outstretched like he was some sort of messiah awaiting the adulation of his disciples.

"That's what you get for lying to me," King Shimon lowered his arms and clenched his fists. Even in the dark Liana could see his reddened cheeks. "I need the one who can unlock the pillar's power, the power to bring back my wife, my Queen. Otherwise, all these sacrifices have been for nothing!" King Shimon dropped to his knees and let out a bloodcurdling cry of anguish and pain. "I will make them pay for this deceit," he said through grimace teeth before trudging off back toward the stone palace.

Once the king was out of sight, the group ran over to the still body of Luci. Liana shook her shoulders gently, repeating her name over and over. Eventually, to the relief of the group, she regained consciousness to a chorus of "Luci! Are you ok?" But the relief didn't last long. She lifted herself to her feet without a word and threw a small black orb into the ground. Her body dissipated into a black cloud of sand-like dust. The essence flew up into the stream of Orange Aura that poured out the top of The Pillar.

"She's become an Immoral," Liana quietly said. "The emotionless expression, uncaring demeanour, lack of conversation. The signals are all there. He Turned her."

Saffina turned to Rhonwen. "What was the king doing? Why did the pillar suck in her Good Morality?"

"He's building a bigger army upstairs. That's why Luci turned into that black mist," suggested Joel.

"That, and perhaps he's trying to pry open The Pillar from the inside," replied Rhonwen.

"Open it from the inside? But I thought the Three Trials were the only way to open it now?"

"The Three Trials is the only *right* way to open it, but Tenebris must have found another way. A much, much darker way."

"And just what is that other way?" Joel asked, nervously.

"This would only be a guess, but when someone's Good Morality is separated from their physical form in the presence of the pillar, it seems that the pillar is providing asylum to that morality. However, an object can only have a limited capacity, whether that be in our Realm or in the Morality Realm. I think King Shimon has been sacrificing citizens' Good Morality and plans to break it open from the inside as it goes beyond its capacity."

"You surely don't mean this thing is full of people's Good Morality spirits?!" Joel's softer side showing again.

"That's the real reason for the curfew, so he can make a sacrifice each night," said Saffina.

"And if anyone breaks curfew, they're the ones to get

Turned," continued Liana. "A perfect cover story for the king as an excuse to why people go missing." She then realised how quiet Seff had been through the whole encounter. "How come you're so quiet?" she said, hand-on-hips, an eyebrow raised.

Joel, full of emotion, lashed out at the boy, "I think it's time we questioned him on what exactly he and the king were discussing earlier this evening."

34
CHANGE OF PLANS

'*His Morality just imploded into an Aura of black! Look, Cas, over there, he's rematerialised. The kid is Orbing! I haven't seen that since being released from the Tomb of the Transcended. This is bad news, Cas, very bad indeed. We have to keep a very, very close eye on Liana. She's not prepared for how quickly things are starting to turn dark. Heck, I'm not sure if I'm prepared for it either.*'

Seff pulled a Black Orb out of his pocket and cracked it against his chest. "So long, Swyreites!" he remarked somewhat gleefully. Joel jumped forward to try and grab him but ended up only catching an armful of air as the boy dissipated into a black cloud and raced away from the group.

"So that's how he got away from us so fast," said Joel, annoyed he couldn't stop the boy from disappearing. "What are those Black Orb's?"

Rhonwen stepped forward, first studying the position where Seff had been standing, before looking around to see if she could spot where he had disappeared to. "Just like the

Dagger of Red can cut away an Aura and be captured into an orb, a Reaper can capture Bad Morality into an orb. Its ability, as you have witnessed, is a short-distance boost to speed by way of temporarily turning someone's physical form into an aura. Just before the orb is cracked, the user must choose where they want to travel to by looking at their destination, so they will always re-appear within their own field of vision. The Sentian's call this Orbing," she explained. Joel kicked up a cloud of dust in frustration at Seff getting away. Saffina comforted him.

Liana stepped up to the pillar and examined it as close as she could without touching it. She closed her eyes and concentrated as hard as she could on happy thoughts and friendships, just as her birth mother had taught her, to try and enter the Morality Realm. But she couldn't, her ability of Sight still eluded her. The thought that hundreds of Moralities were trapped inside the pillar, and she could do nothing about it overwhelmed her. Liana sobbed into the palms of her hands and collapsed onto her knees.

Rhonwen crouched beside her and lowered the princesses' hands from her reddened eyes. "Come now, child, we must carry on with our plan."

"He took Luci's Morality because we deceived him. She was caught in the crossfire. All those people above us right now, they're not living life as they should be because this city has been destroyed in the hunt for my Spirits," Liana yelled, angry with resentment and pressure of being 'the one'.

"The only way to make things better now is to beat The Three Trials and get your Spirit."

"And then we hunt my next Spirit and come across the next devastated city."

CHANGE OF PLANS

"Guys," interrupted Saffina, trepidation in her voice, "We gotta go."

The group followed Saffina's gaze and saw a mini army headed towards them. "That little rat must have snitched on us to the king!" guessed Joel.

"Run!" shouted Rhonwen.

"Why? Liana could take them on her own with her Red Aura," Joel shrugged.

"I thought the moral choice was a nonviolent one, Joel? What happened to 'talking it out'?" Saffina said, taking the chance to highlight the hypocrisy from his earlier statement in the chicken coups.

"Had to get the 'I told you so' in, didn't you Saff?" Joel rolled his eyes. "But in all fairness, maybe we wouldn't be here if we went with your approach."

"Why, how kind of you to actually admit that," Saffina said with stuck up sarcasm.

"Okay, argument over, are we running or not?!" Liana said, rushing the group for an answer as they watched the mini army march towards them.

"We don't know the extent of King Shimon's power as a Reaper. By the very essence of being a Reaper, he has ties to Tenebris himself. That in itself is dangerous. We can't risk anything, we can't risk losing Liana," Rhonwen insisted, with an earnestness in their voice. "Go!"

The three friends took off in the opposite direction as fast they could. The approaching army chased after them. After just a few steps, Liana stopped. Rhonwen was not with them.

"Rhonwen!" she screamed. "Why aren't you running?"

"Does it look like I can keep up with you?" she lightly patted her stomach. "I'll be there when you need me," she called, cupping a hand to her mouth to ensure Liana heard her.

"Isn't there a Visendi way of Orbing?!" Liana shouted back, but a simple shake of the head and the impending herd of soldiers gave her the answer she needed.

The three friends vaulted the wall with their aura's and left the king's army, and Rhonwen, behind.

~

Saffina pulled herself out of the small hole that was the cave entrance and brushed down her shirts and trousers. Above ground it had been raining again and the wet muck of mud and tiny gravel sloshed between her fingers as she wiped. "Now I know why you look so grim," she said to Liana.

Liana didn't answer, instead she stared up into the night sky, thankful that the clouds that had delivered the rain had moved on, and the colours of Mikana's three moons could be seen through the streaky remnants of the few clouds that remained.

They set off in the direction of Franklin and his wife's lighthouse, the only safe place Liana could think of as they ran from King Shimon's soldiers. The ground beneath their feet turned from squelching mud to knee-high sloshing of moss and swamp water. As they waded through, a Jackdaw flew low overhead and settled on a rock ahead. It waited patiently for the friends to wade out of the swampy water and hit muddied grass once again.

"I wonder who this is from?" Liana said aloud.

"Maybe it's from your mother, Candela?"

"No, she sends duets for long distance messages." Saffina

and Joel shared a confused look with each other at Liana's matter of fact, yet odd, reply.

Liana held her arm out in front of her for the Jackdaw to rest upon so they could look into each other's eyes. A blue stream of aura light connected their two foreheads and the words of Master H sounded in her head.

"I know you're here. I always knew you wouldn't be kept away. Your Spirits are yours, and yours only, to obtain. Nobody else's. This mission of negotiations was always going to be in vain, but being cooped up in this stone palace would have done you no good.

Remember our last training back in Swyre. The Five F's. Remember you told me that 'Friending' has always been your weakness? That may have been correct in Swyre, but out here where you are not the heiress to this throne, it has been a strength. Use the friends you have made to retrieve your Spirit." The blue stream of light dimmed, and the Jackdaw flew away.

"Who was it, what did it say?" asked Joel.

"It was Master H. He said to 'use the friends you have made to retrieve your spirit'."

"You mean you actually managed to make friends other than us?" joked Joel.

"Haha, very funny Joel. Come on, let's get to the lighthouse and meet some *new* friends of mine," Liana joked back, but before they set off, the voice of a person saying 'Hello?' from behind the rock made Joel jump out of his skin so much, he lost his footing on the muddy ground. In an attempt to try and save himself, he reached out and grabbed a handful each of Liana and Saffina's clothes and pulled all three butt-first into the swamp water, covering them all in stinking wet moss.

"Jeez, Joel!" cried Saffina and Liana.

"S-sorry," replied Joel, flicking a clump of green sludge off his hands back into the water.

"I'm sorry, I didn't mean to startle you all." Joel and Saffina instantly recognised the voice now, whose figure was bent over offering a helping hand.

"Prince Kendrix!" Saffina replied coyly. She took the prince's waiting hand and pulled herself up with his help. The prince didn't extend the same offer to Joel, whilst Liana had already pulled herself up out of the pungent water.

"How did you get away from Amara?" Joel said accusingly, suspecting foul play. The prince was still supposed to be restrained in Rhonwen's shop, being watched over by the warrior.

"Even warriors and mercenaries need to sleep," he responded with a twang of arrogance in his voice, which just annoyed Joel even more. "Next time you apprehend a real enemy, I suggest you search them more thoroughly." Kendrix held the middle of three cufflinks on his military jacket between his thumb and forefinger and pulled. A small, golden blade only as long as his middle finger slipped out from between the seams.

'Amara's going to be furious!' Liana chuckled to herself, before turning her thoughts to the Kendrix's words *'real enemy'*. "So, what made you come up here?"

"Looking for the princess," he responded in his usual brief tone.

"So, you thought you might find her top-side?" replied Joel, in an accusatory manner.

"I hoped I wouldn't," Prince Kendrix hesitated, somewhat uncharacteristically, "but, I think I found her," his gaze motioned to the crowd of Immorals in the distance. A solemn look on his face. "This is terrible for Allicalidantè. If we've lost the princess whilst under our protection, war will surely follow with Queen Adriya. In our state, it won't be much of a fight."

"Yeh, I'm sure it's just the city it's terrible for," Joel said with jealousy under his breath.

"I have been monitoring their numbers for some time," the prince continued, ignoring Joel's remark even though he had heard him. "I need to be candid with you Saff, if I can call you that," the prince took her by the hand. Joel's jealousy increased and a large ridge formed between his eyebrows as he frowned. "As the princesses closest friend, I must trust you with this information I'm about to tell you, so that you can try and reason with your entourage before it gets out of hand but..." the prince flinched again before continuing, "I believe my father has something to do with the demise of our city. I knew there was a reason why he wouldn't accept your deal, he knows more about The Pillar's power than he's letting on, but so do you all. It's the reason why I activated the pillar. I don't know what I was expecting to happen, but I needed to see the reaction of your entourage. Turns out the princess has been hiding some extraordinary things from me."

"Yeh, we know, all about your deceitful father," said Joel, pulling Saffina away from his grasp, earning him a displeased look from Saffina at being manhandled. "So how do we know you're not in on it too."

"I can assure you I'm not."

"Prove it."

"And how am I supposed to do that?" Prince Kendrix moved to within an inch of Joel's nose and eyeballed him, puffing out his chest at the same time. Joel stood his ground. He'd like to think to himself it was because he'd become more courageous over the last year, but it was more to the fact he had his Red Aura Screen to call upon as a safety blanket.

"Show us your hands," said Liana, pushing in from behind her friends.

"And who's this giving me orders?"

Liana lowered her unrecognisably maroon hood. Despite the grime on her skin and clothes, her vibrant indigo hair almost seemed untouched by the dirt. Prince Kendrix was for once at a loss for a direct response.

"I'm the real Princess Liana Langton. The girl who came with Saffina and Joel was someone we found to pretend to be me. I was the one with the powers who saved you from the pillar, not my double. My mother believed it to be too dangerous for me to come here. My double's real name is Luci, she's the daughter of a winegrower back in Coryàtès. They have a vineyard on the outskirts of Swyre."

"I wondered how her knowledge of wines was so good when we talked," the corner of the prince's mouth raised as he recalled the pleasant conversations he'd shared with Luci in their secret meetings.

"Now, show us your hands," Liana demanded again. The prince obliged, sliding off his royal navy gloves. The trio were relieved to see no black mark. "We're headed to the lighthouse, come with us, we have a lot to plan, and I think you can help."

35
THE LIGHTHOUSE

'I-I can't believe it. I-I won't believe it. My sibling by spirit, why would you let yourself be captured like that? Why would you willingly give yourself up to a Reaper? I will never get the sight of your morality being cast from your physical being and sucked into the pillar out of my head. I can only imagine how many spirits are in that colossal structure.

Damn it, I should have done something! I should have protected her.

What is it, boy? The pillar is pulsing. Yes, look! It's like it has a heartbeat. Maybe this was part of her plan all along? Rhonwen is the protector of this Founding Temple after all. I hope she knows what she's doing, I haven't even had a chance to reunite with her. I was all ready to say: 'Hello Rhonwen, how are you? How long's it been? Only 213 years? Never…'

Yes, Cas, I know it's a lame joke. Come on, we have to get back to the lighthouse before anyone realises we're missing.'

The sea-facing side of the lighthouse paintwork was weathered in thousands of small chips from tiny stones that had been kicked up by the waves crashing against the cliff below. Discolouration of white and brown in the brickwork indicated a build-up of salt damage to the lighthouse, which looked like it hadn't been repainted in a good decade or so. The lantern room above remained unlit to make the building appear abandoned like the rest of the city. Liana pounded her fist against the red door, which in contrast to the white brickwork, looked brand new as the moonlight shimmered off its glossy finish. A series of sliding, clanking and clicking on the other side could be heard as various different types of bolts and locks were undone.

"Nice to see you again, Liana," said the familiar, friendly face of Franklin. "Please, come on in."

Liana hadn't realised how harsh and cold the salty sea air was outside until she stepped in the doorway. It was pleasantly warm inside - a cosy kind of warm. She looked around the circular, ground floor room as the others followed her inside. There was a small, empty desk and chair furthest away from her. A single rack of shelving beside the desk had stacks of neatly rolled up parchments. Judging by the size of them, Liana assumed they were maps or mechanical drawings, probably of the surrounding seas and the workings of the lantern room. She'd seen similar looking paperwork before in Vivek's study when she had tutoring sessions with him. Recollections of how she, and so many others, had been betrayed by someone so close bubbled up into her thoughts. She knew he must be involved in some way.

"This is Joel, Saffina, and Kendrix," Liana said, introducing her friends and the prince to Franklin. "And this is,"

"Franklin Rozier," said the prince, finishing off Liana's sentence for her.

"You know each other?" Liana asked.

"Not personally, but Franklin's reputation as being one of the greatest Chantrah players in the land precedes him," replied the prince.

Franklin bowed to his monarch. "Pleasure to meet you, your highness."

"I've seen this man come runner-up in the Tournament of Tournaments for Chantrah two years running." The prince held up two fingers to emphasise his point. "You know, I always thought you purposefully lost those games."

"Well now, why would I have done such a thing? Come all, follow me, I'll show you around," said Franklin, leading the way.

"You know what one thing I've enjoyed leaving behind?" Joel let out a loud sigh which seemed to echo all the way up the lighthouse and back down again. "Spiral staircases."

"I second that," Saffina said, puffing out her cheeks.

Liana shrugged, "I'm kind of used to it by now."

The group trudged up the stairs. Roughly every fifteen steps was a small arched window, barely larger than Liana's head. The first floor of the lighthouse was the kitchen area. It was a simple layout, a table just big enough for two, a fireplace, sink and a stove. The same style arched window sat above the sink, the bare minimum of moonlight shining in.

The next floor was the bathroom. Liana was surprised to see a freestanding bath in the middle of the room. "Feel free to use it," Franklin said to Liana. The longing look on her face for a wash must have been obvious.

"I'm definitely taking you up on that offer," said Joel, overhearing the comment.

"I second that too," Saffina said, agreeing with Joel again.

The final floor before the gallery was a living area-bedroom combo, and it was also the smallest. There was a single-sized cot, an armchair and a Chantrah game board on the floor.

"My wife, Meredith, sleeps in the cot with our baby boy. I sleep in the chair." Franklin felt the need to explain their sleeping arrangements. He picked up a couple pieces of parchment that were tucked under one corner of the board. "I of course spend a lot of time devising new Chantrah plays." Franklin wafted the folded-up bits of paper and slid them into his coat pocket like they contained top secret information. "Meredith is a cartographer, so she likes to spend time on the ground floor looking at the lighthouse's old maps. She's the genius who found the hole in the rocks that leads to the crater. Without her knowledge, she and I would never have gotten out, and you'd never have gotten in."

As if on cue, Franklin's wife appeared descending down from the gallery cradling her babe. She was the cleanest person Liana and her friends had seen since leaving Coryàtès. It made the princess want a bath even more.

"Hi there," a broad, homely smile stretched across the cartographer's dainty face. Her long, blonde hair curled down either side of her body all the way to her hips, beautifully framing her curves. Her eyes were almost as blue as Liana's. "It's an honour to have royalty of two different lands in our temporary home." She stood with Franklin and linked arms with him. Liana could feel a sense of hope in Meredith, like her presence in their home was the light at the end of the tunnel for them after all they'd been through.

The familiar sounding pitter-patter of tiny footsteps trotting down the steps had Liana excited. Pushing himself between the legs of Saffina and Joel, the wolf-like white-furred face of Cas jumped on her, sending her falling back into the armchair. The jubilant dog proceeded to lick her face gleefully.

"Have you been a good boy?" Liana repeated over and over in a baby-talk tone, smushing and rubbing his soft cheeks and ears. After a few more minutes of fuss, Cas broke off and circled a small pile of blankets on the floor at the foot of the single cot before curling up. "Thank you for looking after him."

"He's been good as gold, your highness," replied Franklin. "It's been nice having him around. Bit of extra company. He's been such a good boy, sometimes it's like he's not even here."

"I see, I'm no longer enough company for you, hey?" joked Meredith. The pair chuckled together in a way only a couple truly in love do. "What can we do for you, anyhow?"

"We need your help," answered Liana. She was desperate to get straight to the point so they could return and save Rhonwen, and she knew the best way of doing that was by retrieving her Sacral Spirit. "Specifically, your help, Franklin."

The group all chipped in to update Franklin and his wife on the situation in the crater. How the negotiations with Coryàtès were just a front to get Liana into the city. How the pillar is in lockdown. How King Shimon is a Reaper and has been sacrificing Moralities to try and bypass the Three Trials and break it open from the inside. How they left Rhonwen behind and not knowing if she is still alive or not.

"And you want my help to beat the pillar at Chantrah?"

"If you're as good as they say you are, you're our best option in that trial."

Meredith held her husband's hand tightly, their fingers locked in and intertwined. They both knew the dangers involved in helping Liana.

"Assuming I agree to help you, there's still one problem," Franklin broke his grip from his wife's hand and made his way to the room's small arched window. He squinted and looked into the distance towards the hoard of Immorals amongst the orange field of tulips. It was an automated routine of paranoia.

"Well, what is it? What's the problem?" Saffina said impatiently. Franklin returned to his wife's side and clenched her hand once again.

"We've seen the game board unfold, but no one's ever managed to play. There's no pieces. After a while, the pillar just folds back up on itself."

"Any thoughts on how we might go about solving that puzzle?" asked Joel. Saffina dejectedly shrugged. The room went into a thoughtful silence.

A short while later, Meredith broke the silence. "You all look extremely tired. We all need to rest. You two can have the cot," she said, pointing to Liana and Saffina. "You, have the chair," she said, pointing to Prince Kendrix, "And you, have the blankets," pointing to Joel.

"Gee, thanks," Joel replied sarcastically, looking at the clumps of white dog hair stuck to the dark green throws. Saffina elbowed him in the ribs for being ungrateful. "Sorry, the blankets will be fine," he added, although not very convincingly.

Despite their urgency and desire to save Rhonwen, the group didn't argue with Meredith's observation of their tiredness. They knew they needed to be mentally switched on if they were to save her.

"I think we'd all like to clean up first, then we'll rest," Liana said on behalf of her and her friends. Tomorrow was going to be another difficult day.

36
PROCLAMATION OF LIES

'There's no way I'm letting them out of our sight, Cas. Meredith and her child can either stay here or come with us, but we're going with Liana. I just have a sense that we're going to have a part to play in making sure all of this works out as it should.'

"I can't believe we washed last night and we're still wearing these foul-smelling clothes," complained Saffina as she sniffed the pits of her shirt in disgust. Her nose scrunched up at the concoction of smells ranging from swamp water to mud, fish and who knows what else as it wafted into her nostrils.

"We'd stick out like a sore thumb if we returned clean and preen," Liana said as she, Saffina, Joel, Franklin and Kendrix crouched behind the corner of a building in a side alley which had a clear view of the main road in the crater which ran alongside the boundary wall of the pillar.

"Where does that phrase even come from? I mean, does a sore thumb really stick out that much? I can think of so many things that would stand out more than a sore thumb. I mean, what if you wore gloves to cover it up?" Joel's observation about the simple phrase seemed a little too close to home for the prince, who slapped him round the back of the head for his inconsideration to the recent revelations of his father. "Ow!" Joel reached for the point of impact on his crown and rubbed it to numb the pain. "Jeez, sorry. I didn't mean to offend."

Saffina rolled her eyes at the boys. Liana was less than understanding. "Cut it out you two," she snapped. "I don't care if you get along or not, we need to work together, you got it?" They both went silent.

It was sunrise in the crater. The few streaks of natural sunlight that shone through the great canyon entranceway reflected off the black gloss of the pillar. Despite the early morning hour, it seemed the whole of the crater's population was making its way to the stone palace. The mass of people meant the crowd was walking at snail's pace along the road. "Where's everyone going?" Liana asked herself, before seeing a familiar face amongst the many faces. "Hood's up everyone, follow me." Liana, Joel and Saffina, all wearing their once maroon but now muddied Shroud Clan robes flipped up their hoods to conceal their faces (and hair, in Liana's case). Franklin and Kendrix flipped up the hoods of their brown poncho-like coats. Prince Kendrix was less than pleased about the attire, but the two ponchos were the only clothing with hoods on that Franklin could lend him. Of course, Joel took great joy in the matter when Franklin revealed that Kendrix was wearing Meredith's poncho. Franklin would have offered the prince his, but Meredith's poncho didn't fit him so they were left with no choice.Liana was becoming more and more sure that the prince would have Joel's head after all this was over. The group soon merged seamlessly into the mass of citizens.

"Hey," Liana whispered to the girl next to her. She pulled back her hood slightly to reveal her indigo-blue hair, careful not to show it to anyone else.

"Hey!" came an excited response. It was Wyn, the eldest orphan that Rhonwen took in. Liana put her fingers to her lips and shushed her before she accidentally blurted something revealing out.

"Where's everyone going?"

"The king has requested everyone to the front of the palace. Some big announcement. Everyone's hoping we're finally going to be able to get out of here!" The hubbub and buzz in the crowd seemed to indicate that Wyn wasn't the only one with this thought. Whatever the real reason for the king's proclamation, it certainly wasn't going to be one the citizens hoped for. The group plodded on to the steps at the foot of the stone palace where everyone was gathering.

It didn't take long for the population of the crater to finish gathering and for King Shimon to appear. He made his way to the edge of the top step, clutching a large, brass, horn. He raised it to his mouth and began to speak.

"My fellow Dantians," Liana was surprised at how amplified the king's voice was through the horn. "It has been many months since we were forced into this place. As you all know, despite my disputes with Queen Adriya of Coryàtès, I reached out to her as our nearest neighbour in a bid to help us out of our dire situation." *'That's a lie, we reached out to him.'* thought Liana. "Over the past few weeks," the king continued. "We have been holding talks and negotiations on forming some sort of deal between our two monarchies. All I have asked for is some periodic supplies of food, drink, maybe some materials. Basic needs of any Mikanan's survival. Needs which any compassionate ally would gladly support. But it seems Queen Adriya and her Table do not think as compassionately as we do. For their part of the deal, they only have eyes on the powers that the Pillar of Sanctuary contains." A wave of murmuring swept through the crowd. "That's right, they are only interested in having power and allowing them to have that would be yet another threat to what remains of Allicalidantè. I cannot allow them to conduct this research and take away what makes the Pillar of Sanctuary special, this is why these talks have not yet come to a conclusion. But it seems, they were not willing to wait any longer." King Shimon then paused for dramatic effect. He's an accomplished speaker, Liana thought, much like her mother. It goes with the job description. During the pause her great uncle Sir Tarak and Master H were dragged out from the doors of the stone palace, their wrists and ankles cuffed. "Princess Liana Langton, and her friends Saffina Greymore and Joel Ellwood have gone missing, and so has my son, Prince Kendrix. I believe the Coryatès children have him hostage somewhere so that Sir Tarak Langton and his clerk could use him as a bargaining chip in the negotiations and force me into signing whatever they wanted under duress of my son's kidnapping." The crowd's murmuring turned into a raucous discussion. "I will not let that happen," the king raised his voice over the hubbub of the crowd. "Even though they have my son, I will not give up on what remains of Allicalidantè. My son is strong, and so are we, and we will find our way out of our peril with or without the help of Coryatès." The stirred-up crowd cheered their king. His speech empowered their pride as Dantians. "There is one more thing!" the voices of the crowd quietened again. "Princess Liana and her friends Joel Ellwood and

Saffina Greymore must be found at all costs. If we can turn the tables on Coryàtès, we can hold them to ransom instead. Finding them is in all of your interests!"

Wyn turned to Liana. "Is it true?"

"No, he's lying. Yes, we need the power of the pillar, but it's the only way to save you, to save all of you. I can't explain it all now, but I believe King Shimon is holding Rhonwen like he is my great uncle and Master H. There's guards all over the boundary wall and now everyone here will be looking for us, but my friends and I need to get to the pillar. Will you help us? If you trust Rhonwen, you must trust me."

The orphan took a moment to consider Liana's words. "We'll do it. I'll get the others to help. I trust you."

Liana breathed a sigh of relief. She had made new friends here.

37
VERTIGO

'Honestly Cas, I didn't think Meredith would come with us either considering her child and all, but you heard her, she knows something's not right too. Just keep your wits about you, we don't want any of those Immorals getting sight of us.'

"She went that way!" A high-pitched screech at the back of the crowd interrupted the King's proclamation. Everyone turned to look at the source of the shout and saw a small child pointing towards a flash of red light.

"That's her! If you want your troubles in this place to be over, catch her and bring her to me!" shouted the king to his citizens, who didn't need to be told twice and moved like a herd of wildebeests towards the flash of red, including the king and his guards. Liana, Saffina, Joel, Kendrix, Franklin and Wyn were left standing at the bottom of the palace steps.

"My orphan brothers and sisters have scattered themselves throughout the crater. That should keep my fellow Dantians busy for a while. I just hope we gave them enough of those little red orb things."

"Enough to give everyone the run around for a while before the king realises it's a diversion. Thank you, Wyn." Liana embraced her new friend, which was a rare honour, as she wasn't much of a hugger. A royal handshake was usually the extent of friendly physical contact she allowed, but somehow the connection seemed to seal their newfound friendship.

The distraction only solved their first problem - getting rid of the guards who watched the only entrance through the border walls. Their next problem was getting inside without using any Aura powers and attracting attention to themselves.

"Any ideas how we get in?" Joel asked the group. "A human pyramid maybe? I volunteer for the bottom!"

"Right, 'cause that would mean you'd be left behind and wouldn't face certain death at the hands of the pillar," Kendrix pointed out, before muttering "coward," under his breath.

"I heard that! I'm no coward!" Joel pushed Kendrix in the chest. "Don't you know I fought in the Battle of Coryàtès? How many battles have you ever fought in?"

Kendrix frowned and his eyes narrowed, before Saffina angrily stepped between them. "Stop your bickering, both of you!"

"Doesn't matter anyhow," Kendrix reached inside his shirt and pulled out a silver key that was dangling on a chain around his neck. "I have the key to the gates. Only my father and I have one. Looks like you'll be joining us in our time of peril after all," the prince strutted arrogantly past Joel, purposefully shoulder barging him aside as he moved toward the border wall entrance.

"Let it go," Saffina whispered in Joel's ears, whilst placing a gentle hand on his tightened fist. He took a deep breath and relaxed his clenched hand. "Come on, let's get this over and done with so we can all go home."

Kendrix slotted the simple silver key into the gate's equally plain cast keyhole and turned it one full circle anti-clockwise. Aside from the shopkeeper's creations, there really were no other intricacies produced in the crater. The scraping sound of a metal bar sliding followed by the clunk of a deadbolt notified the group that they were now free to enter the pillar's vicinity.

"Wait for me!"

"And me!"

A short, round man and a tall, slender man with a long face came bouncing around the corner. A Kalimtar and a flute strapped to their respective backs.

"Monty... Mack...?" Liana raised a bewildered eyebrow. "What are you doing here?"

"This bird told us to come."

"Said you needed us."

"So here we are."

"We came." A Jackdaw sat perched happily on the shorter man's shoulder. "It said Mack needed to bring the bird to you."

"And Monty!"

"But it sat on Mack's back!"

"It's not even on your back!"

"No, but it rhymes!"

"You can't lie to make up rhymes!"

"A little lie hurt no one!"

"But better to tell none!"

"You're just jealous of me and my bird!"

"I am not, you lying turd!"

The Jackdaw had clearly had enough of the musical duo's rhyming squabbling and glided to the dusty floor, before hopping over to Liana's feet. It peered up at her and tilted its head sideways, waiting for an invite. She obliged and held out her arm in front of her. The Jackdaw flew up and transmitted its message to her. Liana spoke the words aloud as they entered her head so the group could also hear the message. *"The duet will come in useful to one of your problem's. Remember our games. See you soon, chosen one. Rhonwen."*

"Looks like your musical friends are coming along too. The more the merrier!" Franklin said with open arms. The now group of eight stepped through the gates and crossed the boundary threshold towards the Pillar of Sanctuary. When they arrived, they unconsciously formed a line in front of the pillar in height order. The exception being Monty, who was clearly the tallest of the group, but he maintained his usual stance beside his duet partner Mack, breaking the perfect order.

Another flash of red lit up the crater from beyond the boundary wall. This flash hung in the air a little longer, and the scarlet tint gave the crater's atmosphere a red sunset-like ambience, striking across the faces of the group like an impending doom was imminent as they gazed up at the massive structure.

Liana, standing just off centre of the group, reached out her hand. "Here goes…" She placed the palm of her hand gently on the glossy surface. It was cold to touch. She removed her hand slowly and noticed that her fingerprints remained imprinted only for a second before fading away, like a window cleaner had come and wiped them off.

A pulse of red aura spread from where she had placed her palm. "I've never seen it do that before," observed Kendrix as the pulse spread across all four surfaces like a shock of red lightning before fading back to its solid glossy black. A red etching of the outline of a door then appeared around the area where Liana had touched, as if it were being engraved in front of their eyes.

"Welcome," a faceless voice resonated from the pillar. The edges of the pillar pulsated an orange light in time with the voice. Liana recognised the voice immediately and could tell it was clearly modelled off Rhonwen's tones. "This is interesting," it continued, as if the pillar was a sentient being with its own thought processes and opinions. "It seems I have been touched by both the Restorer of the Spectrum and the Guardian of Light. You are one and the same. The scriptures never suggested this would be the case." The voice paused, as if it needed to ponder some thoughts. "Who knew that such burdens would fall upon a single soul, such a young one, too? Well, if this is how Aurora sees the solution, I will not argue. Enter through the door to avoid being crushed and we shall begin the Three Trials. If the feelings of my aura's are correct, and Aurora's words are true, then you will be the one to finally restore the Neoteric Temple to its former glory."

The door swung open, wide enough for the group to enter in pairs, and so they entered two by two. Liana and Franklin, Saffina and Joel, Kendrix and Wyn. Monty and Mack were the last to enter and the door swung shut behind them. A thin stream of orange light flowing up a column in the centre of the room provided the only light. The rest of the room was pitch black and even with the glow of the stream of orange light, the group couldn't see past their own noses. Even without being able to see each other's body language clues, Liana, Saffina and Joel had the same thought and called upon their own Red Aura's to light up the room. To the group's surprise, they still couldn't make out the edges of the room, but at least they could now see each other.

"Considering this is a temple for the God of Dawn, it's awfully dark in here," Joel quipped just in time before the ground started to shake violently causing everyone to fall to the floor, with exception of the three lit-up best friends whose Visendi training helped them maintain their balance. "Feels like we're going up?" Joel's voice shook as the room shuddered around them.

~

Liana shielded her face at the dramatic change from pitch black darkness to bright white light. Her eyes took several seconds to readjust, and as she took in her new surroundings, all she could do was scream.

The bright white light around her wasn't from a sun, a moon, or a flame, but by White Aura's. Liana was in the Morality Realm and surrounded by the desperate and confused faces of those who had been touched by the Reaper. The translucent figures pushed and shoved each other to get close to her. There were so many faces crying out they covered up the distinct Moralities of the rest of her group. She became overwhelmed with sorrow, with pain, with empathy. *'Is this what it means to also be the Guardian of Light?'*

In contrast to the Turning process Vivek had practised on Coryàtès which was gradual, suggestive and manipulative, these Moralities had been ripped from their physical bodies. Vivek's process was to make a person gradually believe in the wrong ideals. More often than not they would only end up with the person not caring about anything, hence the term 'Immoral'.

But the way a Reaper Turns? It's more of a rip, like having a poorly made shirt torn off roughly in a fight. It was brash, brazen and traumatic.

As the desperate faces spun around her, squeezing and pushing each other to get nearer to her, two faces she recognised appeared before her. The faces of Rhonwen and Luci hung in front of her.

Luci looked so scared and frightened. Liana thought of the arguments she'd had with her over the last six months and felt a wave of guilt roll over her. The doppelgänger was just a girl from a vineyard doing the right thing for her Queen and city. No amount of training could have prepared her for this. For her Morality to be ripped from her physical being. For her physical being to be just another Immoral vessel for Vivek and the Sentians to abuse.

Rhonwen's shining white face was surprisingly neutral. Liana could only assume that King Shimon had Turned her after they fled and left her behind. She also realised the consequences that had on the Three Trials. The Third Trial required a Spectra Child's Morality as sacrifice. With Rhonwen already having been Reaped, it would mean Liana would have to be the lamb to the slaughter for the Third Trial. *'But what would that mean for the prophecy? If I become Immoral, I surely cannot be the Restorer or the Guardian'.*

"Do not doubt yourself, child," Liana jumped as Rhonwen's Morality spoke. No matter how much their mouths and tongues moved, none of the other spirits appeared to be able to speak. "This has happened for a reason," Rhonwen continued. "I appear to not be like the other spirits in here. Perhaps it's because I am one of the seven Spectra Children. When my spirit was ripped from my body, my physical self did not Turn.

It lays motionless in the same cell as your great uncle and Master Hayashi.

Master Hayashi wants me to pass a message onto you: *'Don't forget our last lesson together.'"* Rhonwen's face then faded away into the blur of other faces fighting for attention.

Confused and in emotional turmoil, Liana begged and pleaded to herself to leave the Morality Realm. In that moment, she also made a promise to save the trapped Aura's, no matter what.

∽

"Liana, Liana? Are you okay?" Saffina shook her friends' shoulders with vigour. The princess's eyes had turned white, but the upturned eyebrows on her face and heavy breathing suggested her trip to the Morality Realm wasn't pleasant. After a few more shakes of the shoulder, Liana eventually returned to their world. "Are you okay?" Saffina repeated.

"Um, yeh, I'm fine. At least, I am now."

"You looked petrified!" Joel placed a reassuring hand on her back. "What happened?"

"The Moralities that the king has taken, they're trapped in here, and they're scared, in pain. They were unwillingly ripped apart from their bodies. It was terrifying but I have to help them. I have to."

"Sounds awful," Joel said, stating the obvious.

"We will help them." Saffina rubbed her friend's arm, watching a tear slowly descend down her cheek. "Let's get these Three Trials done and we'll do whatever we can." Liana wiped the tear from her face and nodded. She became aware that the ground was still shaking, and the group were still ascending.

Some moments later, the ceiling above parted. If the sun was able to break into the crater, light would have flooded in, but instead the small amount of available light gradually introduced itself like a nervous pet meeting a new owner for the first time. The group eventually reached the top of the pillar and surveyed the view.

"Is-Is anyone else afraid of heights?" Wyn was visibly shaking in fear.

"There're not even any walls or fencing to stop you falling off. It's just straight to a ledge," even Kendrix sounded a little nervous at being up so high with no sort of safety barrier. He tentatively shuffled to the edge and hesitantly peered down. The height of the drop made him feel a bit queasy with vertigo.

"Do we know if our Aura Screen's would protect us from this height?" asked Saffina.

"No idea, but I'm not willing to test it out," replied Joel.

"Monty doesn't like this,"

"Neither does Mack," the duo huddled together well away from the edges.

"Look, the gameboard is unfolding," Liana pointed at the ledge closest to her. "Guess it's time for the first trial. I hope you're ready, Franklin."

38

THE FIRST TRIAL

'Whoa boy, steady on your feet, get low to the ground until the shaking stops, just like Meredith is doing!

Yes, I think I know what's happening and it's magnificent. I never had the chance to see it in real life before I got entombed, but I always wanted to, I just thought it would be under more joyous circumstances.

Finally, the shaking has stopped. We should head inside and move into a prime position.'

The sides of the pillar touched the dusty ground. A big plume of dust puffed up following a dull thud. Another flash of red light sparked in an alleyway near the stone palace. 'Probably the last one', Liana thought, who'd be counting loosely. 'I hope they didn't catch up to the kids. They can hide now. The king won't have missed the sight of the pillar opening.'

"So, what happens now?" Joel said, peering over the edge.

"No idea. No one's ever played. The board unfolds. Sits for a few minutes, then folds right back up," explained Franklin.

"Must be missing something," Saffina shrugged. The group

looked around at each other, searching for some inspiration. "Anyone got any ideas?"

In the distance, Liana could see the king and his guards standing at the gate. She knew whilst the gameboard was down he wouldn't enter the boundary walls, but she wondered if the game board folded back up like it always had done, would the group descend back down into the pillar? They'd be ripe for the taking, and so would the Moralities trapped in the pillar if the king got his hand on Liana and Turned her, bursting it open from the inside for the ultimate reward of one of her Spirits.

"Liana, why don't you try saying something to start the game," suggested Joel.

"Like what?"

"I don't know. Something like, 'let the games begin!'"

"Really?" frowned the princess.

"All right then, how about 'I command my Spirit to release the pieces!'"

"Release the pieces?!" Liana and Saffina laughed. "You are such a kook; you know that right?"

"I don't see anyone else coming up with any suggestions." Joel huffed and folded his arms childishly.

Liana, not wanting to hurt her friend's feelings, stepped to the edge of the pillar and stretched out her arms. "I command my Spirit to release the pieces! Let the games begin!" With no surprise to the group, no game pieces appeared below. After a few moments the pillar started to shake again, and the board began to fold back in. Liana let out a frustrated cry.

"Fine, it was a stupid idea!" Joel flung out his arms and caught Mack, who then bumped into Monty, causing him to drop his Kalimtar and the metal prongs to ping.

Before the usual round of 'Jeez, Joel!' the gameboard

paused its enclosing process. "Did anyone else see that?" Liana asked.

"I did," confirmed Saffina. "It hung for a moment, paused."

"Yeh, just at the moment when…" Liana and Saffina spoke together and simultaneously looked towards Monty who was picking up his fallen Kalimtar.

"Monty, play a tune," Liana said excitedly. He, of course, obliged and plucked the silver prongs in a delightful twinging and twanging.

"Mack, play your flute, join in." Saffina directed the second member of the duet. The duo's music aired across the crater. The combination of being at the pinnacle of the pillar and in the confined space of the crater created a beautiful acoustic for their instruments. "It's working! The board is laying back down!" Liana joyously declared. Another puff of dust rose from the ground as the game board lay flat once more.

Then, to everyone's surprise, a flagpole popped up out of part of the boundary wall. A navy-blue banner unfurled itself and displayed the Allicalidantè symbol, the Bandera de las Artes. As the duet continued their music, more flagpoles popped up at orderly positions all around the rest of the boundary wall.

"Now I get why Candela and Rhonwen sent Monty and Mack to us," Franklin said thoughtfully. "Beating the game isn't the First Trial. This is the First Trial. The music, the atmosphere, the pre-game build up. There's more to games and arts than just the performances themselves, it's about the entertainment, and that's what Allicalidantè was always the greatest at. No wonder this is the First Trial. It's been right there on our flag the whole time," Franklin pointed to the nearest banner, highlighting the flute player.

After the series of banners had finished popping up around the boundary wall, the floor began to shake once more but this time it was more than just the pillar or the game board, the whole crater seemed to be shaking. Bits of stone started to break away and tumble down the crater's cliff faces. The shaking became more violent, causing the wooden beams and makeshift bridges that connected the upper levels of the dwellings to come away from their fixings and crash to the streets below. Every Dantian, including the group atop the pillar, fell to the ground as the crater rose from its sunken footing.

The vibrations carried above through to the fake aura floor. Immorals scattered due to the quake below their feet and fled beyond the outskirts of the tulip field they'd been residing in.

The pace of the climb quickened, causing the vibration to become even more intense. "Hold on!" Liana screamed to her friends. The flat, glossy surface of the pillar meant there was nothing to hold on to. She noticed Joel, who was laying closest to the pillar's edge, had started to slip away.

"Help!" Joel screamed over the noise of the rumbling. His legs fell over the edge, and he was desperately trying to grip onto the smooth surface, but the lack of friction made this almost impossible.

"Hang on! I'm coming!" Liana screamed back. She managed to commando crawl to him and grab onto his wrists, but a heavy jolt made Joel fall back even further, pulling Liana with him. He was now fully over the ledge. The only thing stopping him from falling was his friend's grip.

"Pull me up! Pull me up!" Joel panicked. He wasn't prepared to be the one to test whether a Red Aura Screen could protect him from falling such a height.

"I-I'm slipping too!" Liana began to panic as well. Her

hands were beginning to sweat and her grip on Joel was loosening. The vibration didn't relent, and the grip continued to become harder to keep.

Just as Liana thought she'd also be pulled over the edge, she felt a hand grasp around her ankle. She managed to peer over her shoulder and saw the hand of Saffina latched onto her. Peering further back, her new Dantian friends had formed a human chain, with Kendrix anchoring the group, his arm wrapped around the quartz tube that housed the spouting aura stream.

"It's okay, Joel," Liana stared into Joel's eyes. "It's going to be okay," she repeated. The sincerity and certainty in her voice calmed his panic. He couldn't see the human chain that had formed behind her, but the look in her eyes was enough for him to believe she was right.

As the top of the pillar reached the point of the fake floor, the aura beam stopped emitting its orange light and the fake floor dissipated. The field of orange tulips rained down onto the Dantians in the crater like confetti at a wedding. Petal leaves floated peacefully toward the ground in stark contrast against the rumbling of the crater's movement and tumbling of any loose rocks. If the Immorals hadn't scattered beyond the tulip field, they would have fallen to their death, but all had gotten away in time.

The fallen Dantian's shielded their faces as they adjusted to the rising morning sun. They hadn't had direct sun contact in months and this moment somehow felt like they were being blessed.

The crater had risen out of its pit and reached ground level. The human chain of friends pulled as one and Joel emerged back over the top of the ledge. He attempted a thank you but he was breathing so heavily the words barely came out of his mouth.

Before anyone could catch their breath, the roads encompassing the boundary walls began to crumble and shake, and up rose huge stands of seating. The stone bleachers fully surrounded the game board and created a magnificent looking arena. More flag poles popped out around the newly formed stadium, alternating with straight beams of orange light that shot upwards, emblazoning the low-light dawning sky.

Fizzles of Orange Aura swept across the rows of seating and created plump, padded cushions ready for spectators to sit comfortably. The stadium seating became separated in two by colour, horizontally across the gameboard. Half of the stadium's cushions were coloured the navy blue of Allicalidantè and the other half a scarlet red. Out the top of the flagpoles, trumpet horns also fizzled into existence from the sweeping Orange Aura. Any dust that had settled on the gameboard was dissolved, leaving a pristine, clean surface as the aura circled back round to the pillar.

The group found their feet, taken aback by the transformation in front of them. "It's glorious," Liana said, awestruck.

"Oh my, never in my days did I ever think I'd see it," Franklin said, overcome with awe. "This is Estadio de la Alegría. I've only seen drawings in historical manuscripts. It was said to have been destroyed almost two hundred years ago after the banning of the old religions. Only in my dreams had I ever believed I would be standing here amongst its glory," he turned to Monty and Mack. "Please, play a song that is befitting of this magnificent structure."

Monty and Mack sounded out an imperial tune. Their music echoed through the flagpole trumpets that not only amplified their notes, but also accompanied them in brass tones for all to hear.

The Dantians from the crater began to filter into the navy-blue side of the arena. Immorals filtered into the scarlet-red side of the arena. The numbers of each were small, far fewer than the amount of seats available. Once everyone had seated, a flash orange light projected from the top of the pillar and filled the spare seats with fake, cheering spectators.

"We cannot have a half-filled stadium now, can we?" said the voice of the pillar through the trumpet sound system. "Congratulations on passing the First Trial. Now it's time for the Second Trial."

39

THE SECOND TRIAL

'No, wait, please! Rhonwen if that's you in that pillar I beg of you don't do this! What are you doing? You can't take Meredith! Cas, what have we done? We should never have allowed her to come with us. Look at the danger we've put her and her child in! Let's pray to Aurora that her husband is as good as they say, or I shall never forgive myself.'

"Many skills are required to play the game of Chantrah: strategy, foresight, analysis, problem-solving, practise, to name just a few. The Restorer of the Spectrum and the Guardian of Light must be well versed in these attributes if they are to succeed in ridding Mikana of Tenebris and his devotee's. The Second Trial has no puzzle to solve, what you see is what you get. You must play, and win, a game of Chantrah. The only twist is, you must play against your adversary." The Pillar's voice echoed through the arena. Its framework pulsed orange as it spoke.

'At least this part of the Three Trials is pretty much as anticipated,' thought Liana. "I have a question," she asked, surprised that her own voice also echoed through the trumpeting sound system. "I want someone else to play in my place."

"You wish to nominate a proxy?" The Pillar went silent for a few moments. "But you cannot demonstrate these skills unless you are the player. You must play."

"But why must it be me alone to possess all these skills? I can't be everything to everyone. I can't be the best at it all. I have to have whatever's necessary and that sometimes means trusting friends, new and old, and putting them in harm's way no matter how hard that is."

"It is clear in the H'WA. Aurora names a chosen one in each of the two Realm's. Only the chosen ones can banish Tenebris and his Sentian's."

"But does it say they do it alone?"

The Pillar went silent once more as it considered Liana's answer. The arena's spectators also settled down after minutes of non-stop cheers and chanting. A suspense hung in their air waiting for the pillar's response.

"I have studied the H'WA again cover-to-cover," it began.

'Jeez, fast reader!' Liana thought to herself.

"The H'WA does not say the chosen ones will be alone in their undertaking. You may nominate a proxy in your place."

Liana did an uncharacteristic squeal and jump of joy, before quickly composing herself. "I nominate Franklin Rozier as my proxy." A roar from the Dantian's in the crowd erupted at the sound of the famous Chantrah player's name. "So, where are game pieces?"

A bolt of Orange Aura shot out from the top of the pillar and probed Liana's forehead. The bolt temporarily stunned her but disappeared as quickly as it had appeared. Streams of Orange Aura stretched from the pillar like a cranefly's legs into the crowd. The wispy light reached out and began lassoing people from their seats. Despite the struggles of those lassoed, there was no breaking free from the aura. It lifted them up and placed them on the gameboard. The streams of light then headed to the top of the pillar and wrapped themselves around Kendrix, Saffina, Joel and Wyn.

Wyn screamed as she was grabbed. Joel and Saffina tried casting their Red Aura's, but it was rebuffed by the orange rope-like aura. Kendrix shifted and struggled as he attempted to slice the light with his cuff-link blade, but it was to no avail. The ropes of light placed them gently onto their own square on the gameboard. Wyn had been placed in the outside-left wingman position. She looked across the rest of the people who had been plucked with a frightening realisation. All of her orphaned brothers and sisters had been chosen: Kali, Brent, Zach, Xabi, Taylor, Roberto, Savannah. As well as Kendrix, Saffina and Joel, the rest of the players that had been chosen were Meredith - with her baby cradled in her arms, Amara and Seff. Every piece on the gameboard knew Liana. Kendrix and Meredith were positioned in the most powerful Shooter positions, prime targets for Vivek.

Franklin called out, mortified by the danger his wife and child were in. "How dare you! How dare you!" he screamed at the pillar beneath his feet over and over.

The three jumper positions were made up of Saffina, Joel and Amara. The orphans took the nine Wingmen and Infantry roles between them.

"Typical, just when I thought I might get to sit this one out," said Amara, sarcastically.

"I'm havin' nothin' to do with this guff," piped Seff, who was standing in the outer right Infantry position. "I'm outta here." As Seff moved to step outside of his square a wall of

Red Aura blocked him. The boy fell backwards onto his backside. "Aw man."

"What's the big idea?!" Liana shouted at her feet to the pillar below. "You're using all my friends as game pieces?"

"I'm putting your argument to the ultimate test. Can you stand by and watch your friends put themselves on the line for you?"

"You're a Founding Temple, aren't you supposed to be on my side?"

"The Neoteric Temple is in lockdown. In lockdown, the Neoteric Temple trusts no one. Only the chosen ones can prove themselves."

"Argh!" Liana stamped her feet in anger at the pillar below her. Not that it would cause any damage, of course.

The pillar then reached out with its ropes of orange aura again, this time plucking spectators from the Immoral side of the arena.

Amongst the random Immorals that were chosen was Yasmin, Eugene, and King Shimon. King Shimon and Yasmin were positioned in the important Shooter positions. Eugene was placed in the Jumper square directly opposite to his sister, Saffina. After the pieces had been chosen, the pillar grabbed Vivek from the crowd and placed him atop the pillar.

"No way, no way!" Liana clenched her fists and readied her Red Aura.

"Well, well, it's been a while," Vivek's arched, grey eyebrows frowned menacingly. A Chesire grin spread across his face. His fingers interlaced together as he straightened himself up and walked with purpose toward the princess. Liana noticed the absence of the clickety-clack of the stick that usually accompanied him, and his hunch, was no more. Tall and straight-backed, the old clerk became an imposing figure.

Vivek stopped at the half-way point of the platform and cautiously tapped the space in front of him. A wall of Red Aura flashed and dissipated. "You're fortunate this Aura Screen stands between us, 'chosen one' of the Visendi."

"No, you're the fortunate one," Liana said with grit and determination. The stakes had risen. It was no longer solely about passing the Three Trials and regaining her Sacral Spirit Orb, it was about preventing Vivek from acquiring it. "Where's Tarak and Master H?"

"I've no idea." shrugged Vivek. "I wasn't the one using them as collateral for your capture. You'd have to ask our resident Reaper." He pointed down to King Shimon with his ageing, bony index finger of his left hand.

"Why are you up here anyway? Surely a Reaper outranks a creep like you."

"Oh darling, you have no idea what I've become," the toothy smirk on his face lingered.

Liana was rooted to the spot, frozen. She flashed her Red Aura in anger but remembering the affects her emotions had on her friends back in Castle Langton, she regained control of it quickly. If they were to succeed, they had to beat this trial properly. "I am most definitely *not* your darling."

The framework of the pillar lit up and the sound of Rhonwen's voice boomed through the airwaves. "To decide who goes first, I have hidden an orb in the hoods of Franklin or Vivek's clothing. You have to guess which hood the orb is in. If you get it correct, the Visendi shall have the first move. If you are wrong, the Sentian's move first."

'Great,' thought Liana. *'All I can do is guess. There's no skill involved in this. Just randomly pick someone'*. "Franklin," she said decisively.

"Incorrect," replied the pillar immediately. "The Sentian's have the first move."

Usually at this point you'd expect a cheer from that half of the arena, but since that was populated by Immorals, a roar of hideous laughter reverberated instead, along with taunts such as "Lights out for you!" and "Where's your sun God now?"

"Damnit," Liana stomped.

"Don't worry, I've got this," Franklin reassured the princess.

"The usual rules of standard Chantrah apply. No distracting or communicating shall take place between the competitors or the chosen one. Any cheating will result in swift punishment. Is this understood?"

Liana, Franklin and Vivek each responded with an "Aye".

"Let the game commence!"

Vivek stepped toward the ledge of the pillar and called out to one his Immoral pieces in the front row to move diagonal right.

The game had begun.

∼

Franklin had positioned his Infantry pieces defensively either side of the pillar. All were covered by a Wingman or Jumper. Considering he had never played on a board with the four middle squares unusable due to a giant pillar sticking out of them, he was feeling pleased with his efforts so far, but was not taking Vivek for granted. Liana had told him earlier in the lighthouse how intelligent the former clerk was, how he had developed new technologies and was well versed in the sciences. He had no doubt that this intelligence would transfer into this game of strategy, and it had proven to be so far, with Vivek's pieces also well positioned and covered. The game was poised at a point where pieces would begin to be taken, and the positions of pieces for the next two, three, four and more moves would become crucial to avoid being the loser in key positions and pieces.

But for Franklin now, he was faced with a tough decision. A decision not just about game pieces and good moves. He knew what his next move should be. It was one that would put him at a tactical advantage. If this was a normal game of Chantrah in a normal tournament, he'd have already played the move. Right now, though, he was hesitant. He didn't want to play it.

"We both know what your best move is here," Vivek said sinisterly. "Come now, play it already. I want to see what happens."

"It's ok," Liana said as she held Franklin's hand. The gentle touch made his eyes water with sadness. The corners of his mouth trembled. "If you can't do it, we'll find another way. I won't blame you."

"No," he replied gently, but firmly. "What we are doing here is bigger than me. I agreed to help, and that's what I will do."

"No talking between players!" Rhonwen's voice sounded out, chastising the two competitors and Liana stood atop the pillar. "The next violation of this rule will result in immediate loss of the game."

Franklin released his hand from Liana's grip and drew a deep breath. "Kali, forward-left," he ordered. A shimmer of red-light in front of the youngest orphan indicated that the Aura Screen for the square front-and-left of the youngest orphan had dispersed. Kali stepped into the next square. Liana heard the Chantrah Master mutter the words "I'm sorry," under his breath.

Vivek ordered his next move quickly and with no hesitation. "You, take control of the square in front of you." Vivek ordered one of the Immorals, a Jumper, into the square where Kali had just moved into. Liana couldn't bear to watch. A tear rolled down each of Franklin's cheeks as he watched Kali's eyes fill with fear, like a rabbit who'd seen a rabid dog. Her body began to shake in terror. She turned to her left and to her right. "Zach, Taylor, help me! Please!" She begged with her neighbouring orphans in the squares next to her, but they were helpless.

"The Sentian's take the first piece!" announced the pillar, and as it did, the dusty ground beneath Kali fizzled into a red aura which dissolved and vanished. The young girl fell through the floor with a disturbing scream. She was gone. The ground reappeared and Eugene moved into the square that Kali had vacated.

The Dantian half of the arena fell silent once more. Now that they had seen how the taking of pieces worked, the crowd's mood had changed from enthusiastic to worried.

∼

The loss of Kali had opened up the board for Franklin and he now found himself two pieces up with no further losses, but the game was still tightly poised. Vivek's Wingmen were well positioned defensively, so Franklin would have to trade pieces in the middle of the board to push up. He ordered Saffina to jump to the square in front of her. The person standing in that square was her brother, Eugene. She hadn't been this close to him since the Battle of Coryàtès, but this wasn't the brother she grew up with. Somehow, he'd been

Turned differently to the other Immorals. Other Immorals could wander off freely if they so wished, but they tended to stay with whoever promised riches or comfort. They congregated with whoever they saw as the most likely winner. Eugene on the other hand was more like Vivek's puppet. No control of self-thought at all. That didn't stop Saffina from hurting inside as she watched the ground vanish beneath her brother and swallow him. Not for the first time, she had no idea if she'd ever see him again, or if he would ever return to his old self. She stepped solemnly into the now vacant square in front of her.

"Yasmin, front-left four squares. Take her." Yasmin eyeballed Saffina from across the board and grinned with sadistic pleasure. One-by-one the Aura Screens of the squares in front of her disappeared and as they did, Yasmin took one, long stride into the next square. The move seemed to last forever for Saffina, but they were soon standing face-to-face as the last Aura Screen dissipated.

"As much as this will give me great pleasure in witnessing, I only wish that the princess stood where you are now instead."

"This isn't the end," Saffina said defiantly, before she felt her feet go light and her heart got yanked up to her throat, seeing just a blur of Yasmin's torso and legs disappear out of sight as she fell to her fate.

Liana desperately wanted to scream out from the pillar, but heeded the warning of the pillar and kept her anguish to herself. She could only hope that Saffina's words would turn out to be the truth.

∽

Vivek made an impressive play, taking Taylor, Xabi and Zach for only the loss of one Immoral Infantry. Despite Yasmin, a Shooter, being at risk in such an advanced position up the board, he decided to cover her position with his second Shooter, King Shimon.

Franklin decided, with the endgame being exposed due to Vivek's adventurous play, to trade Shooter's. He pushed Prince Kendrix up to take Yasmin, who disappeared with a raucous cheer from the Dantians. They may not have personally known Liana's childhood adversary, but they'd already made up their minds that they also did not like the girl. Vivek pushed King Shimon up to take his son, Prince Kendrix.

"How could you do this, father?"

"You really haven't figured it out, have you?"

"What's there to figure out? You betrayed your people. You lied to them. Turned into this… this thing."

"I did it for us!"

"For us?! How many of our people have you sacrificed so you could get your hand on the power inside that pillar?"

"It was never about the pillar's power."

"I don't believe you."

"Please, son, you must. I'm not who you think I am." King Shimon held out his arms as if to welcome his son.

"That mark says you are exactly who I think you are," Kendrix pointed to the black mark on his father's palm.

"It was a means to an end. A necessity to get back what was taken from us."

"The things you are fighting with are what took everything from us! They Turned our people! Forced us into this damned crater! How was joining them going to help us get The Dantè back to how it used to be?"

"I don't mean the damned city, boy! It was never about the city!" The Black Aura of the mark on the king's hand spread through his body. Veins bulged in sickening darkness from his wrists to his neck, stirred on by emotions of anger and painful memories. "It's about your mother. It's always been about your mother. My Queen."

"My mother? But, she's gone, father."

"But what if I could get her back?! What if the powers inside that pillar could return her to us? Look at what this structure can do, look at what it's doing right now! I just wanted Jayne by my side again. The pillar took her, all I wanted was for it to bring her back to us. That old man, the one they call Vivek, promised we would get her back if I took a special vow to his god, so that's what I did. In exchange for the powers inside the pillar, he would make it happen, all for the sacrifices of some others."

"So you sacrificed hundreds of innocents for the return of my mother? Do you hear yourself? How immoral that sounds?"

"They were curfew breakers! Thieves! Troublemakers! Jayne's life is worth more than every single one of them delinquents."

"I loved one of them!"

"Loved?! You've known her for barely even a month! I knew my queen for three decades. Don't talk to me about love!"

"You speak as if I did not also love my mother. You're not the only one who's lost someone in this," Prince Kendrix turned his back on his father in shame. "You are not the man I thought you were." Those were Kendrix's last words before he fell below ground. King Shimon flung out an arm in a bid to try and catch his son, but only grabbed a fist full of air. A sudden jolt across his back forced him into the empty square as he was hurried by the pillar.

Franklin's next move took Vivek by surprise. A sweeping move up the board with Wingman Roberto left Amara exposed, but it attacked the only piece protecting the endgame square. Vivek chastised himself for missing his opponent's move. He was clearly in the losing position now, but as ever, he was not without a plan. The old clerk's eyes turned a glossy black, his body stiff and motionless. To everyone else in the arena, it would seem like he was just in deep thought about his next move, but Liana was close enough to see differently.

"Hey! Hey! He's cheating!" she screamed, stamping her feet on the pillar floor. Before even Franklin could turn around to see what the princess was complaining about, Vivek had returned to his natural state.

"No act of cheating has taken place on the gameboard," The Pillar announced.

"He's planning something, I swear!"

"Quiet, chosen one, or your proxy will incur the loss."

Liana balled her hands into fists in frustration. *'What did he do?'* she wondered to herself. She didn't have to wait long for an answer. On the gameboard below, her and Franklin watched in horror as Seff took out a Black Orb and smashed it onto his chest. His body evaporated into wispy specks of black aura and moved through the Aura Screen with speed and ease, reforming in a square the opposite side of the board.

"The chosen one, if she still is the chosen one, and her proxy have a cheating player in their ranks. This defaults the game. The Second Trial has been won by the Immorals. This result means the pillar shall return to its lockdown state."

The fault cracks that marked the outline of the crater vibrated violently as the Neoteric Temple began to lower itself and reset the gameboard. The pillar reached out to the remaining game pieces and placed them back into the crowd.

"Oh no, not again," Joel uttered to himself.

40
A VISENDI CORONATION

Saffina called upon her Red Aura as she dropped down from the game board above, but to her surprise, she hadn't needed to.

As she landed on her back, she sprang back up into the air. She righted her body position, so her feet were below her again and looked down to see a glowing net of Orange Aura below her. With each bounce she got lower, until eventually she bounced no more.

Kali, Taylor, Xabi and Zach were all sitting in the middle of their respective square nets, pondering what they should do.

"Are you guys okay?" she shouted to them.

"Yeh, we all good!" replied Kali. Saffina breathed a sigh of relief. Kali was so young it was hard seeing her disappear into the darkness. "What'ya think we should do?"

"Guess we just wait until the game has finished," shrugged Saffina. "Anyone tried moving nets yet?"

Each orphan shook their head. None had wanted to test if

the Aura Screen that contained them within their square remained active below the surface.

Saffina stood up and balanced herself precariously on the springy aura net. "Guess I'll give it a go then…" On the count of three, she launched herself forward into an empty square and to her relief, wasn't rebounded back. "Ha-ha! We can move again!" The four orphans whooped and cheered and sprang toward her.

As they huddled together, another scream from above rained down as Yasmin fell onto a net square. She soon stopped bouncing and her gaze quickly set upon Saffina and the orphans. Her straight jawline curving mercilessly into a smile.

"I guess we're outside of the game rules now," she said with menace in her voice.

"Stay behind me, kids, I'll protect you," Saffina stretched her arms out and ushered the children behind her. She called upon her Red Aura to shield them from any attack Yasmin may make.

"Remember, you're not the only one with an aura," Yasmin smirked as she tried to call upon her own shield, but instead the red light flickered a few times and disappeared. "What's going on?" she said, looking at her hands as if they were the problem, before trying again and getting the same result.

"Seems to me like you've annoyed Aurora. Can't imagine why," sniggered Saffina.

Yasmin continued to try and bring out her aura, but to no avail. A few moments later the figure of King Shimon was bouncing in a net of aura beside her. Saffina couldn't help but muse at seeing a member of royalty end up in such an ungraceful position. Then it dawned on her the new danger she and the orphans were in.

"Not to worry. If I can't take care of you, our Reaper here will," Yasmin said arrogantly.

The king steadied himself in his net, Black Aura still pulsing through his veins. "What's the matter with you?" he asked Yasmin.

"Seems like my Visendi abilities have faded. But if that's the case," Yasmin paused in thought before turning to the king. "Try and Reap me," she instructed him.

"Reap you? But why?"

"Just try it, damn it!"

The king complied and bounced somewhat awkwardly onto Yasmin's net and placed his hand of swirling Black Aura onto the centre of her chest. "I don't understand, nothing's happening." He lifted his hand away and placed it back to try again, but still nothing happened.

"Just as I thought," Yasmin announced with unpleasant arrogance. "If Aurora's spirits have lost faith in me and I'm no longer officially a Visendi, then I must have finally been accepted into the Sentio Tenebris doctrine," her eyes shifted to Saffina and the orphans, flecks of black appeared in the white of her eyes as she leered with pure evil intent. "And that comes with its own special abilities which I'm desperate to try out."

As Yasmin readied herself to launch an attack of Sentian power, the aura net below them vanished and they all fell with a heavy bump onto a hard and glossy stone floor. Before they could regain their feet, the walls began shaking violently and clouds of dust rained down from above, catching in their throats as they all gazed upwards, causing them to choke.

"The gameboard," coughed Saffina, "It's moving. It's coming down. It's coming down right on top of us!"

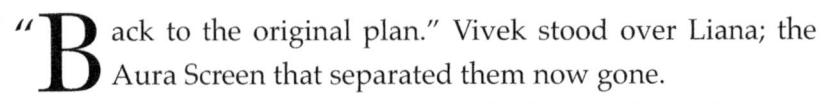

"Back to the original plan." Vivek stood over Liana; the Aura Screen that separated them now gone.

"I won't let you sacrifice me," replied Liana defiantly.

"Oh no, I couldn't risk sacrificing you. Although your Morality would certainly be enough to finally crack this pillar open, but if you are the Guardian of Light, then I can't imagine the temple would take too kindly to the one who murdered you. No, I'll take him instead," his bony finger pointed at Franklin. "You were a worthy adversary in this game. You should be honoured to be my final pick for sacrificing."

The arena, still shaking violently as it moved, had already sunk half-way.

"I won't let that happen," Liana shouted over the rumbling noise.

"And just how are you going to stop me?" Vivek cackled.

A sudden jolt as the arena neared its destination caused Liana to fall. She felt a dull pain in her side as she hit the floor and grimaced. She felt for what had caused the pain. It was the Jewels, and remembering she had them on her, she had an idea. She slipped the intricate gold chains over her fingers, the black backplate almost fully covering the back of her left-hand.

"So, you have the Jewels already," observed Vivek. "No matter, without your next Spectra Orb they are useless."

"I wouldn't be so sure of that," Liana unsheathed the Dagger of Red with her right-hand and popped the Spectra Orb from its handle. Using the dagger's blade, she sliced the orb open to empty the Red Aura she'd stored in it before making a dash for the orange beam of light and launching herself into it. The beam of Orange Aura caught her as she jumped and the princess floated in mid-air, her body's frame glowing.

Liana placed the empty Spectra Orb into the sunken hole on the Jewels backplate. As the orb was placed into its holder, the princesses head was thrown back and her arms were thrown sideways into a crucifix pose. The Spectra Orb began to fill with the dancing, orange light.

A vine of orange light wrapped itself gently around Liana's right-hand, producing a tickling sensation that made her drop the Dagger of Red. Once the vine of light stopped moving, it transformed into a matching handpiece. A second vine of aura wrapped itself around her neck and shaped itself into a three-stranded gold necklace with an orange orb pendant. A final vine coiled around the crown of her head, creating a golden tiara, with an orange orb set in the centre. The princess felt a wave of power flow within her.

"It is official now," Liana spoke in her usual speaking tone, but her words somehow projected loudly across the arena. "The Neoteric Temple has crowned me the Restorer of the Spectrum."

Vines of orange light projected from Liana's Orange Aura and planted themselves around the clifftops like spider legs. The ground stopped shaking and the arena stopped lowering, before the vines began to pull the sunken crater back to its arisen position. More vines projected from Liana's figure, grabbing the human game pieces and placing them back into the crowd before the squares of the gameboard below fizzled out, revealing Saffina and the other taken game pieces on the stone floor below. The fake crowd fizzled out as the pillar transferred the control of its power to the princess.

Vivek, seeing the Dagger of Red lying on the floor, seized an opportunity to take out Liana. He scrambled across the floor and gathered the blade. "I can still defeat you," he cried and aggressively thrust the dagger towards Liana's floating figure, but another vine shot out from the princess and grabbed his wrist, lifting him off his feet by one arm.

"Not today you can't," replied Liana, flinging the former clerk from the apex of the pillar. The princess fell from her levitated position, collapsing in a heap. The surge of overwhelming power had made her weary and exhausted.

Vivek's body tumbled the long drop downwards, but as he neared Yasmin, Saffina and the glossy stone floor below, his form dissipated into a black whispy cloud. His body reformed just as he hit the floor, rolling several times as he landed.

∽

"Vivek!" Yasmin shouted, running over to her mentor. "Are you okay? Can you hear me?"

"Ugh," he grumbled, pushing himself gingerly to his feet. "I'm fine. Plus, I still have this," he added, raising his hand that was still clenching the Dagger of Red. "Let's say we raise the stakes a bit." He pointed the tip of the blade into the crowd where Meredith and her child were seated. "Immorals, get that woman!"

On Vivek's orders, the Immoral half of the stadium charged through the terraces into the less populated Dantian half. They punched and kicked their way through the crowd, not interested in killing, only interested in carrying out their order. Prince Kendrix and Joel did their best at rebuffing as many as they could, but they were soon overrun and the woman and child had quickly become the hostage of Vivek and his army.

They lowered Meredith over the arena wall onto the glossy

stone floor below, still with the child in her arms. Yasmin moved towards the shaken and scared mother, but was rugby tackled to the floor, pinned down by Saffina.

"How low do you have to be to take a mother from a child?" Saffina said with anger.

"Oh, we aren't taking a mother from a child. We're taking a mother *and* a child." A disturbing grin spread across Yasmin's face. She moved her lips closer to Saffina's ear and whispered. "And you're going to let us, because we both know deep down how jealous you are of Liana and that you secretly want her to fail," a wisp of Black Aura floated into Saffina's ear as Yasmin spoke.

Saffina unpinned Yasmin and stood in confused silence, allowing the newly ordained Sentian to retrieve the hostage safely.

"Saffina, what are you doing?!" shouted Joel from the crowd. "Saffina! Saffina!" But she just stood there, watching as Yasmin brought the mother and daughter to Vivek for their sacrifice.

"King Shimon, would you like to do the honours, or shall I?"

"You should have the final sacrifice, Master," replied the king.

"Excellent, I was hoping you'd say that." Vivek raised the Dagger of Red above Meredith's head, poised and ready to strike.

41
A SENTIAN WARNING

'They have Meredith and her child! We can't just sit back and do nothing. Liana is down, Joel and Kendrix are fighting off Immorals in the crowd, Yasmin has somehow incapacitated Saffina. It's down to us now, boy.

Good, I'm glad you agree. Then let's go, and if anything happens to us, it's been a pleasure riding along with you, buddy.'

The Dagger of Red shimmered its red tint as the sun dawned above the horizon, it's never-blunting blade ready to cut through anything in its way. This time, it was the flesh of a mother and child. A crying mother, shielding her child away as best as she could from the horror that was about to happen. A squealing child, squealing not because it wanted food or sleep, but because it recognised the upset in its mother. An unspoken bond of emotional alignment.

Vivek released his arms and the blade sliced cleanly through the air. The squelch and crunch of metal on skin and bone was of little consequence to Vivek. He had killed others before, watched the life drain out of their eyes, but it was the first time he would see it in a person so young. He was not so much as disturbed by what that may look and feel like, as intrigued.

But as Vivek removed the dagger from the flesh it had penetrated, the weeping of mother and child could still be heard, their bodies lying on the ground beside the victim of the blade.

The white fur of Cas now stained in his own red blood. His canine body lay motionless.

～

"Castiel!" Liana screamed in emotional anguish as she peered over the ledge of the pillar. She'd watched the whole event happen. Cas bounding in from the terraces, pushing Meredith and her child out the way just as Vivek struck with the Dagger of Red and instead stabbing the heart of Liana's trusted companion. Tears wetted her cheeks.

"He saved my wife and child's life," said a shocked Franklin, before wrapping his arms around the teenage princess. "You asked him to protect us, and he did. He's a hero."

Their moment of grief was quickly interrupted by a creaking underneath their feet. Cracks of shining white light splintered across the faces of the pillar.

"I've done it!" shouted Vivek from the foot of the pillar. "We've fed this damned pillar with enough Moralities. Now I can finally get my hands on the *real* Spectra Orb."

The pillar began to ooze, and the black gloss surfaces began to melt in on itself into a goo of black lava.

"Liana…" Franklin said nervously as they were left standing on a small tile of pillar which was becoming smaller and smaller.

"I got this," said Liana, and with a twist of her hands a familiar vine-like rope of Orange Aura grabbed Franklin around the waist. Another two planted themselves on the ground beside Meredith and gently lowered the princess and the Chantrah Master to the ground. Franklin immediately cradled his wife and they sobbed with relief together on the floor.

Liana fell to her knees and stroked Cas behind his ears. She immediately welled up at the absence of his panting from the delight of his sweet spot being rubbed.

"It's all gone," came the shocked voice of Vivek from behind her. On a pedestal in what was once the centre of the pillar, sat an empty Spectra Orb. The former clerk picked it up and examined it, before smashing into the floor in anger. "You've ruined my plan again!"

"That's kind of the point of being a chosen one, isn't it?" countered Liana.

Vivek grunted, before an evil smirk crossed his face. "Maybe there's another way to stop you and the Visendi."

A hand grabbed Liana by the shoulder and spun her around. A second hand pressed against the centre of her chest, and she felt a sudden jolt. King Shimon was attempting to Reap her.

The colours around the princess flickered until everything turned greyscale. Around her, a contrast of bright white figures was set against deep black figures. She gazed down at the hand resting upon her chest and saw her own Morality fighting against the attack of King Shimon.

A dark figure moved beside the king. Liana knew in the physical world this was Vivek, but here in the Morality Realm he looked different. A tall being of black flames. The same being that was locked in a cell, until Liana in her dream gave him the power to escape.

"I told you we'd meet again, Guardian of Light," said the low, coarse, echoing voice of the flaming man. "That's right, you know who I am."

"Y-you're Tenebris, aren't you?"

"Indeed!" he said, raising his arms joyfully. "I am Tenebris himself, riding the Morality of the man called Vivek. It may not yet be complete freedom, but it is better than the cell I've been imprisoned in for millennia."

"H-how?" she stuttered again, unable to hide the fear she had of the imposing being.

"Someone hasn't read the Scriptures of the Visendi and Sentian beliefs, have they?" The being cackled, finding Liana's lack of knowledge on his race amusing.

"Get away from her!" The words of warning came from a familiar voice. A voice Liana thought she'd never hear again.

"I don't think you can handle a war in the Morality Realm just yet," said another familiar voice.

"Rhonwen, Gilroy!" Liana breathed a sigh of relief at seeing their Moralities.

Ruff, ruff!

"Don't forget this one," smiled Gilroy.

"Cas!" exclaimed an excited Liana, her fear temporarily turning to joy.

Tenebris sped across the ground to face up to Liana. The black flames that licked her face were not of heat but gave off the same sinking and hopeless feeling in her stomach from when she found herself in his cell.

"Unfortunately, your friends here are right. I am not yet strong enough to take out three Spectra Children in this Realm, but I will be. Soon, your Morality and this planet will be mine." The black flames retreated, leaving just Vivek's dark frame.

Liana looked down at her chest. King Shimon was still attempting to Reap her Morality. She turned to her three fallen comrades by her side. She had a rekindled desire to see through her predicted destiny.

Sensing Liana's new-found determination, Vivek could see imminent danger. He smashed a Black Orb onto the ground and a portal of dark energy opened up, swirling in the same dark flames that engulfed Tenebris's figure. The Sentians closest to the portal dove into it and out of sight, before Liana unleashed a blinding dome of white light across the arena.

The Moralities that had been imprisoned in the pillar floated back to rejoin their bodies. The fighting in the terraces stopped. The Immorals that had been Turned or sacrificed caught their breath and lowered their fists.

"Kendrix. Kendrix?"

"Luci!" shouted the prince as he shoved his way through a crowd in front of him. "Luci, I thought you were gone!" The pair hugged each other tightly.

"I guess you know I'm not Princess Liana then?"

"And I don't care," he said, pulling her in for another hug.

Liana heard a faint whimper at her feet, followed by the scrabbling of paws on the floor. This gave the princess the biggest moment of joy. "Cas! You're alive! You're okay! Come here boy!" the hound lapped at her face as she rubbed him behind the ears.

After a few moments enjoying each other's attention, she looked around for Rhonwen and Gilroy. Cas sniffed the ground beside her and circled it. Liana felt a pit of dread in her stomach. She closed her eyes and controlled her breathing.

"You're not coming back, are you?" she said. Her ability of

Sight had returned as she spoke to Rhonwen and Gilroy in the Morality Realm.

"I sacrificed myself as part of the trials to unlock the temple. You see, I never said anything about the Trials needing to be done in order," winked Rhonwen. "And the temple knew all along Vivek cheated, it just wanted to give you the right nudge to unleash your Morality. But, to answer your question," her tone switched to a more sombre note. "No, we're not coming back. It appears us Spectra Children are different. It seems we can continue as conscious beings in the Morality Realm, and so our bodies don't call us back."

"So, you're not dead then?"

"Depends on your definition of dead, I guess."

"What will you do?"

"Watch over you, of course. The war between the Sentians and Visendi is just beginning, and it will be fought both in your realm and the Morality Realm."

"Well, I hope you're still going to respect my privacy!" said the princess.

"Of course we will," replied Gilroy, despite knowing he'd already intruded on it once in her chambers back at Castle Langton.

"We'll come up with some rules when things have settled down, shall we?" winked Rhonwen. "For now, let's help get Allicalidantè back on its feet again. Starting with returning the Neoteric Temple to all its former glory."

With a wave of her hand, the Estadio de la Alegría shimmered, and the crumbling old stone crumbled no more. The flags, the banners, the cushion's that had all become torn and ripped in the melee returned to their glorious colours, as if new. "The Neoteric Temple will be returned to its former glory under the stadium. When we were outlawed from practising the religion for hundreds of years we had to hide somewhere, and where better than underneath a stadium full of chanting spectators? If you head down into the crater now you will no longer see a stone palace facing a sea of leaning buildings and haphazardly built mezzanine floors, but a wondrous hideout full of Visendi entertainment. That reminds me, I must show you how to play Aura Ball one day."

"Sounds like a great place to hold a Visendi tournament. My friend Benji and great uncle Sir Tarak have been wanting to hold an inter-Coryàtès tournament for months. It would be great to get The Dantè involved too!"

"Well, I think after the events of today, Allicalidantè will be converted into practising the ways of the Visendi. I'm sure when it's back on its feet, and if a few more monarchies come on board, Prince Kendrix would be delighted to host a Visendi tournament."

"Sounds like something to look forward to," Liana bounced excitedly at the thought.

"We will need all the things to look forward to as this war progresses, but for now, we must say goodbye Guardian of Light and Restorer of the Spectrum. Until we meet again."

42
HOMEWARD BOUND

The RNC Ascendancy lowered its walkway onto the Dantian harbour. Admiral Remi marched down the damp slope.

"Nice of you to join us whilst we're right in the thick of the action," Sir Tarak said sarcastically as he greeted the admiral.

"Rather be out in the open seas where my only worry is seagulls pinching my dinner than whatever you've been in the mix of. Been sitting out on my deck in the cool ocean breeze with my nice stash of booze and food. Hope the cuisine in the stone palace was as delightful," the admiral replied knowingly, with equal amounts of sarcasm. Sir Tarak couldn't argue with her reasoning, he and the rest of the entourage were particularly looking forward to eating something other than tough chicken, stinking fish and tiny potatoes.

"I must say, I am very proud of my pupil today," Master H. bowed before Liana on the precarious timber-built harbour. "You remembered my teachings."

"I did?" Liana raised an eyebrow.

"You don't think so?" her mentor questioned.

"Depends which of your many teachings you are on about, oh wise one." The sarcasm was also catching on with Liana. Master H plonked her on the head with his staff for her insolence. "Ouch!" Liana rubbed her scalp.

"Our last session of course," Master H's brow furrowed.

"The Five F's," the princess paused trying to recall them all. "Fight. Flight. Freeze. Flop and… Friend."

"Correct, and I believe you used them all in your time here in The Dantè."

Liana thought back to her time in the city, how she'd fled a group of Dantian's rescuing Kendrix from the pillar, befriended a group orphans (and a musical duet), fought off Vivek (again), froze at the sight of Tenebris.

"I guess you're right, but I don't remember using the flop technique? Seems a pretty daft approach if you ask me, pretending to lose."

Master H. turned away, laughing, as he made his way up the ship's walkway.

"I don't get it. What's so funny?" Liana shouted after him.

A strong hand landed on Liana's shoulder. "Well, you did lose quite an important game of Chantrah. I'd say that was quite a big flop," joked Amara.

"I didn't lose, Vivek cheated, and I wasn't even the one playing!"

"Putting your faith into a proxy is something I'd never do! Always control what you can, that's what I say," said the warrior, puffing out her chest and slamming a fist against her heart before also making her way hastily up to the promise of good food and wine aboard the royal ship.

"I'm good, but even I can't beat a cheater," said Franklin,

his arm wrapped around the waist of Meredith who was cradling their baby. "Thank you, Liana, for saving our city."

"Aye, thank ya princess!" shouted Kali from behind the couple as the rabble of orphans scurried down to the harbourside from the cobblestone street.

"It was a team effort," Liana smiled. "By the way, has anyone seen Seff?"

"Nah," the youngest orphan shook her head. "We think he must have skedaddled with the wrong'uns. We might not've liked him much, but I don't wanna see him turn out like that Yasmin lass." Kali rubbed her nose with the back of her hand as let out a small sniffle thinking about him.

Liana squatted down so the orphan was looking down at her. "If that's the case and he has gone with Vivek, it won't be the last time I see him. When I do, I promise I'll do my very best to bring him home and put his misguided morals onto the right path." The orphan wrapped her arms around Liana's neck and hugged her tight. "What will you do now?" the princess asked Franklin, raising herself back up from her squat.

"Well, we've decided to take on caring for these children. Now that we can return to the abandoned part of the city, we're sure we can find a place big enough for us all." The children looked delighted at the sound of living with Franklin and his wife. "There's a lot of rebuilding to do to get the city back on its feet, although there aren't enough of us to make it the same, thriving theatre of games and arts as it was before…"

"But we'll get there with the help of our new allies." The interruption came from the voice of Prince Kendrix. "The city of Allicalidantè will stand side-by-side with the Island of Coryàtès in whatever destiny has for us." The prince held out his hand and the pair shook on his words.

"I'm sorry I couldn't save your father," Liana said with a tone of guilt in her voice.

"After my mother died, I don't think anyone could have saved him," Kendrix fiddled with the ring on his finger as he reflected on his family's past. "My father masked his inner turmoil for so long that Turning him into the thing he has become must have been easy."

"I promise we will return with as many supplies and resources as we can spare, including labour."

"Anything you can offer will be greatly received," Kendrix bowed.

Liana gave a gentle nod of the head. "Although there's something I must ask in return," she said.

"Ok, let's hope this request won't require another four weeks of negotiations," joked Kendrix.

Liana chuckled, "So do I, since all I'm after is an invite to your coronation of course!"

"My coronation? I guess I hadn't given that any thought. My father is still technically alive somewhere, but is most definitely unfit to rule," Kendrix paused in thought. "Terms accepted. You will be first on the invitations, but I'd like to add something else to these impromptu talks," he turned around looking longingly at Luci, who was jokingly pushing and shoving Joel and Saffina. "I'd like Luci to stay here, by my side. Would you be able to handle the diplomacy involved with her parents?"

Liana smiled inwardly. Knowing Luci was staying with Kendrix would make her life back on Coryàtès both easier and happier. "I'll have my mother see to it as soon as I return."

Liana's doppelgänger bounced over towards them. "What's going on?" asked Luci cheerily, observing the huge grin on Kendrix's face. The prince guided her away and out of earshot from Saffina and Joel to tell her the news, which was greeted with a big kiss on his cheek and arms flung around his neck.

"Let's get on board," Liana said to her two best friends. "I'm dying for some cheese."

43
TAKEN

"That's so cool!" exclaimed an excited Joel as a radiant orange light seeped through the gaps of Liana's clenched hands.

Liana had taken the quartz from hers and Amara's makeshift head torches that they'd used in the secret passageway to get in and out of the crater and, using her special ability with the Jewels of Orange and her Sacral Spirit, transformed them into a brand-new Spectra Orb. Using the Dagger of Red, she cut a piece of her Red Aura from herself and filled the new orb with its dancing, glowing light.

"Back on the pillar," Liana started to explain to her friend, "I came up with the idea that I could simply empty my Red Aura out of my old Spectra Orb and use it to catch my Orange Aura, knowing I could craft a new orb for my Red Aura once I'd attained my Sacral Spirit with the Jewels of Orange," she said, mapping out her thought process for jumping into the beam of orange light.

"Your brain's certainly gotten a bit quicker these last few

weeks," praised Joel. "Hey, look!" he said, pulling out his own case of Aura Orbs and picking up a newly lit one. "I gained my Sacral Core too, look at my cool Orange Aura!"

"Nice!" replied Liana.

"Isn't it weird how so far we've only seemed to be able to Ascend ourselves after you've gained your spirits."

"Yeh, guess it is. I'm sure we'll find out why sooner or later," said Liana, pondering the observation.

"Anyway, I'm gonna go below deck and get some more crackers and cheese, you want any?"

"No, thanks," she replied, looking curiously towards the bow of the ship. Joel skipped away excitedly at the thought of more food.

"Hey, you ok?" Liana stepped up beside Saffina who was standing at the bow of the RNC Ascendancy, gazing out to the open waters.

"Uh-huh," replied her friend without any conviction at all.

"Well, you sure just persuaded me you're fine!"

"Sorry, I'm not really in the mood for talking."

"Wanna tell me why?" Liana tried to put a reassuring arm around her friend but got shrugged off.

"No. I really just want to be left alone," Saffina shifted a step sideways.

"Is it to do with Eugene? We didn't find him afterwards, so I assume he went with Vivek through his portal. We will rescue him, you know."

"No, it's not to do with my brother. Anyhow, I've already begun to lose hope for him."

"Don't say that, think of all the people I've Unturned at the Battle of Coryàtès and here in Allicalidantè."

Saffina bowed her head, contemplating the fate of her

brother and how long he'd already been Turned, pondering if even Liana could return him to the brother she once knew.

"There's something else though, isn't there?" Liana speculated. "Something to do with what really happened between you and Yasmin down there? I know you wouldn't just let Meredith get taken like that. It's not you."

"I don't know, okay. I completely froze. I've been playing it in my mind over and over. I just don't know."

"It wasn't your fault."

The cool sea breeze felt chilling against a single tear that ran down Saffina's cheek. "Well, it feels like it."

"Hey, Meredith is fine. You're fine. We're all fine. That's all that matters," Liana shifted a step to be hip-to-hip with her friend.

"That's not the point," Saffina's curly hair bounced in the wind as she swivelled to face Liana. "Next time we might not be fine. Next time a child might die."

"We're only teenagers ourselves, Saff. Look, this burden is mine. All these titles I've been given are for me to bear. If you feel like you can't pitch in for the next Artefact and Spirit hunt, sit it out. No one's forcing you to help."

"And that's just what you'd like isn't," snapped Saffina before running off towards the deck.

"Saffina, wait, what are you talking about?" Liana called after her, but before she could chase down her friend, a swirling black circle of energy exploded into existence next to her, halting the princess in her tracks. She stared curiously into the dark abyss, black flames circling the portal. "What the? No, it can't be," but before she managed to finish her sentence, an arm reached out from the circle of energy and pulled her with a jolt inside, but not before she let out a cry of help to her friend.

Saffina slipped on the wet deck as she spun around, just in time to see Liana's legs disappear through the collapsing portal. "Joel!" Saffina screamed. "Joel, someone, help!"

∽

"And then she disappeared, dragged in by someone, or something," explained Saffina, standing before the fully occupied Queen's Table, minus Liana.

An oppressive-like silence hung in the room. Master H stroked his handlebar moustache, Priestess Yi fiddled with her green strand of hair, Sir Tarak finger-tapped the table, Benji rocked on the back two legs of his chair and Admiral Remi ran her fingers through the feather of her brown, tricorn hat that was resting on the table in front of her.

Queen Adriya addressed the room. "Does anyone have any idea where my daughter may have been taken?" The question was met with more silence. "Okay then, does anyone have any thoughts on how we can find out where she's been taken to?" The room remained silent.

"We could send out flocks of Jackdaw's," suggested Priestess Yi. "All over Mikana, one of them will surely seek her out."

"And what if she's been pulled from the physical realm into the Morality Realm?" asked Queen Adriya.

"To my knowledge, I don't believe that's possible, her physical form would always remain here, yet we know her physical form was pulled through the portal too," Master H guessed, still stroking his moustache. "Plus, it would take several flocks of Jackdaw's some considerable time to find Liana, even if they manage to find her. She could be well hidden, out of reach."

"We could get messages out to the other major monarchies of Mikana?" suggested Sir Tark. "Surely wherever she's been taken, there will be a trail of Turnings?"

"It would be a good starting point," agreed Queen Adriya. "The Jackdaw's would be the quickest way. Master Hayashi, Priestess Yi, make the arrangements now. It's all we've got until we pick up a trail."

The door to the Queen's Table burst open. "Wrong," a strong female voice echoed into the circular room. Candela, Liana's birthmother, strode into the room, her vibrant indigo hair flowing in behind her, sending an emotional blow to all in the room as they were reminded of their lost princess.

"Candela, do you have information on the Founding Temple's and other Spectra Children?" asked Priestess Yi.

"And," added Queen Adriya, "of my - our - daughter?"

"Both, in fact. I believe she's been taken to the Athenaeum Temple," declared Candela.

"The Athenaeum Temple?"

"Yes, the Founding Temple of the Yellow Aura," Candela clarified.

"And why do you believe this?" Queen Adriya continued her questioning.

"Because the Spectra Child tasked with safeguarding it is missing," Candela shifted her weight nervously.

Queen Adriya could tell she had more information to divulge. "And - spit it out," she said, pressing the Spectra Child.

"There's something else missing too," Candela gathered herself.

"Let me guess, the Artefact and the Spirit Orb are missing from the temple too," assumed Benji, chipping in.

"Actually no, well, I'm not sure. It's something else."

"Well then, hurry up and tell us what it is!" urged an impatient Sir Tarak.

Candela motioned towards the knight. "Do you remember the burnt foetus shaped mark on the lava-surrounded rock upon which you found Liana?"

"Yes, of course. After all these years I've simply dismissed its shape as a coincidence," he said, his finger-tapping sped up nervously.

"Nothing is a coincidence where Liana is concerned. That burned shadow in the rock was not made of any physical heat or fire."

"Then what made it?"

Candela took a deep, deep breath before answering the question. She spoke with an uncharacteristic but noticeable tremble. "It was made by Liana's Immoral Spirit."

Liana will return in:
Scriptures of Yellow

GLOSSARY OF TERMS

Allicalidantè/The Dantè: The capital city of King Shimon's monarchy

Artefacts: Special objects crafted to help protect the Founding Temples. Gifts Liana special abilities if used with her matching Aura Spirit

Aura Orb: an orb housing a Visendi's aura

Aura/Aura Spirits: the reward given to a Visendi for being well versed enough in an Inner Core

Aurora Visendus: The religious following of the God of Dawn. Translates as 'To See the God of Dawn'

Aurora: The God of Dawn

Coryàtès: the home island of Liana, ruled by the Langton monarchy

Founding Temples: Following her devastating conflict with Tenebris, Aurora left Mikana in the hands of the first Visendi. Each went their separate ways across Mikana to spread the word to the few remaining tribes of the world and formed the Founding Temples

Immorals: Those who have been Turned to Bad Morality but do not practise the ways of either religion. Easily manipulated to take sides if they see benefit for themselves.

Inner Core: the measure by which one attains their aura spirits.

Mikana: The planet this story takes place on

Morality Realm: A realm where a person's morality spirit exists

Morality Spirit: One's morality, either Good, Bad or Speckled (whilst being Turned)

Peeling: The act of stripping someone of their aura using the Dagger of Red

Quartalitium: a mineral formed combining Quartz and Cobalt creating a blue-tinted glass and is Coryàtès most tradable asset

Queen's Table: The governing body of Coryàtès. Current members are: Queen Adriya, Princess Liana, Sir Tarak, Admiral Remi, Benji, Master Hyashi and Priestess Yi

Root Core: The first Inner Core of the Visendi. Successful ascension gifts one the use of a Red Aura

Sacral Core: The second Inner Core of the Visendi. Successful ascension gifts one the use of an Orange Aura

Sentians: Those who follow the Sentio Tenebris religion

Sentio Tenebris: The religious following of the God of Darkness. Translates as 'To Feel the God of Darkness'

Sight: The ability to see into the Morality Realm

Spectra Child: The child of two transcended Visendi. Only six can exist (until Liana was born, making seven). Rarest and most powerful of Visendi.

Spectra Orb: an orb housing a Spectra Child's aura

Spirit Orb: an orb housing a mixture of a Visendi's aura and morality

Swyre: the capital and sole city of Coryàtès

Tenebris: The God of Darkness

Transcended Visendi: A Visendi who has ascended all levels of their Inner Core's

Turning: The act of manipulating one's Morality from Good to Bad. Can be done quick or over time

Visendi: Those who follow the Aurora Visendus religion

RETURNING CHARACTER LIST

Admiral Remi: Commanding Admiral of the Langton Navy

Agatha: Housekeeper of Langton Castle

Amara Langton: Unruly sister of Queen Adriya. Former general in the Langton army, now a freelance mercenary.

Aurora: The God of Dawn, the god and teachings who worshippers of the Aurora Visendus follow.

Benji: A former navy chef who now runs a butcher's in Swyre. Merchant's Guild Leader for Swyre.

Candela: Liana's birth mother and Indigo Spectra Child.

Eugene Greymore: best friend of Yasmin, Saffina's brother. Got Turned by Vivek in the lead up to the Battle of Coryàtès.

Gilroy: Entombed in the Tomb of the Transcended as the Red Spectra Child and guardian of the Dagger of Red.

Liana Langton: Our heroine and the never-before-seen 'Seventh' Spectra Child who was freed from the Tomb of the Transcended on the Day of Darkness. Adopted into the Langton royal family after being found by her great uncle Sir Tarak. Also known as 'The Light from the Dark', 'Restorer of the Spectrum' or 'the chosen one/the one'. On a quest to regain her Aura Spirits and put an end to the darkness of Tenebris once and for all.

Master Shiro Hayashi: the priest in charge of the Shrouded Temple of Roots, a Visendi Founding Temple. Liana's Visendi mentor, also referred to as 'Master H' or the 'Old Priest'.

Myra & Dimitra: friends who sought refuge in Zagan's camp from their homeland

Priestess Yi Lang: Taught the Visendi ways underground

whilst the religion was still outlawed. Now the Priestess of the Tulip Temple in Swyre.

Queen Adriya Langton: Reigning monarch of the island of Coryàtès who adopted Liana into the royal household

Saffina Greymore & **Joel Ellwood**: Liana's best friends after the princess stopped them getting bullied by Yasmin Thornfalcon when she first met them in school.

Sir Tarak Langton: Liana's great uncle, Queen Adriya's uncle. Found the princess after Mount Indigo erupted on Coryàtès. Commanding Knight of the Langton Army.

Tenebris: The God Darkness, Aurora's adversary and foe in the Aura Wars.

Vivek Tenebra: former clerk and aide to the Langton monarchy. Betrayed the family for pursuits of power.

Yasmin Thornfalcon: Liana's childhood antagonist.

Zagan Thornfalcon: Father of Yasmin and former Master of the Mines. Partnered with Vivek in a bid to destroy the Langton's and claim Coryàtès for himself. Was banished from Coryàtès by Queen Adriya.

ACKNOWLEDGMENTS

Huge shout out to everyone who's here! Thank you for reading book one and coming back for book two. I've always said, even if just one person bought and enjoyed book one I would continue writing, so I'm thrilled you have returned to see Liana's journey continue. There's so many of you that got behind me in this side venture of mine, especially my work colleagues who jumped straight onboard to show their support. Sue W, James E, Tom D and Stirls (hope you enjoyed your cameo), to name just a few, thank you.

As ever, a huge thanks goes out to my wife Sabrina and our children, Jensen and Mina, who somehow allow me the time to write amongst everything else we have going on in our lives. To my dad, whom this book is dedicated to, thank you again for being my proofreader and number one supporter with everyone you come across. Mum, for being the glue that keeps us all together.

As you can see, Inessa Sage of Cauldron Press has done it again with a magnificent book cover and formatting. I can't wait to continue working with you again.

See you all for book three!

- Simon.

ABOUT SIMON PITTMAN

"There is something eternal about publishing a book." Says Simon, who is by trade a Learning & Development professional, and a family man who lives in Dorset, UK with his wife Sabrina and his children Jensen and Mina.

Simon didn't discover his passion for reading until his thirties. Cyberpunk, Virtual Reality and Sci-Fi genres are typically his favourite genre for reading, but as an author, it's the limitless creativity of fantasy writing.